# *Bits of Blue*

Kay D Johnson

Johnson, Kay D
Bits of Blue

ISBN 978-0-9952658-9-9 (pbk.)

Also by

*Kay D Johnson*

Life on the Lawn

*First Page Last Page*

MARKED

*In the Hunt for the Perfect Martini*

Lovage

*An Angel Named Topaz*

The Last Motel

Acknowledgement

I would like to thank the City of Belleville Fire and Emergency Services, Belleville Ontario for their advice on the anatomy and behavior of fire, but mostly in believing me when I said it was only research for a book and not my plans to recreate the plot in real life.

Also, D. P. Lyle, MD, for his endless advice on the forensics of a murder scene.

And to the master himself, Stephen King, for reminding us, that deep down inside, we all have the capacity to do whatever it takes to survive — and writing about it, is truly satisfying.

# Part 1

There they were again, those tiny floating stars above her head, dancing wildly out of control. He had hit her, his anger and frustration, released on her as it had many times before. The beatings were coming more often, each one getting more and more violent than the previous. Tess stayed on the dining room floor curled up in a ball, protecting her face and chest from whatever vicious action he was to throw her way. For the first time, she feared for her life — he'd gone too far.

The beatings started shortly after the accident. An incident that she thought was singular because of his heavy drinking at the time. It never changed. He continued to drink heavily, and when he wasn't crying and depressed, he was angry and violent, venting his frustrations out on whoever was handy. The dog had long run away from his torturer, but she had stayed. Tess had no choice. Where was she to go? She had no money, no family, no friends, therefore nowhere to escape to.

It was a situation he had made sure of, early on in their marriage. She realized, when it was far too late, that he had actually been brainwashing her right from the start. Even on their second date, he began the slow, insidious task of removing her friends and family from Tess's life — isolating her from them through excuses and exclusion. Eventually, even her closest friends gave up trying and left her to his manipulating strategies.

Within a year, he was all Tess had, a fact she was reminded of every day. He didn't allow her to work or leave the house without him being present, totally controlling her life and inevitably her thoughts. Each evening he would drill her as to her activities of her isolated day. She learned to lie artfully, carefully choosing the right words, trying her best to please him and calm his suspicions. But if her answers didn't suit his liking or he considered them a threat, she was quickly reminded that her place was by his side, serving him only and that all others had abandoned her, not caring about her any longer. Verbal threats were an everyday occurrence, but never a violent hand. The spoken abuse had become part of the daily routine between them. She realized now how long he had restrained himself — for that she was grateful.

It began early that afternoon, when Morty had seen a TV commercial depicting a plate of thick juicy meatloaf. He announced with his customary roar that he wanted meatloaf for supper. With mashed potatoes smothered with gravy and buttery carrots, just like he'd seen on TV. Tess cringed, both at his demanding bellows and at the fact that she had none of those ingredients to make such an elaborate meal. Except for the potatoes. Much to her disgust, they always had a large bag of potatoes. Now she would have to make a special trip to the grocery store for the ingredients just for that meal. An extra trip that they could neither afford or later utilize for other meals.

But what was dreadful for her, was that she would have to bring up the fact she would need to leave the house without him. She could already feel her neck and shoulders tense up as she formulated what she would say to Morty. As always, she would have to ask his permission to venture out into the world on her own. Then she would have to convince him she wasn't running away or meeting up with another man for a quick round of satisfying sex. It was the same inhuman treatment she had to endure each time she needed to leave the house alone.

Tess decided to take a chance, stepping beyond the rigid rules Morty had laid down in his house. She decided to twist the situation around, using Morty's own strict constraints to avoid the entire situation. She made her voice a soft whisper, filling it with vulnerability, "Oh Morty, do you really want meatloaf? That means I'd have to go out to get hamburger and carrots." She emphasized the word out so he'd think twice about letting her out of his sight — and his grasp.

Unfortunately, Morty took it the wrong way, as an insult to his worth. "So, I'm not worth the effort?" He slapped the arm of his brown vinyl recliner, "You'll do as I tell you, woman!" The next hard slap made Tess's entire body jerk with fear. He dropped down the foot rest by its lever, "I pay for the food around here and you'll do as I tell you." He grabbed his cane and shook it angrily at her, "You'll go to the store if you know what's good for you!"

Tess cowered into her kitchen chair, making herself as small as possible while he continued with his orders. "Yes, Morty."

"You'll go get the stuff for my meatloaf, you hear me? You dumb ungrateful bitch!" He placed both hands on the chair's arms, "Without me, you'd have nothing! Not even that ugly sweater on your back." He struggled to get to his feet. "Without me, you'd be nothing. No one wants you.

You're nothing. You're lucky I let you live here!" Not being able to get out of the chair on his own, he slid back down into the seat with a hard Plop, "Now get me another coffee." When she didn't instantly jump to her feet to serve him, he smacked the arm again, "I ... said ... NOW!"

As always, she did as he demanded. She moved quickly to pour him a fresh cup, adding just the right amount of cream and sugar to please him. She then carefully presented it to him at full arm's length, placing the handle within his reach, yet leaving her arm itself just out of his grasp. As soon as he took the handle of the cup, she yanked her arm back, tucking it safely behind her back. She took two steps backward, placing herself out of his reach from the chair. She waited until he took a sip. Waited for his approval, or whether she had to correct her blunder. She made his coffee the same way every day, but some days it was okay, and other days it infuriated Morty, sending him into a state of rage.

"Good, you finally got it right." He calmly placed the cup on the small table beside his chair and exhaled while his eyes narrowed at her. He sat quiet for a moment, eyeing her up and down, then exploded at her, "What's wrong with you? Get dressed and go get some hamburger. I ... want ... my ... fuckin' ... MEATLOAF!" He repeatedly hammered the arms of the recliner with both fists, throwing a tantrum where he sat. "Get! You stupid useless BITCH! Get out of my sight!" Tess's body knotted into a tight terrified ball, frozen where she stood. When she didn't move fast enough, he gnashed at the air with his teeth, like the crazy man he was. That made her scurry for the stairs, one, to do as he said, and two, to get away from him.

Morty hadn't always been fanatical and violent. It was the accident that pushed him over the edge, forcing his violence to the surface. With only frustrated interaction with the outside world and losing his position of authority, he felt powerless and for the first time in his life, at the mercy of others. A fact that infuriated him. His previous needs to boss and control those around him were now thrust upon the only person left in his life — Tess.

The accident happened while he was at work. She often wondered if it was indeed a true accident. Or was it his fellow workers who had also endured enough of his bullying and found a way to put an end to it. Forklifts didn't normally run full steam into a person, pinning them at the waist to the wall.

It happened on a Monday, a day she would never forget. It was the day her life was forever altered.

The phone rang at ten o'clock, not the usual time of her one and only allowed phone call from him. At first, she hesitated to pick it up, but when Vivian's voice came over the answering machine, Tess rushed to the phone. She listened shakily as the factory nurse informed her that her husband had been injured by one of the company's forklifts and was just then sent to Memorial Hospital by ambulance. Vivian's voice was a mixture of concern and confusion. Vivian informed Tess that Morty insisted that she call his wife to have Tess take a taxi directly to the hospital and that she wasn't to talk to anyone, but him or the doctor. Morty's odd behavior concerned the nurse, prompting her to ask if everything was okay at home. Not knowing how to answer her question without possibly getting herself in trouble with Morty, Tess quickly made her goodbyes and hung up the phone. As Morty had always commanded, what happened in his home between him and his woman, was no one else's business.

When she arrived at the hospital, her husband's boss was at the admissions desk filling out forms. By the expression on his face, Bruno was obviously perplexed. He admitted he realized that he knew nothing about the man who had worked for him for over twelve years. He handed the forms to her, relinquishing the duty and excused himself to return to the factory. Tess quietly sat in the corner, filling in the blanks Bruno didn't know, which turned out to be most of the information.

After a two hour wait, the doctor finally told her that the operation wasn't as successful as they'd hoped. Morty would be paralyzed from the waist down, and he would spend the remainder of his life in a wheelchair. She sat still for a moment, her head racing with fear. Eventually, she timidly asked only one question.

If he worked hard in physiotherapy, would he walk again?

After a brief explanation, she went to the waiting room pay phone and hunted down Bruno at the factory. Within ten minutes, she had her answers. Yes, he would be receiving a disability pension, and he was indeed covered under his medical plan for such rehabilitation therapy. Hanging up the phone, relief relaxed the tension in her neck and shoulders. *It's going to be all right,* she told herself. They'd have money to live on and her husband, with hard work, would walk again.

Except, that's not what happened. He didn't want to work hard; he didn't want to walk again. Instead, he sat in his wheelchair, ordering her around. Bullying her from his comfortable red cushion, bellowing to be served instantly and properly, the way he had taught her to do it. And Tess did it — not giving a second thought as to what was truly taking place. In her mind, she knew without his disability cheques; they would either starve to death or freeze come winter. She did it out of necessity, needing his signature to cash those cheques.

Using his meager pension and careful planning, she managed to pay the bills, purchase their food for the month and as he demanded, buy his favorite liquor. Three heavy and rather expensive bottles of brandy. He justified his heavy drinking with claims that it stopped his nightly pains, helping him to sleep. A benefit she appreciated as well — the faster he went to sleep, the less she had to deal with him and his non-functioning libido. Eventually, to save money, she switched to a cheaper brand by pouring it into the empty expensive bottles while he slept. To her way of thinking, he didn't notice, and he still got the same 'high' as before. To her, it meant she could buy better foods like real — not canned — meat and the occasional bunch of fresh vegetables. She liked steamed green beans and sautéed baby carrots with a touch of dill. A dish she rarely got to enjoy.

However, as time went by his drinking became more prevalent. Instead of starting at eight o'clock, he demanded a drink with his dinner and of course, one for after dinner, *like the rich people do*, he touted. She wanted to remind him that they were not rich people and that the money that paid for the brandy was being taken out of the food budget. Yet, she didn't. She knew what would happen if she did. A drawn-out string of insults and accusations, bellowed at the top of his lungs, along with anything he could get his hands on thrown at her. Books, ashtray, remotes, and once a lamp. Anything that would punish her for being stupid.

After an angry fit of unsuccessfully chasing her through the house in his wheelchair, it occurred to him that if he could walk again, he could get at her — then she would pay for her disobedience. He demanded physiotherapy the very next day, insisting he wanted to walk once more.

Each week she shopped, while he went to physiotherapy. And each week, he would grill her about her conduct while she was out of his view. Adultery and scheming to leave him for a younger or healthier man were the usual allegations she had to contend with. Tess defended herself to his satisfaction, and in the end, he'd let it go with a harsh warning.

To her happiness, he was getting stronger. That's what the physiotherapist said to Tess when she returned to collect him after his session. Soon he would be able to walk a few steps on his own. A miracle she claimed with praying hands. Soon, with more hard work from Morty, they wouldn't have to come in for additional sessions. He could do the routines with his wife at home.

Morty didn't see his wife cringe when the therapist joked, "With more hard work, you will be up out of your chair and chasing your pretty wife about the house with your cane in no time." Tess's breath caught on her final words. The woman had no idea that the exact words she used to jest about her future, was sadly the horrible truth. The perpetual knots in Tess's stomach painfully tightened when Morty smiled at her, his evil eyes narrowed, warning her of his plans — and her impending abuse.

However, what Morty was oblivious to, was the fact that Tess was also getting stronger. With each shopping trip, she met more and more people. Nice people who treated her fairly and with kindness. No verbal abuse, no threats. Then there were the men who looked at her, smiling their intentions. At first, she pulled her clothing tightly together concealing her femininity. But as time went on and she became accustomed to her own body, she let them look, enjoying the feeling of being desired.

It felt wonderful to walk and talk freely in the real world, to not have to watch every word said or every little action done, in fear that it would be misconstrued as something other than it was. She even dared to have lunch at a diner instead of at the hospital's cafeteria. Pastrami on rye with chocolate milk tasted heavenly on Tess's tongue. She liked the freedom his therapy brought her, and now it was going to be taken away. As much as she wanted the physiotherapy appointments to continue, she was powerless to stop them from being discontinued. She prepared herself to return to the life she had before the therapy, the loneliness and isolation — and just him.

As unconsciously predicted by the physiotherapy nurse, within no time, he was chasing her about the house, attempting to catch her, swinging wildly with an angry cane and fists, all aimed at her.

That night he did it again, hitting her so hard, she fell to her knees with the pain. Blackness and stars danced through her bashed brain. Except for this time, he was drunker than usual, this time when he swung, the force of the hit made him fall, landing squarely on his own ass. To her relief, he couldn't get up. Between the booze and his disabled body, he was unable to pull himself to his own feet. As much as he stretched, his cane was out of reach. Tess saw it as an opportunity to get away, if only momentarily. She pulled herself out of her curled ball and ran into the other half of the room, the kitchen. Her injured head swirled the room around her, so she clung to the counter for stability. She heard him bellow at her to come to the dining room and get him up off the floor — then he'd show her more of the same, just to keep her in line.

His words sent a shiver down her spine, a sign that the abuse would never end — unless she ended it. But how? If she left, she wouldn't have anywhere to go or money to go with. He was the one who signed the cheques. He was in command of the finances. At that very moment, Tess Logan understood her life.

She had NO life.

It was all him — and none of her.

She heard the words 'stupid ugly bitch'. Within seconds, blood began to boil through her veins. Her head throbbed with the pressure, and her face stung where his fist had hit her jaw. Touching the heated spot of her skin with her fingertips, she hopelessly admitted to herself that he would never change, she would be under his spiteful supremacy for the rest of her life. Morty was in control of everything — or was he?

Angered blood rushed through her ears, pounding like a taunting drum, egging her on to finally do something, anything, to stop his tyrant rule over her. Scattered thoughts and pain whirled through her mind, straining her distraught body, forcing her lungs to heave for air. She grasped the sides of her head, her fingertips digging into her temples, *Enough!* She screamed in her head. Without thought, her hand unconsciously reached for the butcher knife stored neatly in Morty's wooden knife block, its handle clenched tight in her fist. It was now or never for her. If she backed down now, she would never be able to live with herself; she might as well give up completely and drive that very same knife into her own chest.

He repeated the trio of insulting words yelling them at top volume. With the knife in hand, she stormed into the dining area and pointed the knife at his face, "Shut up! Just shut up! You miserable old bastard! Shut! Up!"

He covered his face with his hands, attempting to protect it from the eight-inch blade. That's when she saw it, the fear in his eyes. He was afraid of her.

The pendulum of power swung ever so slightly in her favor, and she was its witness. 'NOW!' she told herself. She thrust the knife closer to his throat, her voice firm and low, "From now on you'll stop yelling at me. And from now on you won't hit me. And from now on no more booze and you'll sleep on the couch." She leaned in closer, narrowing her eyes at him, "And from now on, *I'm* in charge." But the power swung again. She saw the spark of darkness return to his eyes. He was laughing at her with his eyes. Her blood thundered in her ears, her mind whirled wildly, her face stung, and her heart broke. He was not going to change — ever. She had no choice but to get out.

But when she turned to leave, he grabbed her hand, pulling hard back towards himself. She pulled in her direction with all her strength, unwilling to let go of her eight-inch protective weapon. They struggled back and forth, neither one of them giving up the fight. Suddenly, for some unknown reason, her mind told her, *Let ... Go!* Instinctively, she opened her hand and released her grip. Morty's combatant pulling now released its energy, forcing the blade to slash deep across the width of his own neck, slicing both the jugular and artery in his throat. The immediate pain made his hand spasm open; the knife dropped in his lap. Out of instinct, she grabbed the knife, holding it above her head, ready to strike if need be. Volumes of pulsing blood gushed heavily from the gash, emptying the entire contents of his body. Eventually, it slowed to a trickle of vivid scarlet, throbbing from the lengthy wound, sending tiny wet waves down the side of his neck. The profuse sprays of blood trickled down the white glossy wall. Blood frothed wine-red from his mouth and nose. The tension of his pain faded from his face as he lost consciousness, rapidly followed by muscle spasms. She couldn't move, frozen by shock and fear created by the sight in front of her. She listened to his last escaping breath, gurgle bubbles in the dripping blood. Her arms slowly sank to her sides as she watched the pool of red grow larger and larger around his head and torso. The muscles in his body wilted as his life left him limp and pale.

She stood absolutely stunned, still scrutinizing him for signs of life, the knife still dangling from her hand. She focused on his chest measuring it against the line of his collar, waiting for it to move up and down with his breaths. The kitchen clock ticked away time as she waited for his chest to expand. It didn't move. In the time that it took to make herself react, his blood flowed slower until it became a dawdling trickle. The knife fell from her hand, clattering across the wooden floor. The sound and smear of blood it left behind, pulled her out of her horror-struck trance, bringing her back to the reality of what had happened.

She fell to her knees, kneeling in the blood that pooled on the floor beside him. She shook his shoulder, trying to rouse him, "Morty! Morty, you son of a bitch, wake up!" His body shook flaccidly and slumped into another lifeless position. She shoved him again, "Ass hole, screw you!" She was hoping to provoke him into reacting with another punch in her direction.

No fists came.

Neither did any movement.

Tears of horror filled her eyes. Overwhelming panic set in. She blinked hard to clear them away. Once more she shook his body to revive him, but his flesh felt flaccid to her touch. At that moment, it finally registered in her mind that her husband was dead. She pulled her hands away from him to wipe the tears from her face, only to see the bright red blood smeared upon her palms. Unconsciously, she wiped the blood away on the belly of her blouse, the wet red liquid sticking the material to her flesh. She didn't notice the soggy sensation on her skin. Her mind was still focused on the body before her. The weakness in her legs ached, forcing her to shift sideways, sitting down on the floor with a hard thud. Simultaneously, she screamed and wailed, allowing her emotions to explode and convulse from within her. She wept hard, her body shuddering with each breath exhaled until she had no more to give. Now with all emotions released, she curled into a fetal ball, her body and mind numb with the devastating shock - Morty was dead.

The clock ticked. Time passed as the blood thickened and dried dark crimson at the edges of the bloody puddle.

As she lay motionless on the cold floor, questions continued to creep through her mind. What actually happened? The violent scene ran over and over in her head. Was she the one who slashed him? Or was it an accident?

She thought about the seconds just before the knife severed Morty's throat.

No, she didn't do it.

She was only protecting herself — it was Morty who wouldn't let go. It was because of his controlling stubbornness that he slit his own throat. As far as she was concerned, it was an accident and not her fault. And that's exactly what she would tell the police when they came to examine the body.

She immediately sat up. "Oh, God! The police!" Total fear knotted her stomach tighter. Resting her head in her palms, she held it tightly in her hands, thinking hard for answers. There was no way she was calling the police. They would arrest her for sure, blaming her for his death. That realization quickly brought her out of her numbness.

She stood straight up from the floor. At that instant, Tess realized that she was in trouble, deep trouble. She would have to find a way out of this; she wasn't going to prison for killing Morty, even though it was in self-defence.

She looked at him, stuck to the floor by his own blood. Even in his death he still managed to annoy her by dirtying her floor. The very floor he demanded shine so brightly, he could see himself in it. The floor she spent hours washing and waxing on all fours, buffing to a mirror-like shine. She didn't do it to please him; she did it in order to avoid another round of name calling. Or worse, a beating for being lazy and disobedient. Painful memories of his daily abuse weld up inside, rushing to the surface, feeding her impulse.

She kicked his leg.

Half bent over the lifeless body; she screamed at his face, "Prick! I'm glad you're dead."

Inside, her heart turned cold towards the corpse that lay at her feet. After all those years of abuse, she suddenly deemed he deserved to die a more painful death. She kicked him again, his body jolting with each strike of her foot. All her pent-up frustrations and fears rushed out in a violent outburst. Vindictively she kicked his legs and torso repeatedly, ending her savagery by stomping on his hand — the very hand that beat her virtually every day for months. She kicked him until she had no strength left, each kick releasing a tiny bit of anger and resentment. Those intense emotions rushing through her, wave after wave. Exhausted, she staggered backward, running to the kitchen sink to throw up in its spotless stainless steel. She wretched until there was nothing left, her stomach aching from the violent thrusts. She leaned her elbows on the edge of the sink, gasping for air, praying the gagging would stop.

Splashing water on her face, she recovered from her fit and returned to stand above the corpse. Ashamed of her own violence, she covered her face and wept away her remaining torment.

Empty of emotion, she made peace with his dead body, forgiving him as well as herself. "You'll never hurt me again," she whispered through the slats in her fingers, "Never."

Her mind, psychologically confused and chaotic, decided from that moment onward, it was just a dead body and not her husband. It was her way of coping with her strained moral code. In her head a switch clicked, turning off that emotion, the emotion of caring.

This was a strategy she had taught herself many years before. Tess learned that if she felt nothing, it couldn't hurt her. As she had done during and after every beating from Morty, she turned her conscious mind off, removing herself from the physical and emotional pain he inflicted. She allowed that surreal state to flow into her mind, embracing the relieving numbness it brought.

It was just a dead body and not her fault.

She told herself it was time to stop being illogical and emotional; it was time to take care of matters. She sat herself down in her favorite kitchen chair, the tablecloth white and ironed wrinkleless the way Morty wanted it. What was she supposed to do now? She couldn't leave the body sprawled in the middle of her floor.

Her floor. That was the first time she called it her floor.

Morty always called it 'my floor' as though she never mattered when it came to the house they lived in. She squelched the urge to kick him just one more time and focussed her mind back to the problem at hand. What to do with the body? It was summer, with the days humid and hot as hell itself — not exactly the best weather for storing a dead body on the dining room floor. Then a familiar sound hummed in her ears. It was the sound of salvation.

Her freezer had come to save her.

The idea made her jump to her feet with relief, but then she slowly sat back down. Morty had made her buy the smaller freezer, not the full-size model as she had wanted. She realized he wouldn't fit. Maybe if she folded him, maybe he would fit that way? She would have to measure to be sure.

In the workshop, she took his measuring tape from its allotted spot on the pegboard and measured the interior space of the freezer. At five foot ten inches, even folded in half, he still wouldn't fit in it, not all in one piece. Her stomach churned at the thought of what she would have to do next.

The bigger question was — could she do it? Accidentally killing him was one thing, cutting him in half to fit in the freezer, that was another. But what choice did she have? If she didn't, she would go to prison. She took a deep breath and prepared herself mentally for her gruesome task ahead.

She searched through his garage for a tool to sever the body.

Jigsaw? Too small.

Circular saw? It was attached to its table, so useless to her.

Chain saw? The spray of fleshy bits would be messy, but faster yet than the circular saw. She checked for gasoline, but the tank was empty.

That's when she saw it from the corner of her eye, the Sawzall. And as she knew, the blade of the reciprocating saw would do the work, and so the name Sawzall implied, it would indeed, saw all.

Pulling it off its hooks, she smiled to herself. Tess recalled that she had scrimped together enough money during the year to buy him the saw for Christmas. She was proud of her diligence in saving the extra money and the excitement of giving him the gift that Christmas morning. Then her smile faded as the uglier memory crept in. She also remembered the not-so-pleasant part of that same morning. He accused her of selling her body like a common whore to pay for the expensive saw. The string of insults ended only after he had consumed his third triple rum eggnog which she thoughtfully served him one right after another.

Somehow the irony of her using that same saw to slice him in half, brought a slight smile to her face.

She gripped the heavy saw tight in her hands and entered the kitchen, being careful not to drop it on her clean floor. Flipping back the white table cloth, she placed it on the table, while she thought about her next move. Had he bled all the blood out of his body or would there be more? She decided on one of his painting tarps as a way to protect the wooden dining room floor from more damage. That too she found neatly folded and stored away in his garage, sitting right in its designated spot.

Back inside, she laid out the plastic tarp, scrunching up the one side directly next to the body. She tried to roll the corpse over onto the tarp, but to her shock, it had gone stiff. With the hours that had passed, rigor mortis had set in. And the corpse was heavier than she thought; its weight dead and inflexible. She finally managed to wedge a two by four she found in the garage, under the body and hoist it over onto the smoothed section of the tarp; the sticky coagulated blood stretched long gooey threads from body to floor. To her relief, its head faced downward. The vacant eyes wouldn't haunt her when she sawed it in two.

Using her foot, she unraveled the other half of the tarp over her floor, protecting it from any blood or flesh that might be spilled or splattered by the Sawzall. The corners in place, she plugged the Sawzall in at the wall. After tugging it to full length, she was startled to discover that the saw's cord wasn't long enough to reach the tarp area. Putting down the saw, she tried to pull the tarp closer. With her slender size and the dead weight of the body, she couldn't get it to budge. She would need an extension cord. In the garage, she went from cord to cord, examining their ends, only to learn that all the cords had two-prong receptacles with safety guards, instead of the required three prong ground for the Sawzall.

She would have to borrow one from a neighbor.

She looked down at her hands and clothes, both smeared with dried blood. She would have to make herself presentable before venturing out into the neighborhood.

As she showered, she was mesmerized by the red swirls in the draining water. The pattern flowed faster and faster, the more she scrubbed at the smears on her hands. The swirls blurred through her tears, crying was all she could do to release her heartache. When the water ran cold, she realized she had been in the shower so long, she had emptied all the hot water from the tank. She slowly climbed out of the tub and made her way to the bed, unresponsively drying herself off. In the distance, a dog barked, pulling Tess out of her numb trance, forcing her to move on with her plans.

Changing clothes, she developed the long list of lies she would tell the neighbors if they asked any questions. Lying came naturally to Tess these days.

As the wife of an abuser, quick lies became a defensive strategy. If someone questioned her about bruises or her timid behavior, and her lies didn't cover up the suspicion of abuse by Morty, she got hit twice as hard when Morty got home. In fresh, clean clothes, she felt presentable enough to go next door to Jenny's house. But only after she secured the house completely by locking the windows, as well as the doors. Only then did she realize that it was well into the night. Putting her bloody clothes into the washer, she read the kitchen clock — 3:22 AM — much too late to disturb Jenny, an action that would definitely bring on questions she didn't wish to answer.

She would have to wait until morning.

# Part 2

Tess, exhausted both mentally and physically, lay motionless on the bed. On her side of the bed. She couldn't bring herself to actually sleep in the middle of the bed, the luxury spot she thought she would use if Morty ever stayed away at night.

He never did. He always came home, even in the worst Canadian weather. Morty was there beside her each and every night. In one of his yelling fits, he told her that he didn't trust her enough to stay away even for one night. He accused her of finding some man to replace him in bed, performing depraved sex acts on him like the whore he knew she was. The accusation hurt just as much as his fist did. She had always been faithful to her husband — partly out of love, but mostly out of fear.

The LED digits from the alarm clock cast an eerie light throughout the room. Shadows darkened, while the walls shone shades of reflective scarlet. The night's events spun through her mind, rolling over the details of what had happened — and worse — what was yet to come. The perpetual knots in her stomach tightened as she planned the next step in freezing the dead body laying in the dining room.

Her eyes finally closed, but her thoughts kept repeating the lie she would tell in the morning. She hated the fact that she would have to lie to Jenny's face. Tess genuinely liked her. She was kind and always ready with a joke or two. In this case, she had no choice, but to betray Jenny's trust and lie to her. She had to borrow the extension from Jenny since she was the only one Morty allowed his wife to talk to in the entire neighborhood. In Morty's mind, she was a busy single mother, so there were no men around to steal Tess away from him.

Finally, darkness crept into her brain, allowing her to fall asleep. But it was not a restful slumber. The night replayed in her mind, pulling her back into her bloody reality. After only three hours of tossing and turning, her nightgown wet with sweat, it clung to her body. She lay staring at the ceiling waiting for time to slowly pass by. The clock read 7:36 AM when she finally gave in, getting out of the bed to start the day. She showered and dressed again, trying to waste more waiting time. That brought time to just after 8:30 AM, still too early in the morning to knock on Jenny's door. She then passed the time by briskly pacing the length of her bedroom, rehearsing her lie and any possible answers she needed to carry it off. At 9:00 AM, she checked her reflection in the mirror and prepared herself for the first task of what would be a long, trying day.

As she descended the stairs, she was affronted by the smell that had crept into the air, filling the lower half of the house — the body was beginning to decay in the humid August heat. Its pungency triggered the memory of the time she had mistakenly left a dish of raw hamburger in direct sunlight on her kitchen counter. It was that same stench of rotting meat that invaded her nostrils and churned at her stomach. Sometime during the night, the body had released its body fluids, the yellowish liquid oozed from the mouth into a pool on the tarp. This too, she added to the decaying stink. Tess swallowed hard, trying to keep her stomach down. She covered her mouth with her hand, gagging and choking back bitter bile. The sooner she got the body into the freezer, the better. She left for Jenny's straight away. Time and heat were not on her side.

Tess stood in front of Jenny's back door, her heart pounding hard in her chest. She had to appear calm, as though nothing out of the ordinary was happening. She took a deep breath before knocking four times. She stared at the door's peeling paint and waited — but no one came to answer the door. She opened the blue screen door, its squeaky rusted hinges added to her nervousness. She knocked again, this time a little harder than before.

Still no answer.

Panic set in, her heart drummed louder in her ears. Fear fired question after question through her frantic mind. What if Jenny wasn't home? What if she was gone for the day? Would someone else smell the body before Jenny got back? What if she couldn't get the cord from her? Where would Tess go next? She didn't know anyone else in the neighborhood. She was never allowed to associate with anyone besides Jenny. She mentally cursed Morty for his controlling ways, for turning her into a social recluse. Instantly, her hatred of Morty's domination turned her fear into fury. She rapped hard on the wooden door with her white clenched knuckles.

Jenny's voice yelled down the back hall, "Hold your horses — I'm a comin'!" She stopped to peek through her kitchen curtains, surprised to see her rarely seen next door neighbor. Jenny's door opened as wide as her smile, "Well, hello Tess. Long time no see. I haven't seen ya in awhile. How ya been keepin'?"

Tess swallowed hard, gathering her courage as well as controlling her nervousness, "Good. How's the little ones?" It was a tactic Morty had taught her — if you didn't want to say much about yourself, ask about them. People are always happy to talk about themselves.

"Oh growin' like bad weeds in good soil. You want to see them?" She pointed over her shoulder with her thumb at the mob of children sitting on the floor watching TV and running tiny cars around in circles.

"Oh no, don't bother them. They're playing so nicely." She peered over Jenny's shoulder pretending to care about them. "I was just wondering if I could borrow an extension cord. Turns out all of Morty's cords are two-pronged, and they got that annoying safety thing-a-ma-jig on them. He sent me over to see if you have one that has three prongs." To Tess's way of thinking, if Jenny thought Morty sent her, it meant Jenny believed Morty was still alive and not a dead corpse lying on her dining room floor.

"Oh, yah sure, come with me, I got a twenty-four-footer in the garage." Over her shoulder, she yelled at the kids, "Billy, you watch the little ones. I'm going out to the garage for a minute." In the background, they heard a muffled what-e-ver. Meaning at thirteen, he heard his mom, and he would do as he was told — but he wouldn't like it, not one little bit. Jenny slipped past Tess and headed for her detached garage, "Tess, don't mind me asking, but what's Morty need with an extension cord? Ain't he in a wheelchair?"

"It's for his Sawzall. And actually, he's been doing real well lately. The physiotherapy has done wonders. He's decided that maybe if he took his time and was careful, he could put in that wall nook I've been wanting. I'll finally be able to put my cookbooks away." Another lie to remember.

Inside the half-light of the garage, Jenny handed it over, carefully slipping the strands over her neighbor's arm, "There ya are. Well, that's nice to hear he's doing so good." She pushed out a sigh, "Hell of a thing he's gone through."

"M-o-o-o-m, the twins are fighting again, and they're not listenin' to me!" Billy's voice bellowed from the back door.

Her eyes rolled back in her head, "Christ almighty. Excuse me for a minute, would ya?" Tess politely nodded she understood. Jenny yelled over Tess's head, "Tell them to smarten up, or I'll come in there and whack 'em one." The door slammed as he repeated Jenny's commands. She turned her attention back to Tess, "Sorry about that. They just get so bored over summer break with nothing to do except drive each other ... and me ... crazy."

She shrugged, "Kids." Tess draped the loose coils of yellow cord over her shoulder, "Morty's working in the living room, so if you hear any loud sawing, I'll apologize now. Morty should only need this for two, maybe three hours' tops. I'll bring it right back after that."

"Don't worry about the sound. We're going out for the day anyway. And just leave it hanging on the back door knob, and I'll take it in when I get the chance." She wiped tiny beads of sweat from her forehead. "I'm taking the pack of banshees to the park so they can bust loose without bustin' up my house. Then we're heading to the river for a picnic. The breeze is cool there this time of day.' She pinched her blouse and shook out her body heat, "Weatherman says it's goin' up to 33°C along with a humidex of damned near 41°C." The door opened again, but before Billy could whine, she held up a finger halting him to stop. "We most likely wouldn't be back until at least suppertime."

In her head, Tess gave a sigh of relief. That was the one concern she had. If she made too much noise, someone might get suspicious and start asking questions

— questions she didn't want to answer. But it was the other half of Jenny's conversation that concerned Tess. With the temperatures, Jenny predicted, in no time at all, the body would soon smell worse than this morning.

"M-o-o-o-m! They're at it again!" Billy hollered out the squeaking screen door.

Jenny disappointedly shook her head, "Looks like I got to go and stop world war three. Like I said, hang it on the doorknob when he's done." She turned to walk away then stopped for a brief moment, "And Tess, don't be such a stranger. If you can stand the kids, come over for a cup of tea. I'm here most mornings, and frankly, it would be nice to talk to an adult once and awhile. Okay?"

The thoughtfulness of those words hit Tess's heart hard. Jenny honestly liked her. Someone wanted her company. Morty was wrong. People did like her. To her, the simple gesture was completely overwhelming. She forced herself to inhale deeply through her nose, holding back her emotions. If she let go of them now, she would never be able to recover enough to hide the truth from Jenny. Instead of answering, she simply nodded her head that she would. And oddly enough, that wasn't a lie. With Morty's controlling self out of her life, she could not only visit for tea but whenever she wanted.

The screen door slammed behind Jenny, and her yelling began. To Tess that was a wonderful sound. It meant she was busy with her kids and wouldn't be over to check up on her doings. Tiny beads of sweat formed on her upper lip, reminding her that the longer she took, the more the body would smell. Time was of the essence. If the smell reached the rest of the world, she would be found out for sure. She was determined to conceal the body.

She was not going to prison.

The opening of her own front door churned her stomach. Between the smell and the flies that hovered over the body, she immediately dropped the extension cord to cover her nose and mouth. She ran to the window and was about to open it, then quickly realized that fresh air wasn't a possibility just yet. If she opened the window, the smell would indeed escape, but it might also attract unwanted attention. She would have to endure the smell until the body was in the freezer. And only then would she open two windows, just a thin crack, allowing the stench to seep out slowly as to not alert those outside her house. It was best that she got the sawing over with and the halves in the freezer. That would stop the odor altogether.

She set her mind to the task. She had determined that turning up the edges of the tarp would stop any spray from ruining her floor. Carefully, she positioned two kitchen chairs on either side of the plastic sheet, attaching the corners to the tall back spindles with duct tape. With the plastic wall in place, she stopped for a moment, her heart racing in her chest. It was the moment she had been dreading. In her head, she once again convinced herself that she could do it — would have to do it — to save herself from prison.

Survival, she reminded herself, was the only option she had. She convinced her mind it was only a body and nothing more. Like a dead animal that needed to be disposed of and quickly before rot developed, ruining her health and her beautiful wood floor. She swatted away the fly that buzzed about her head and turned her focus to the Sawzall lying beside the body.

She plugged the cord into the saw, then into the wall. Picking it up, she tested it ensuring it was indeed in working order. To settle her nerves, she slowly inhaled deeply. She held her breath and pulled the trigger, the loud rattle of the metal blade startled her so much, she let it go, letting it fall to the floor with a thud. Automatically, she knelt to examine the damage in the narrow shiny planks. To her relief, the tarp stopped the wood from being gouged. She pulled the trigger of the Sawzall again, studying its juddering metal blade. Soon her ears and nerves became accustomed to the clattering sound and vibrations of the weapon. It's only a corpse, she mentally reminded herself, while steadying her shaking hands. Taking a deeper breath, she held it and aimed the blade at his torso, her hands trembling harder than the saw itself shook. She couldn't do it. Her finger released the trigger. The rattling noise stopped. The saw in her hand sank to her side. She couldn't do it. Her heart broke inside her chest.

The reality was, it was not just a dead body.

It was Morty — and her husband was dead.

Grief and self-torment overwhelmed her. She burst into heart-wrenching sobs, releasing the pain that had been building inside her. The pain that she had been suppressing deep into her soul and psyche, rushed out all at once. She fell to her knees, shuttering with the release of each sob. How could she do it? Cut her husband in two and freeze him. He wasn't an animal that needed disposing of — he was a human being, not an unforgotten creature with no past life or possible future. He was the man she met and fell in love with so many years ago. He was the man who loved her when no one else did. The man who taught her how to structure her life and control her emotions, making her the person she was today — a survivor. When a fly flew into her cheek, the tiny sting changed her perspective.

Control and Survive were the two words that stuck in her head. Control, she needed to get herself under control and do what needed to be done to survive. He'd approve of that; she convinced herself. In her mind, she believed that in some absurd manner, Morty would appreciate her thinking of him as just a body, disconnecting herself from what he called her female emotions. It was the same methodology he lived by when he was alive.

The sound of Jenny's car doors slamming, pulled Tess out of her state of remorse, reminding her that the outside world was still a threat. She wiped away her tears and calmed her nerves. She pulled the Sawzall into her lap and told herself this is what he would have wanted her to do. Deep in the darkness of her mind, she let her ethics go, setting her thoughts to betraying her own moral code. With saw in hand, she took the time to decide where she should bisect the body. Rummaging through memories of her high school health class, especially the skeleton that hung in its corner, she determined that under the ribcage and above the belly button, would be the best cut line. She would miss all the larger bones, except the spine, making cutting less difficult and more importantly, the hideous task being finished faster.

She braced her butt against her heels and pulled the trigger. The Sawzall blade pulsated back and forth, rattling loudly through the house. She held the blade's edge, touching the body but the teeth caught in the cloth of Morty shirt, strangling the saw to a stop. She slowly released the trigger and leaned the saw against his body. Once the material was untangled, she pulled back the cotton shirt to expose the reddish flesh of the torso's back. Starting the saw, she aimed the blade in the direction she wanted to cut. She couldn't bring herself to watch, so she closed her eyes tight. She felt it tug at the tissue as she pressed it onto the muscle. She pushed harder into the flesh, hoping to speed up the process. But doing so, nearly pulled the saw from her hands, forcing her to open her eyes, so she didn't injure herself.

What she witnessed startled her. Bits of flesh had flown up from the Sawzall blade and landed on her arms and hands. The tiny chunks of pink made her skin crawl; panic overcame her. She dropped the saw and shrieked while she frantically danced about, wiping off the flecks of flesh. Finally, all the bits she could see were wiped clean. Her heart hammered in her chest, her light-headed mind reminding her that it was best that she remain calm and returned to the bisecting. Bright yellow rubber gloves from the kitchen drawer covered her hands and forearms as she pulled the trigger, continuing her work. This time she watched what the saw was cutting. The blade slowly sank in further, gnawing at the side of Morty's thick muscle. But the gloves interfered with the trigger, so reluctantly, she abandoned them to the floor.

Minutes seemed like hours as she wriggled the blade, cutting into the firmed flesh. She disconnected her mind and conscience as to what she was actually doing with the saw. It was the only way she could continue with the gruesome work. Eventually, she became accustomed to the bits of tissue that flew from the body, merely brushing them off her face or arms when she released the trigger to change sawing positions. It was the flies that bothered her most. Their relentless attacks on her face and forearms. Those too she overlooked, concentrating on where she was aiming the blade.

Her psyche remained in that detached mindset until she reached the abdomenal cavity. Over time, Morty's stomach had swollen with gas, and when she pierced it with the blade, all the accumulated gasses escaped through the incision. The body deflated slightly with a soft inaudible rush of air. It was the intensity of that putrid air, which pulled her out of her deadened trance and back into reality. The sudden sight of the mangled body and her bloody hands; forced her to face the truth of her inhuman act. Her insides lurched, and Tess twisted away from the corpse, throwing up on her wooden floor. Even after she had emptied her stomach, she continued to dry heave and shake uncontrollably. Sweat wept from every pore as the bile burned it way out her throat. Her breathing became erratic, turning deep breaths to gasps, followed by dizziness. Knowing she would pass out, she slowed both her breathing and her heart rate by concentrating on the sound of the freezer running in the garage. Oddly, the steady tranquil hum soothed her.

Finally bringing herself under control, she took the time to switch off her ethics, numbing her mind completely so that she could return to her grisly undertaking. At last, the blade had sliced through the flesh, leaving only the task of severing the spine, releasing the upper body from the lower. Inhaling a deep, purposeful breath, she braced herself against her heels, shoving down hard on the Sawzall. It shuttered with the hardness of the bone, bouncing slightly in her hands. Determined to finish, she clenched the saw firmly, stabilizing the blade against the bone and pressed down harder, leaning her whole body weight behind the tool's square handle. Slowly the teeth of the blade gnawed away bits of bloody white. Her arms ached at the strain of the saw's weight and the tension to hold it straight. To cope with the pain in her wrists, she narrowed her eyes and began to concentrate on the blade itself. Her breathing went shallow; her hands burned with the hefty amount of exertion she was placing on the saw. If it took any longer, she was sure she would lose her grip. Abruptly the blade severed through the last bit of bone, removing the counter support of the saw blade. With the pressure of her weight pushing downward, she collapsed hard on top of the still running saw and mangled flesh. She automatically released the trigger and frantically shoved herself off the body. She was covered in bits of white bone and pink flesh; her hands smeared bloody red. The sight of it all, startled her, pulling her out of her numb trance. Without thinking, she scooted away backward until her ass slammed against the wall. Tears filled her eyes and her body drooped with her breakdown. She sobbed uncontrollably, her face resting in her bloody hands. Time passed. Her crying eased. Tess wiped her cheeks removing the wet tears along with dried crumbs of flesh.

Tired and unresponsive inside, she stayed leaning against the wall staring at the corpse before her, mangled and halved. She knew what she needed to do next, but her nerves weren't willing to move her own body. She leaned her head back and closed her eyes to rest before attempting the next stage of her undertaking. She felt her body slowly slide into a deep state of shock. Her body and mind were shutting her down. Tess drifted out of consciousness. A black void replaced her thoughts of blood, tissue, and bone.

It was the booming crash of thunder that woke her. At once her eyes popped open, blood rushed through her ears. Still unsure of what the noise truly was, she immediately jumped to her feet and searched from window to window. Outside, the hot, humid weather had broken into a full-blown summer storm. The savage winds whipped at the trees, while torrential rains pulverized vehicles and plants alike. Recognizing that it was only a storm, her heart stopped pounding, slowing its pace with the relief. No one was outside banging on her door, wanting to come in for her — she was safe for now. Nevertheless, it was a reminder that it was essential the body was placed in the freezer and that she complete the cleanup before someone did come to her door.

As she had planned that morning, she placed the faded rug from the front hall beside the lower half and pulled that half onto it. Using the mat's fringed corners, she tugged it across the room, down the three steps into the garage, stopping in front of the freezer. In her head, she prayed that it would fit and that she wouldn't have to use the saw again.

She leaned over the body and lifted the freezer lid. It was filled to the brim with frozen packets of cheap ground meat and loaves of white bread. Those she removed, tossing into a pile on the floor. She would store what she could in the refrigerator's freezer compartment. The rest would have to be thrown out. After she had removed the meat packets and bread, all that was left was a blue plastic tub. Opening the lid, her heart sank at the sight of its contents.

Peas.

Fifty single serving packages of frozen peas.

She detested peas.

They were for Morty's mashed potatoes. For some peculiar reason, Morty wouldn't eat mashed potatoes without peas mashed in first. A lesson she learned by fists and threats of death if she dared to serve him potatoes that weren't tinted green.

Tess loathed peas.

"Bastard!" Infuriated by the sight of the bags, she grabbed one after the other, heaving them across the room, some splitting on impact, scattering tiny green balls in all directions. Fury pumped adrenaline through her veins, its energy giving her the muscular power to pick up the body's half and jam it down deep in the bottom of the freezer. She slammed the lid and shrieked at it — at him, "Rotten bastard!"

Angrily, she dragged the empty rug back into the dining room. She positioned it beside the tarp, slapping it into place. Next, she yanked the upper torso onto its center. "Bastard!" she screamed in his face, his eyes smoky and frozen into a haunting stare. Sadistically, she hauled it into the garage, Morty's head thumping down each wooden step. In front of the freezer, she stopped, propping up the lid, grunting hard as she lifted the upper half, flipping it into the freezer's opening.

It didn't fit.

The shoulders were too wide.

She tugged and shoved at it, trying to make it slide all the way down inside. It didn't budge. That infuriated her even further. Impulsively, she climbed up and stood on top of the body. With fists clenched by her side, she stomped on the torso, attempting to force it into the confines of the white box. It only budged an inch or two before stopping, wedged and unwilling. Its resistance fully enraged her. Even in death, Morty was still a nuisance. Losing all self-control, she completely flipped out. She jumped up and down using both feet, hammering it down inch by inch until it was below the lip of the freezer's rim. She jumped down onto the garage floor and spun around, furiously slamming the lid hard, angrily turning the key, locking the body inside. She tugged the lid upward to make sure it was indeed locked up for safe keeping. Safely locked away from the outside world. She stood staring at the large white rectangle, her mind telling her that he was finally in his frozen tomb — out of her dining room and out of her life.

Time passed slowly, the tension easing from her muscles and her heart rate slowing its pace. A smile slipped across her lips. It gradually turned into a grin that turned into a soft laugh. The longer she stared, the louder her laugh grew. She found herself laughing hysterically with tears rolling down her face. It was over. He was tucked away safe and sound where no one would find him. She was finally free. Free of the fear that someone would find the corpse and put her in prison for the rest of her life.

But best of all — she was free of him.

She stepped back, squishing peas under her feet. The sensation reminded her of the bits of flesh she had wiped off her hands and arms. Specks of pink flesh still adhered to her white wall. That image pushed her onwards, on to the last part of the job, cleaning up the mess still waiting in her dining room. Along with the rug at her feet, she would need to clean the blood and tissue still clinging to her floor and wall. She still hadn't decided what to do with the tarp. Should she clean it and store it back in the garage or dispose of it in the trash?

But first, she wanted to rest, just for a moment or two. The tugging and lifting of the heavy dead body were exhausting work for her tiny frame. Her back muscles ached, and her hands burned with the stress of pulling the weight by the corners of the mat. She went back inside to sit in her kitchen chair. Feeling weak and slightly light headed, she decided on some earl grey tea for calming and lemon cookies for some sugar-induced energy. After that, she would clean up her house.

Mechanically, she washed the blood from her wrists and hands, leaving the red smeared bar of soap in the dish by the taps. As the kettle boiled, she took out a bag of cedar chips, a jug of bleach and a bucket. She filled the red bucket half-full with warm water, a large glug of bleach and a hand full of wood chips. Hot water would stain the floor, as would cold water. It was a formula she had learned from the many bloody noses Morty had inflicted on her. The mop she retrieved from the closet along with her bag of white cotton rags. The kettle whistled it was ready for her. She sat and sipped her tea while she decided how to go about cleaning up the blood and flesh. With her mind disconnected and numb, her senses shut down as well, the cookies tasted flat and the dark tea weak.

The bits of tissue she would first pick off and then scrub the residue they left behind. As for the blood, nothing but repeated washings would remove it. Most of it was now either dried or a thick coagulated syrup. But what worried her most were the cracks in between the floor boards. She was sure the blood had seeped in the seams, and not even her favorite cleaning toothbrush would be able to get it all out. Tess hoped the bleach would remove any stain without damaging her floor. The floor she had worked so hard on, making it shine mirror clean.

Finishing the last of the five cookies, she set her mind on the work ahead.

She started with the sprays and smudges on the walls. She washed the drips, wiping the smears over and over again until all of it was gone. She examined the wall closely. The blood had left faint stains in the paint - she would have to repaint that section of the wall, covering them up permanently. Emptying and refilling her bucket, she turned her attention to the floor. However, she had to deal with the tarp first, getting its bulk out of her way.

Common sense told her that if she left the bits of tissue on the tarp in the summer's heat, it would quickly smell of rotten meat. Donning her yellow rubber gloves, she rolled the tarp into a ball. She carefully carried the tarp up to her bathroom where she placed it directly into the bathtub. She picked off the chunks, stuffing them into the toilet bowl and once finished, she flushed them away forever.

From the tarp, she wiped away as much blood and fleshy sludge as she could with rags. She ran a trickle from the shower head, providing an ample amount of clear water for rinsing, yet not enough to splash more blood onto her tiles. After that washing, she doused it with bleach and rinsed it lightly. Cleaning of the entire house took priority over anything else, so she carefully folded and squished it, until it was small enough to fit into a garbage bag. Then she added another garbage bag on top, creating a second barrier against any smell that may develop later on. She had decided earlier to store the tarp in the garage until she could figure out what to do with it. She placed it between the freezer and Morty's work bench.

Back in the kitchen she rinsed and washed the pail of rags with hot water and bleach. She was grateful for the cedar chips that floated in her bleach water, their scent mellowing the harsh fumes of the sodium hypochlorite.

With the tarp out of the way, she concentrated on the dining room itself. She placed the Sawzall in the kitchen sink and rinsed away the blood from the blade, casing and handle. Tess picked out the strings of tissue that were caught in the blade's teeth, these she dropped into a white pail. She gently wrapped the cord around the Sawzall and hung it back on its hook in the garage, exactly the way it was when she found it. Jenny's extension cord she wiped by pulling it through a wet soapy cloth, removing the blood which she had accidently dragged it through while sawing. Happy with her final rinse, she hung it on the back of a kitchen chair, waiting to be returned later. But before she could do that, the wooden floor of the living room needed to be cleaned; it took priority over all else.

As before, she started the actual washing by first picking off any fleshy bits and bone chips, placing them in the white pail. She studied the mop. Then the bloody floor and returned it back to the closet. Her little string mop was no match for the volume of blood spilled across her floor. On her hands and knees, she scrubbed at the puddle of blood. The blood had dried in some spots, while in others, it had simply thickened, giving it the texture of gluey wax. After countless washings and draining of the pail for clean water, the majority of the muck was removed from the wooden surface. And after a thorough scrubbing using her favorite toothbrush, no more bodily remnants were visible. A final rinse with bleach to ensure nothing was left behind to discolor later. To be completely sure, she took a fresh wet cloth and wiped over the entire surface. Nothing came up; the rag stayed pure white. However, to her disappointment, at a closer inspection, she noticed that the blood had not only stained the wood slightly, but it had also removed the wax finish, a shiny surface that had taken her months to perfect. Despite that disappointment, she didn't linger long on the floor; it was the fumes that stung her eyes that forced her forward.

Fresh air was needed and fast. Between the bleach, cedar chips and decaying flesh, it was difficult to take in a deep breath without it turning her stomach. Carefully peeking through the curtains, she was pleased to see that due to the thunder storm no one was outside. At long last, it was safe for her to open a window or two, if only a crack. A cross-draft would make quick work of airing-out the stench. She jammed a soup can in the kitchen window and propped up the living room's window with Morty's cane. The sweet smell of rain-drenched air swept through the rooms, pulling the yellow gingham kitchen curtain against the screen. Tess inhaled deep, enjoying the freshness as well as the oxygen it brought.

She opened the door leading to the garage, light from the kitchen fell on the freezer, its white shining brighter then Tess had ever seen before. For a brief moment, Tess panicked — was Morty trying to tell her something from beyond the metal walls, his spirit threatening her.

She chuckled at the silliness of that thought. Although it pained her, she knew he was dead, and he could no longer hurt her. She quietly went about cleaning up the garage. First, she double bagged the rug and put it in the big green trash can. With meticulous attention, she wiped down the freezers white enamel coating. Again, the toothbrush reached into crevasses the cloth couldn't clean. Satisfied with its gleam, she tackled the wooden steps. After several washings and an absolute full-strength bleaching, red stains remained in the wood's grain. She smiled to herself, she had always wanted to stain and wax the steps, but Morty would never let her. It was his garage, and no woman was going to pretty it up, not as long as he was alive. She assumed that the tiny can of mahogany wood stain would cloak the red streaks nicely. That she would do tomorrow after the steps were completely dry.

Inside the smell was dissipating, but not fast enough for Tess's liking. She rummaged through her closet finding the little hidden box of perfumed candles. Candles she secretly used during her baths, when Morty was at work. She chose the lavender scented pink ones and lit them in the living room, dining room and another in the kitchen. The draft from the windows gaps wafted their sweet fragrance throughout the house. Their bouquet helped Tess relax slightly, her neck loosening its held tension.

All that was left to do was to wash the rags, mop and her bloody clothing. These she added to the tiny pile of clothing from the night before and ran the entire load through two warm washings. Finally, with all evidence out of sight, she opened the windows fully, allowing the maximum fresh air in, and foul air out. Forty minutes later and to her happiness, the majority of the cotton material came clean. Unfortunately, still to remain stained and grimy were the white rags, these she soaked in hydrogen peroxide for twenty more minutes, then ran them through a load of scalding hot water. The result — a clean, stain free wash being placed in the dryer before she left to return Jenny's extension cord.

Outside Jenny's house, she quickly and quietly hung the yellow cord on the door knob as Jenny had instructed and immediately returned home. With all the tasks completed, the heavy weight of Morty's death slowly lifted from Tess's body. She could finally slow down. She set her body to rest by stretching out on the long couch, her arm covering her eyes from the dim light that poured in the windows. To her relief, the sweetness of the candles and the fresh air had replaced the stomach-churning stench. Even the cedar chip scent was barely detectable through the lavender's sweetness.

The whole ordeal had been so exhausting, that if she carried on any further, she would no doubt collapse from the heat and fatigue. She needed a nap, even if it was just a short siesta to revive her fading energy. Feeling that all that could be done, was done, she let herself relax and quickly slip into sleep. Darkness filled her mind, emptying it completely and for the first time in over 24 hours, it also relaxed and rested along with her physical body.

But her siesta didn't last long.

She woke abruptly by the hammering of fists on her front door. Her eyes popped open; she sat up stiff and straight. Her heart raced in her chest. Who was at her door and why did they want inside? Had her secret been found out so quickly? But who would know? It wasn't as though Morty would be missed by anyone. It was Tuesday, so he wasn't due for physiotherapy for another two days. And after all, it was Morty who had eliminated the outside world from his life, so consequently, the outside world wouldn't miss him either.

But her question still remained — who was at her door and why?

Both out of fear and pure curiosity, she tiptoed through the living room, to peek through the open window.

She gasped at the sight. It was an OPP officer, and he was about to knock on her door again. She slipped down and sat on the floor, leaning against the wall to hide herself from the police officer.

But it was too late. Being tall, the officer leaned over the railing and bellowed an order through the window's gap, "I know you're there. Just open up, and there won't be any problems."

Tess slowly got to her feet, her answer timid to the point of being apologetic, "Yes officer, I'll be right there." She quickly scanned the rooms. Even to her conscious eyes, there was nothing to reveal that a murder had been committed there. Inhaling deep, she unlocked the door to let him in. But by then there were two officers and both were overwhelmingly mammoth in comparison to her petite frame. Looking up at their faces, she was sure she was going to prison after all. Overpowering fear of what was about to happen rushed blood straight to her head. Suddenly she felt extremely light-headed. Tiny stars danced in Tess's mind, and within seconds, her legs gave way as she fainted, her body hitting the floor with a bony *Thunk*. This left the OPP Officers standing above her, completely baffled by the strange woman's odd behavior.

# Part 3

Down on one knee, Officer Adams lightly slapped Tess's pale cheek, trying to revive her, "Ma'am? Ma'am? Are you okay, Ma'am?"

Slowly, her eyes fluttered open, only to be peering directly into the cop's face. Panic leaped into her throat, constricting her vocal cords. Unable to speak out of fear, she nodded slightly.

"Holy jeepers, you scared us there." He offered his hand, "Let's get you off the floor and into something softer, like a chair." He noted, she was light as a feather, slim and delicate, like a china doll.

Controlling her nervousness, she took his hand, pulling herself to her feet. "Thank you, Sir."

He tipped the brim of his blue-black hat in her direction, "Sergeant Adams, Ma'am. But please, call me Kevin. Everyone else does. And this is Constable Doucette." His partner nodded politely. "Ma'am, are you sure you're all right?" He bent forward lowering his head, looking directly into her graceful face. "You're awfully pale."

His close scrutiny made her anxious, her mind raced for an answer and quickly came up with a logical one, "It's the heat. Looks like it's finally got to me."

Doucette tugged on the collar of his blue-black uniform, pumping in cooler air, "I hear ya there." Over her shoulder, his superior shot him a look that told him he had once again, said something out of line. With the message received, he turned his attention back to the fragile woman standing before him. Kevin couldn't help but notice her eyes. Their intense blue stood out against her fair skin and honey hair. He squashed his attraction to her simple beauty, holding back the urge to touch her silky cheek with the back of his finger. Instead, being the police officer he was, he turned his attention back to the serious situation at hand, "Do you need some water, maybe?"

From across the room, Tess's eyes zeroed in on the white bar of soap sitting by the kitchen sink. Controlling her voice not to reflect her feelings of alarm, she calmly replied, "Oh no, I'm fine now. With the heat last night, I didn't sleep real well. I guess it's finally caught up with me." She wiped the beads of sweat off her upper lip. Sweat that was more from anxiety, than the heat and humidity. "I need to rest, that's all."

The three of them stood silent for a moment, creating an awkward strain between them. It was the Sergeant who broke the unknown friction, "Ma'am, we're wondering if you've seen the little boy from next door. Derek ... one of the twins. He's been missing for over three hours."

Silently, she released her held breath. That's why they were there; to find missing Derek. Not to arrest her. "No, I can't say that I have. I mean, I did see him earlier today at Jenny's, but he was in the house with the others."

The sergeant pulled out his notebook and pen, "About what time was it that you say you saw him last?"

Tess tapped her lip with her finger, pretending it helped her think. She knew the time. She had checked the clock just before heading over to Jenny's. "Let see, I think it must have been a little after 9:00 'cause I went over after listening to the news."

He tried to ignore those pink and plentiful lips by looking in his little black book, scribbling down the details. He slipped it back in his shirt pocket, “Do you mind if we look around? To make sure he ain’t in here.”

Panic sped through her head. Dancing images of the bloody soap bar, the red smeared tarp, the bloody rug and the body in the freezer, whirled together. A terrifying image that was, in a flash, replaced by her being hauled away to prison in handcuffs. What should she do? She worried if she said no, she would look guilty. If she said yes, she might be found out. But before she could answer, they started their search throughout her house. With them busy elsewhere, she hurried to the kitchen, slipping the bar of soap into the sink and ran the water. She wiggled her fingers in the stream of water, pretending to check for coldness. While doing so, she splashed water over the bar of soap, rinsing off the red smears. Relief came as the last streak of red swirled down the drain, leaving the bar completely white. She took a glass from the cupboard, filling it with cool tap water. From the edge of her sight, she watched the two officers walk about, peeking into closets and under tables, any place a four-year-old would hide. She drank from the glass, nearly choking when the younger officer opened the door leading to the garage. Tess drank faster, swallowing harder than before to cover up her nervousness. She casually made her way to the same doorway, sipping water as she went.

Through the open door, she watched as the cop leaned over the freezer to peer behind it. And when he pulled up the lid only to find it locked, she thought her heart would explode through the top of her head. Terror-stricken, she couldn't watch anymore, she headed back to the kitchen for a refill, desperately trying to conceal her reaction. She poured herself another glass of water, her hands shaking uncontrollably. But her curiosity got the better of her, and she returned to the garage doorway. She arrived just in time to witness the young officer begin to move items about the garage. Tess gulped her water, mostly to stop herself from screaming when he picked up the garbage bag containing the bloody tarp.

He peeked and poked about until he was satisfied that the garage wasn't hiding a four-year-old runaway.

But when the Sergeant headed for the stairs, Tess stopped him. Peering over the rim of the glass, her blue eyes flashed at him, "Officer, I don't think you need to check up there. I've been home all day, and I haven't seen hide nor hair of the boy." She stuck the glass back in her mouth and turned the other way to hide her guilty lying face.

He swallowed down the sexual urge her beautiful blue eyes raised inside him, reminding himself to behave as an Officer should. He shrugged his shoulders at her request and let it go. "Aylmer! You find anything?"

Doucette closed the garage door behind him, "Nothing."

"Well, sorry to have bothered you. We'll be looking somewhere else now. And Ma'am, if you do happen to see Derek, please call us or better yet, bring the boy home to his mother."

She nodded her head with concern, "I sure will. Poor Jenny. She must be worried out of her mind."

"That she is. Well, you have a pleasant evenin' Ma'am. Hope you get some better sleep tonight." He was almost out the door, when he turned around, his face serious, "Oh, one more question. What were you doing when you were next door?"

The question startled her. Why did he ask that particular question? And what was she to answer — the truth that would invite more unwanted questions. Or lie and risk being found out later? She told the truth — at least the truth as she believed it to be. "I went next door to borrow an extension cord from Jenny." She was plain to the point, refraining from adding the other details of her lie to Jenny, such as Morty and the Sawzall.

"Fine. Thanks for your co-operation. Again, let us know straight away if you see him." He nodded his goodbye and left out the door.

"Shall do. Good night, Officers." The sound of the door closing behind him was the sweetest sound Tess had ever heard. It was over. She flopped down on her kitchen chair and let out an enormous sigh, relaxing her knotted stomach muscles.

She was still free.

Then she started to chuckle at what had actually happened not more than ten minutes before. An OPP Constable had leaned on top of a dead body locked in her freezer and didn't even know it. Either she was lucky, or he was stupid. But she knew better — he wasn't stupid. If she hadn't locked the lid and he yanked on it like he did, she would have been in prison no time flat.

That night, Tess Logan had been truly lucky.

Slowly, it sank in how lucky she had truly been. And how close she had come to going to prison. She also realized it would not be for killing Morty, but for cutting his body in half. She had mutilated another human being, and for that, she would be imprisoned for a long-long time. It became very clear to Tess that she had to get rid of the body and all other evidence. She closed her eyes while she figured out what to do next. After another three glasses of cold water and much foot jiggling, she formed her plan.

The body would stay where it was, safely locked in the freezer out of sight. The disposal of it would take a great deal of planning and time. She would leave the corpse to last, concentrating on the other items first.

The tarp she would burn tomorrow. She would cut it into strips and burn each one separately along with newspaper and cereal boxes. That way, there would be no chance of it smothering itself, going out, leaving any bits of proof.

The rug, she would put in Thursday's garbage collection. Then she changed her mind. It would be too easy for the bag to rip open, exposing the large blood-soaked rug to Hank, her garbage man. What was she to do? As she thought, she brushed away one of the last remaining flies. "Go away you little pest. Before I smash you to pieces," she cursed the insect.

The words 'little' and 'pieces' formed her next strategy. A slight grin slipped across her lips as the plan took shape in her head.

From her teenage years, she recalled her mother getting rid of an unwanted desk. Using her jigsaw, she cut it into small pieces that would fit in her purse. The pieces were neatly stacked by the back door, waiting to be disposed of. Each time she left the house, she would take several pieces with her, dropping them individually into garbage cans throughout the community. A piece at the grocery store. Or perhaps one in the bank's garbage can and then maybe another at the community park. Eventually, all the pieces disappeared, and no one ever connected her mother to the bits of wood sprinkled about town.

That was her answer.

In the morning, she would chop the rug into sandwich sized pieces and dispose of them like her mother did the desk. Her little blue kitchen baggies would serve nicely as their carrying case to the multitude of local garbage cans. Happy with her plans, she headed upstairs to bed. Sleep was what she needed more than anything else. Food and drink could wait until morning.

Flashing lights shot through her bedroom window, reminding her that little Derek was still missing. It didn't surprise her that he had run away. After all, it wasn't the first time he had done it, and she was sure it wouldn't be the last.

She changed into her freshly cleaned nightgown and climbed on top of her covers. Her nightie clung to her body with the heat and humidity. Within ten minutes, she removed her nightie, letting it fall to the floor. Lying naked on her bed, she relished the cooling breeze from the open window that danced gently across her sweaty skin. As delightful as it was, the sensation also felt — unnatural. Never before had she been able to lay about naked. Not without Morty hassling her for sex she didn't want. Or worse, him telling her that she should cover up because she was ugly and no one wanted to see her naked, disgusting body.

At first, she pulled the bedspread over herself, but after some thought, she flung them off with a resentful grunt. No, she didn't have to cover herself up. He wasn't there to control her and she could do whatever she wanted to. Her defiance made the breeze feel even cooler than before. To accentuate her rebellion, she opened her legs and arms spread eagle, a position she hadn't enjoyed since childhood — more so, since Morty came into her life. A position such as that would have brought on one of his lovemaking sessions. An act that mostly consisted of him mounting her only long enough to release his seed and then roll over to fall asleep. Her satisfaction was no concern of his, a fact she had come to believe and accept. To Tess, sex was merely her wifely duty.

The voices outside drew her to the window. Below, she watched Jenny pace beside the flashing cruiser. Dwayne, Derek's twin brother, stood in the screen door, his little face watching for his other half. Officer Adams talked to her as she walked back and forth, "He's fine. Aylmer said the woman found him swimming by the bridge." He let out a soft chuckle, "Apparently, he was buck naked, cannon-balling off the rocks."

In the darkness of her bedroom, Tess stood in the open window, pulling the curtain up to cover her naked breasts and body as she listened to the commotion below.

"God damned, stupid child!" Jenny muttered under her breath.

"Now, now. Don't be hard on him. He's only a little boy having some summer fun."

Jenny stopped her pacing and turned on him, her jaw set with anger. Her voice a high pitched shrill; she let the cop have it, "Only a little boy? Some summer fun?" Her fist dug into her motherly hip, "Do you have any idea how many times that little bugger has done this?" Before he had a chance to answer, she told him at full volume, "NINE!" Her face was turning deep red, with both fury and embarrassment, "This is the ninth friggin' time he's had some ... summer fun," her fingers quoted.

As if to rescue the officer from her sharp words, another cruiser pulled into the driveway. "There he is now." Jenny stomped towards the car door but Adams caught her by the arm, turning her to face him, "Hold on a minute." He looked her in the eyes, kindness filling his, "Before you go screamin' at the boy, you might wanna make sure he knows you were worried about him and maybe that you love him."

Jenny resentfully yanked her arm out of his hand, "Maybe, my ass. Of course, I love him." She looked him up and down, "What kinda man are you anyway? Saying something like that to a missing boy's mother. Shame on ya." With a rather determined pirouette and her nose held high, she continued her way to the cruiser door.

But to her surprise, the other shorter officer stood beside the door for a moment also, waiting for Jenny's temper to calm down. She exhaled a deep breath and nodded she would indeed behave herself. Aylmer opened the door, revealing a wet, scared little boy sitting in, what seemed, by comparison, an enormous empty black hole of a seat. Neither mother nor child said a word. Jenny simply stuck out her hand. The boy immediately scurried out of the police car and rushed directly to her legs. He clung to her as if she was a life raft and he was a drowning boy. At first, she rubbed his hair and shushed his crying, then knelt down to his level to hug him tightly. They embraced quietly while the officers waited. Jenny let go of Derek and gently pushed him towards the house and his waiting twin brother. Billy had taken his place behind the two boys, while they watched from inside the house.

Officer Adams walked to where Jenny stood. Embarrassed by her own emotions, she promptly wiped the tears from her cheeks, putting up her 'tough single mother' wall once again, "Those God damn boys will be the death of me yet." Soft flashes of distant lightning flittered through the dense clouds. The storm was getting closer by the minute.

Adams snickered, "I hear ya, there. Mine are teenagers and driving me up the wall too. I've had it up to here with their, *give me this, give me that, 'cause I'm entitled to it*, bullshit." He noticed her sudden reaction to his kvetching as if the two situations were comparable on any level. He cut it short with a slight nod, "Sorry, Ma'am."

Dwayne slowly came to where they were standing, carrying the extension from the door knob. Without a word, he handed it to his mother.

Curious about the yellow cord, he asked the boy in his friendliest cop voice, "Whatcha got there, son?"

As all small children do, he sharply shrugged his shoulders, refusing to talk to an adult authority figure, then straight away raced back to the house. Billy held the door open so his twin would have a faster escape from the cops.

Jenny rolled her eyes at her son's rudeness, "Just my extension cord. Tess must have brought it back without me noticing. Apparently, I had other things on my mind."

Feeling there might be more to the situation than just someone returning a borrowed cord, he poked about for more information. "If you don't mind me asking, who's Tess?" His cop instincts were telling him that there was something beyond the obvious, something he had to investigate.

Jenny squinted at the officer, wondering why he would ask such a haphazard question. With her thumb, she pointed over her shoulder, "She's my neighbor." The officer kept silent, a tactic the police often used. For some reason when people talk to the police, they felt the need to fill in the silence. He waited for her to add more details and as predicted, she obliged him. "She borrowed it so her husband could plug in his Sawzall. It's amazing how far he's come since the accident." She paused for a minute, letting the silence hang in the air, then filled in the silence again. "She said he was going to put in a shelf or something like that." She held up the cord, excitedly waving it towards Tess's house. He noticed the tiny streaks of rust in the grooves of the yellow cord, just above the plug. "But can you imagine, a man in a wheelchair working on his house?" She nodded her head in approval, "Yep, he's come a long way since the accident."

Images of Tess's house flipped through the Officer's mind. The cane jammed in the window along with the wheelchair in the corner, with blankets folded neatly in its lap. Then it hit him, why he didn't see it at first. These items didn't seem out of place in a house with its furniture arranged for easy access with a wheelchair. Everything had its place and order. But what bothered him was that there was no husband. Upstairs — he didn't go upstairs. Had that been the reason she stopped him at the bottom of the stairs? Was her husband actually up those stairs or was she hiding something else from them?

"Well, if you're done here, I got kids to scold ..." then corrected with a raised eyebrow, "... and hug." Jenny stuck out her hand, "Thanks again for your help and no offense officer, but I hope I never see you again."

Adams cracked a smile, "Trust me Ma'am, no offense taken. You take it easy on the boy." He put on his best public relations smile, "And Ma'am, if you'd like, I can have one of our officers visit your son. To coach him on safety in the big bad world. Frankly, it'll scare the daylights out of him. Once we tell them about the evils that darkness hides, we find it helps them to stay put at night." From the angle he was standing, he could see the Logan's house from the corner of his eye. A random strike of lightning flashed over the structure, its pale grey exterior drawing his attention. The slight twist in his stomach told him there was more going on in that house than he had seen.

From above, Tess saw the Officer glance in her direction, the street light illuminating his face. Fear washed over her. A heavy feeling, as though she had just met an enemy — her enemy. She stepped back out of the dimly lit square, to hide in the shadows deeper in her bedroom.

The police radio blared out static and garbled words, pulling Adams out of his fixed stare. "Looks like I gotta go. Night Ma'am." With that, he hurried to answer the call.

Yet, with his sixth sense sharp, he stopped at the car's door and looked up into the exact window where Tess stood. He couldn't see anyone in the opening, but he knew someone was indeed, there. He could sense their presence.

She stepped forward ducking aside the window's frame. After a few seconds wait, she peeked around its edge. He was still there staring up at her window, his eyes squinting to see better. Again, she pulled away from the opening, her back to the wall, sliding down it to the floor to hide.

The radio blared that a power line had gone down and civilians were attempting to retrieve a person from an electrified vehicle. He had to leave; he had no choice. Climbing into the cruiser, he promised himself that he'd come back to test-out the hunch he held in his stomach.

Tess listened to the cruiser pull away, its radio still garbling inaudible messages into the night air. Although Officer Adams hadn't done or said anything towards Tess, she was sure the man would be back. She felt it in the pit of her stomach. Unfortunately, his interference was the last thing she needed. He would be nothing but a nuisance, with a shiny gold badge.

In her mind, she began planning what she would do when he came around again. But what she decided, depended on what Jenny had told him. Tomorrow first thing, she would pay Jenny a visit to find out that exact information. Of course, she would disguise the visit as one of concern over Jenny's terrorizing twin, Derek.

She lay on the bed, the cool night from the open window blowing across her bare skin. Flashes of lightning flickered in through the window, exposing her flesh to herself. Her silky skin shimmered a pale blue-white in the fractions of light. The vision of her hardened nipples and long slender legs, shocked her modest morals, causing her to cover herself up with the top sheet, curling up to hug her legs. To distract herself from the sexual image she had seen of herself, she concentrated on how to handle the police if they came back to question her again. As each scenario ran through her mind, she plotted out the next moves she had to say and do, to counteract any questions or actions Officer Adams threw her way. The red numbers on her clock read 1:41 AM when she finally switched on her alarm for the morning. Even though she was still strategizing, her exhausted muscles slowly melted into the mattress, pulling her into well-needed sleep.

Outside crickets counted seconds as Jenny emerged from the house carrying the tangled yellow cord. With the kids finally asleep, she returned it to its assigned hook in the garage. On the trip back to the house, lightning flashed to the earth, and heavy raindrops pelted down out of the darkness. Running out of the downpour, Jenny reached her back door just as thunder echoed through the night. She timidly peered out her screen door, feeling the electric charge in the air. Its friction left an uneasy feeling in her body. Although her family was safe, something was wrong with the world just outside her door. What it was, she wasn't sure, but it scared her enough that she quickly shut her door and locked it, an action she rarely did.

The dense downpour reduced the shafts of light coming from the cruiser's headlights as it made an unscheduled drive by the house of Tess Logan. All night the feeling that something wasn't right in that house stayed with him. Stayed in his gut.

Officer Adams never ignored one of his gut feelings.

# Part 4

Tess woke with a start.

The loud banging of metal doors on a delivery truck, made her body jolt. Then the backing up *Beep, Beep, Beep, Beep,* sound, pulled her out of her slumber and back into her existing world. A world she didn't particularly want to be in any longer.

She lay staring at the dimly lit ceiling, her stomach slowly knotting uptight with that day's reality. She was facing another day filled with the tasks of hiding Morty's death. The tarp needed burning, and she would cut the rug up into pieces, ready for their disposal.

Lord knows, she had plenty of the opaque blue baggies she planned to use. Thanks to Morty's insistence, she had bought them in bulk while they were on sale. She smiled at the fact that in some mysterious way, Morty had thought of everything she needed to cover up his own death. She swung her feet over the edge of the bed and glanced out the window on her way to the bathroom. It was a dull day, the rains finally stopping, but possibly only for awhile, according to the globular grey clouds that hung heavy in the sky.

Tess slowly showered, then dressed in lightweight clothing, hoping they would help against the building heat and humidity. On the way down the stairs, it struck her how abnormal it seemed not to be rushing about. Unlike every other morning in her marriage, she didn't have to cater to Morty's morning needs. There were no socks to find, no shirts to iron wrinkle free and best of all, no gloppy oatmeal to cook on the stove. *I have become a lady of leisure,* she thought with a light chuckle. Her stomach rumbled at how empty it was. Two stressful days of living on tea and cookies simply weren't enough to sustain her; it was demanding more. The thoughts of eggs with bacon and toast made her mouth water. Normally that would be their Sunday morning meal. Served exactly at eleven o'clock so Morty could believe it was what the rich folk called, brunch. She immediately changed her mind with the resentment of having to cater to his fanciful ideas. Instead, she contemplated the combinations of breakfast items she had on hand. Maybe waffles with sausages; French toast with syrup or perhaps a Spanish omelet with extra cheese and tomatoes. Morty hated tomatoes.

Once again, Tess recognized to what degree Morty had interfered with her own sense of being. How she had been shaped to be another repressed version of him. An imperfect version, of course, a fact she was reminded of daily. Just to spite him, a Spanish omelet with extra tomatoes it was.

Devouring a chunk of ripe red tomato, she decided that another cup of coffee would be nice. She was enjoying the sweet pleasure of indulging with two teaspoons of sugar; the same amount she normally used plus Morty's share. She leaned back in her chair, no point in rushing about, she had all day — no, all her life to get things done. Sipping her coffee and deciding what to do with her day, she absentmindedly watched a stray dog out the window, zigzagging down her street. When the dog stopped long enough to hold his nose high, sniffing at the air, she paid closer attention. Locating the scent, his four feet turned to a flurry of white, racing off to find its source. To her disbelief, he was heading directly to her garage. She jumped to her feet and raced outside, only to stop short at the sight of the little dog, his snout to the ground sniffing and snorting at the gap under the metal garage door.

"Get out of here!" she yelled, waving her arms at the dirty Jack Russell. "Go on. Get out of here! Go home!" He stopped momentarily to glance her way, but instead of leaving, the dog ignored her and began digging at the crack with his front paws, frantically clawing a mile a minute. He scratched, then snorted a sniff, and scratched some more, his unclipped nail scraping the asphalt.

"You mangy mutt! Get the hell out of here." She ran at him, clapping her hands and snarling at the top of her lungs in hopes of scaring him away. Unsuccessful, she stomped on the driveway, hammering the asphalt with the loud smack of her flip-flops. It worked. He stopped his scraping and jumped back, his paws pouncing in place, before pushing off with a twist, and he was gone with a yelping sprint. She ran after him, "Get! Go home!" He woefully looked back, then disappeared between the hedge and mailbox. She watched for him to return, but after ten minutes, she was satisfied he had gone. What was he so intent on getting at? She knelt down on one knee and sniffed as the dog did. The unmistakable odor of decaying flesh leached through the thin crack, assaulting her nostrils. The double layer of garbage bags no longer held the odor inside.

Apparently, Tess's day had been decided for her.

Back inside her kitchen, she hastily collected the things she needed. A box of blue baggies, clean white rags and a pail of hot water laced with cedar bleach. Once inside the garage itself, she added several used grocery bags and Morty's heavy duty utility knife to the pile.

She held her breath as she ripped open the double layer of garbage bags, the stench of rotting blood in the dirty carpet rushed out to meet her face. The odor was so intense, she nearly vomited from its pungent slap. She stopped for a second to compose herself. She continuously swallowed down the contents of her breakfast, not wanting to lose the nourishment her body so badly needed. Getting her gagging reflexes under control, she hurried to release the carpet from the plastic so the condensed putrid smell could dissipate in the air.

She tore and tore at the plastic until all of the carpet was exposed and lying in a heap on the floor. She bent over to look closer at the rug. A few tiny white maggots crawled over its surface making Tess's skin crawl. She danced a jig of disgust, checking her hands, arms and her body for others; to her relief there were none.

"Blowtorch. Where's the blowtorch?" She desperately searched through the tools hanging on Morty's pegboard. It wasn't there. After opening the cupboard door, she found it on the top shelf right next to its striker. She turned the knob on the slender tank until she heard the soft hiss of gas. She pressed the handle on the striker, rubbing the flint against the rough metal strip. Sparks flew. A pale-yellow flame shot out, and Tess vigilantly turned the knob, switching the flame to brilliant blue hot. She dabbed at the maggots, each one wiggling under the charring heat until it moved no longer.

Carefully, she unfolded the layers, killing any that she saw. The smell in the garage had turned horrid. Rotting flesh mixed with burning blood saturated the air. The rug lay out flat with random spots of charred maggots and scorched fibers. She wiggled it again, just to be sure she had gotten them all. Nothing moved. She replaced the torch to its shelf, careful not to burn herself on its hot metal tip.

Inhaling to ease the tension in her chest, she braced herself and picked up Morty's utility knife, she examined the rug, determining how and where to cut. The answer was simple; start the first cut parallel to the longest edge and continued from there. Carefully, she positioned the rugs so that when she cut, the knife was facing away from her. She sunk the blade into the soggy fibers and slowly drew it forward. It was harder to cut than she thought it would be. The arch between her thumb and forefinger ached with the pressure she placed on the knife's blade. The rug shook with force as she cut down the first strip, it falling to the floor with a wet splodge sound. To be sure she cut the right size strip, she cut it into sections creating both clean and blood saturated squares. She put one in a blue baggie, sealing its zipper top closure. To her relief, it worked. It fit in nicely, looking and feeling exactly like a thin sandwich. Even the opaque quality of the bag's plastic hid the bloodiness it held inside. It was perfect.

She cut the remaining portion of the strip but did not stuff them in the baggies. If she did that, blood from her hands would smear on their outsides. Not an effect Tess wanted. She cut the next parallel strip, letting it fall to the floor and continued to the next four long strips until the rug lay heaped in a pile at her feet. She pulled Morty's work bench stool over beside it, plunking herself down so she would be comfortable. For the next part of the job, she cut the top strip in pieces, placing each piece on the stack for bagging later.

Music would be nice, she thought, turning on Morty's radio. Twangy country blared from the speakers. She dived for the knob, muting the caterwauling of a broken heart. She adjusted the tuner, finding a station with an upbeat pop song, her foot immediately started tapping. Back to the stool and cutting, she went, humming to the lyrics of an 80's hit she couldn't remember the name of.

She cut the strip across, trying to keep them all the same size and as square as possible. The cramping ache in her hands was so sharp, she had to stop and let them rest before moving to the third strip. Filling its daily quota of Canadian content, the radio drummed out a Corey Hart song. The words didn't register straight away but after the lines 'your fortress cool ice blue' she recognized the song's title as the 'Boy in the Box.' Although the subject matter of the lyric was unrelated to her situation, the sentence did hit home, reminding her of the circumstances in her own life. In some twisted scenario, Morty was her 'boy in the box.' Disgusted by her own thoughts, she jumped to her feet and switched it off, attempting to relieve her heavy felt guilt.

Outside, she heard a familiar sound, the noise of nails scratching against wood and concrete — the damned dog was back.

Angry, she grabbed Morty's wooden mallet off the peg board and ran to the door. She hammered on the very bottom edge. Each initial BANG echoed up the huge metal plane, vibrating it into a thunderous rumble. A yelp exploded from the other side of the door. Tess listened for more scratching, the mallet in her hand poised to wallop the door again. Yet, all she heard was the sound of the little dog's long nails clicking on the sidewalk furiously running away. Looking down at the handle of the mallet, it was covered with gooey blood from her hands. Great! Another thing she would have to clean.

Back to the rug strips she went, determined to finish the chore, then cleaning up the mess she had made doing it. The work became increasingly tricky to carry out. Her hands were tired and weakened. *Two more strips, eight cuts per strip for a total of sixteen more cuts left*, she thought to herself. The small number encouraged her to move forward faster. In no time at all, thirteen more squishy squares were laid on the tall stack. But the handle of the utility knife became slimy with sweat from her palm and the coagulated blood from the rug, making it even more difficult to control. She was slicing off the last piece from the third strip when her grip slipped. The knife jolted sideways, stabbing her in the fleshiness of her left thumb. "Fuck!" She automatically pulled out the triangular blade, sending fresh blood trickling into her palm, to then drip off the tip of her little finger. The knife fell to the floor with a clatter. "Shit! Stupid!" she groaned before clamping her other hand over the small weeping gash. Applying pressure one of her white rags, her heart rate spiked with the terrifying thoughts she may have to go to the hospital if it didn't stop bleeding. Through her arms, she looked down at her clothing, they were covered in carpet fibers and smeared wine red goo. She raced to the kitchen sink and slowly lifted the white rag away from her hand, examining the damage to her flesh. It wasn't as bad as she had first worried. What felt like a wide gash, was merely a thin stab wound. Her fears of having to go for stitches melted away. Tess rinsed the cut under running water until it was washed clean. Once the bleeding stopped, she wrapped it with a massive bandage from Morty's first aid kit conveniently found in Morty's garage. The man had thought of everything, she laughed in her mind. Drips of her blood formed a trail from the garage to the kitchen — another bloody mess to clean. She wondered when those bloody little messes would end.

She sat down and went back to cutting the strips into squares. However, with her thumb cut, it was painful to grasp the material and hold it still enough to slice. It amazed her how liquid and red her fresh blood was compared to the dark, almost sable color, of Morty's. She turned it one way, then the other until she got it in a position that was less agonizing to hold. It took another hour and twelve breaks, but she finished the cutting, piling them at her feet. As planned, she washed the knife and her hands in preparation for the bagging of the squares.

Out in the garage, she opened each blue baggie, rolled the rim over and placed them on the clean part of the floor. With her clean hands, she inserted a bloody square using Morty's pliers avoiding the transfer of blood on the outside of the bag. And if any blood did dare to smear on the exterior, Tess immediately wiped it off with a clean rag. Within twenty minutes, she had them stuffed and stowed away in the kitchen's freezer, laid out in layers for easy separation. Cleaning and putting away all other tools, she next tackled the large bloody spot on the floor, making it disappear with bleach and cedar chips. Tess was finally done. Although the rotting stench was gone, it was hard to tell over the acidic tang of the bleach.

But it was her that needed the greatest amount of cleaning; her clothing covered with red blotches that had soaked through to her skin. All that remained for her to do was one last load of bloody clothing and a thorough washing of her own flesh. In the shower, she washed and scrubbed repeatedly, until the water finally ran clear; she had finally washed it all away.

Sitting on the edge of her bed she stretched her aching back; her hand pressing against its center, pushing the tension forward. Naked, she giving into her weariness, flopping out on the mattress, hoping to rest for just a moment. She closed her eyes, shielding them from the bright light shining through the window with her arm. It was the same sunlight that felt good against her damp skin. A little catnap would be nice, she thought, allowing herself to fully relax. She floated off to sleep quickly, her mind and body melting into the mattress with a soft self-soothing sigh.

She woke to a hard breeze blowing against her exposed skin. Her stomach growled its discontent at not being fed at regular intervals. She rolled on her side, wedging her hands under her head. *What to eat?* she wondered. Mentally, she went through the contents of her fridge and cupboards. Nothing appealed to her. It was all food that Morty demanded and nothing she cared for or craved.

"What do I really want?" she asked the open window.

For the first time in years, she could eat anything she desired. Pizza, Chinese or maybe something from the little Greek restaurant down the street, she told herself. Spaghetti from the pizzeria five blocks over was her final decision. She had seen it on TV one night, its pasta sauce red and meaty. She dressed quickly and locked up before she left on foot. Halfway down the front walk she stopped short, spun about and returned to the house. She went straight to the fridge freezer to fetch a blue baggie, stuffing it into her practical black tote. In her mind, she told herself there was no time like the present to start their distribution. Relocking the door, she plodded down the street, her stomach pulling her to the plate of pasta her mouth was watering for.

After marching down the first block, she slowed her gait, changing her appearance to calm and unhurried. She waited at the traffic light for it to turn green. Her eyes stared at the garbage can across the intersection, and then scanned the surrounding streets. To her relief, there was no one else but a man sitting on the street bench, tucked in the shade.

It was old Mr. Lo, his elderly body hunched over, leaning on his wooden cane. His eyes were closed, and from where Tess was standing, she was sure that even if his eyes were open, he couldn't see the garbage can from that angle.

The light turned green. She stepped off the curb and crossed to where the garbage can was. Appearing as though she hadn't a care in the world, she reached inside her sensible tote, took out the baggie and casually dropped it in the community trash can. Walking away, she could see the blue square from the corner of her eye, sitting on top with the other tossed away trash. Her heart thundered in her chest with adrenaline all the way to Rosa's. Going through the front doors, a wide smile washed across her face.

She had done it.

She had actually accomplished her first deliberate task without a hitch — and no one was the wiser. Feeling rather proud of her bravery, she straightened her back and held her head high as Nina showed her to a table for one. Tess chose to sit with her back to the huge picture window; she wanted to take in the entire atmosphere of the brightly lit restaurant. Being so isolated with Morty, she wanted to see and experience people. It was the middle of the busy dinner hour, and most of the other tables were full of couples and young families. She also noted one other single person sitting in the back corner. The man had his head stuck inside a newspaper, hiding his face behind it. The cook smacked the bell in the kitchen, signaling the chubbier waitress to scurry for the steaming hot plates of food that waited for her.

Outside, the old man's head turned back, facing forward to close his eyes again. His body might have been old, but his eyesight and hearing were as young and sharp as ever.

Nina placed the menu in front of Tess, the red table cloth matching the color of the patterned carpet, "So can I get you something to drink?"

"A glass of wine please?" She didn't bother to open the well-worn menu. Instead, she handed it back to Nina. "And I already know what I'd like to order."

Nina pulled her order pad out and prepared to write her order down.

She smiled sweetly, "I'd like spaghetti please."

"Would that be red or white?"

The question confused Tess. "Red or white spaghetti?"

Impatient, Nina asked the question again. She had tables to serve, and the cook was giving her that 'your plates are up and getting cold' look from the kitchen. "The wine. Do you want red wine or white wine?"

"Oh." Her face flushed pink at her own stupidity. "I'd like red please."

Unfortunately, Nina walked away before she got the chance to ask her if the pasta came with bread, to push the strands about, but more importantly for sopping up any leftover sauce. She wanted bread with it — toasted garlic bread to be precise.

Living with Morty, money was tight. Bread with a meal was considered an extravagance. Morty was gone. And that left one less mouth to feed, meaning more money for food. Good food. Fresh vegetables, better quality meat, and bread with her meals — toasted garlic bread daily if she wanted.

She decided she would catch Nina on her trip back.

Somewhat anxious, she fidgeted with her silverware on her placemat. Lining them up straight with the edge, like she did so many times to fulfill Morty's demands. Disappointed in herself, her shoulder sagged, she was doing it again. Letting him rule her life even after he was dead. She pushed him out of her mind, determined to enjoy her meal without him ruining it.

Instead, she watched the young family by the kitchen door, the mother feeding the little girl in the highchair something strained and green. *God damned peas,* Tess mentally cursed the little green balls. In her youth, she longed to have children, but now she was happy Morty was "shooting blanks," unable to produce even enough sperm to impregnate her. The thought of bringing up children with abusive Morty would have been heartbreaking.

Nina came with her wine, pulling Tess out of her lamenting. "Excuse me, does the meal come with bread?"

"No, that's extra. Did you want some?" From the kitchen, the bell rang again, distracting her further.

"Oh, toasted garlic bread if you have it?"

"Want cheese on that?" Her words came out gruff, merely because the restaurant was packed and they were short one waitress and their dishwasher. Speculation was they were together, cozied up at his place. On-the-job-romances were hell on a small business. Curse words and blame would fly tomorrow, Nina swore on it.

That was something new to Tess, garlic and cheese bread. Her face lit up, her head nodded wildly, "Oh, how wonderful. Yes, please."

Nina frowned at her. She had never seen such exuberance over grated cheese melted on garlic bread. The cook's bell rang again, hammering it with his massive hand. She huffed over her shoulder, "Lord, I'm gonna kill that man if he doesn't stop banging that damned bell." She noticed Tess's face tense and pegged her for a timid woman not used to the ways of the world.

In her business, Nina saw all kinds of people. Nasty husbands, miserable wives, parents who were working seventy hours a week to give their precious brats everything their greedy hearts desired. And then there were people like Tess, quiet and reserved, not wanting to bother anyone more than necessary. It was her face that Nina liked. It was honest and kind yet somewhat vulnerable, the sort of woman that needed protecting from the nastiness of the world. It was that sentiment that brought the pleasantness back to her voice, "Anything else you need while I get the chance?"

She raised her wine glass, "No. I'm good. Thanks." With that Nina sprinted for the kitchen's serving window and the waiting plates.

Tess sipped her wine, puckering with the tartness of its inexpensive vintage, but none the less enjoyed it. To pass the time until her pasta arrived, she went back to watching the other patrons in the restaurant. The baby had finally let the mother eat; busying herself with chasing bits of circular cereal around the tray of the highchair.

The door opened, and Mr. Lo slowly made his way to the counter, sitting gently on one of the swiveling stools. The other waitress automatically placed a glass of ice tea before him, implying he must have been a regular. Tess was sure he had turned his head slightly to peer in her direction.

But why would he do such a thing? She didn't know him personally, nor did he know her. Maybe she had only imagined it.

Then again, what if he knew? But how could he know? She took another deep sip. Great! She was getting paranoid about an old man looking at her. She told herself to stop being silly; it was simply her nerves over reacting. To distract herself, she continued to people watch. Nina went from table to table, topping up coffee cups and asking that infernal waitress question 'how is everything?'

Tess was taking another full sip when Nina reached the man with the newspaper, and nearly choked on it when he lowered his paper shield. It was Officer Adams who smiled that *Yes, he would like another refill.*

Unfortunately, the loud sound of Tess gulping for air drew his attention. With a smile of recognition, he nodded in her direction. Feeling forced to, she waved back with friendly waggling fingers. She felt the heat of her face flushing deep red with embarrassment. She fretfully tapped her fingers on the table top, turning her attention away from the Officer's sightline. Adding to her distress, Mr. Lo had also started to stare at her. Her eyes switched back and forth — first to the officer, then to the old man who was pretending he wasn't looking her way. Unable to pull her eyes away, they froze on the officer, her heart raced wildly. The kitchen bell rang, and Nina walked between them, breaking her petrified spell.

Panic rushed over Tess. She felt the urge to flee immediately. The last thing she wanted was to talk to him. She wasn't exactly sure why, but that man made her nervous. Very nervous. The recollection of him standing staring up into her window from Jenny's backyard flashed in her mind. A strong impulse to run rushed over her for a second time but instead, she sat fixed by her own inner turmoil. Morally, she felt she couldn't leave, her meal hadn't arrived yet, and she didn't have enough nerve to just storm off without paying, sticking Nina with her unpaid bill. She would simply have to stay and endure the discomfort of the situation. Then again, she might be fretting for no good reason, she told herself. It wasn't uncommon for someone to nod and smile at someone else they just recently met. She told herself to relax — that he was just a cop being friendly and nothing more.

Luckily for Tess, Nina brought her the garlic toast giving her something to occupy her hands and her attention. Noticing her nearly empty glass, "You want another glass of wine?" Tess nodded rapidly before biting down on a piece of bread, deciding it best to ignore both Officer Adams and Mr. Lo. The cheese stretched long strings which she pinched off with her fingers, stuffing them into her mouth. She licked her fingers clean of the slippery garlic butter with a grin and a groan of pure self-gratification.

From the corner of her eye, a sudden movement drew her attention. Officer Adams was standing to leave, placing a fiver on his table. He turned and walked in her direction. She panicked again. The quickest solution she could conceive was to shove the remaining chunk of bread in her mouth, in hopes of preventing him from stopping to talk.

However, instead of talking to Tess, he stopped to say hello to the hunched over Mr. Lo. He leaned on his elbows, which brought him down to the old man's eye level, "Hello Don. How are you today? Still keeping the streets free of trouble?" He gently patted the old man's sloping shoulder — a 'man hug' if Tess ever saw one.

The old man chuckled along with him, "Not much happening out there today. I guess it's too hot for punks and criminals." He cast a glance in Tess's direction, then quickly returned to the cop's face. His voice dropped down to an accusing octave, "Haven't seen a thing."

His vague words caught in Tess's throat, and again it constricted, nearly choking her. She grabbed her wine glass and chugged down the last of it, washing the lump of bread all the way down. Her hand on her chest, she swallowed hard clearing her windpipe. What was it the old man had not seen? Had he seen her dispose of the blue baggie? Or was he just doing his best to be an annoying old man? She listened carefully to their conversation, hoping to catch a hint of what he was referring to.

Taking a toothpick from the tiny container by the register, "So those boys didn't show up again?"

The old man shook his head, "Nope! I think I scared them good with this." He brandished his cane in the air, nearly toppling Nina's tray.

"God, damn it! Watch that thing!" she hollered at him.

"I'm so sorry, Miss Nina." He tried to help her by reaching for the tray to steady it — a mistake customers often make.

She whirled it out of his hand's reach, "Don't! You'll only make it worse." she scolded. She stepped out of his range and leveled the tray upright and flat. "Just let me be."

The officer scowled at her, "Hey, take it easy! He was just trying to help you with the tray."

"Look Kev, just keep him out of my way or out he goes."

"He'll behave. Won't you Don?" the officer's eyes went extra wide, telling him to agree with him or there'd be hell to pay otherwise.

The old man's face fell sad, pleading as he nodded that he would indeed behave.

She pursed her lips at the officer and then gave in with a begrudging shrugged, "Oh, fine. But keep that cane down and tucked between your knees ... and the hell out of my way." Immediately, Don did as he was told, hanging the handle on his thigh and tightening his legs around its shaft.

Officer Adams noted that Tess had been watching it all, munching on her bread as if it were popcorn — as though she was at the movies watching a show. With his usual pleasant smile, he peeked around Nina's rather ample backside and grinned in her direction, "And how are you tonight? Better than last night, I hope?"

Nina was laying the plate of spaghetti in front of Tess, "You need anything else, Ma'am?" Tess shook her head no but asked for the other glass of wine that she had ordered.

She was sure she was going to need it before long. "Oh damn, I forgot. Be right back with it."

Kevin was still looking at Tess, waiting for an answer. When she didn't respond straight away, he walked to her table and asked it again. "I asked you if you were having a better day today. Are you?" His face appeared to be friendly however his voice was firm to the point with authority.

She inhaled slowly calmly her nerves. "Yes, everything is just fine," was all she said, trying not to add any other details that might be construed as anything but politeness to a city cop.

"Well, that's good." He continued to stand beside her, waiting for the conversation to carry on. But when she didn't say any more, he pushed it further, "That's the best spaghetti in town. That's Mario's secret sauce made with genuine parmesan cheese, fresh herbs and fresh hand crushed tomatoes. You can taste it. It's better than any sauce I could make."

While he talked, she had twirled a large fork full of pasta strands and purposely stuffed them in her mouth, so all she could do was nod in agreement.

"By the way, we found your neighbor's boy. But I guess you already know that, don't you?" he slipped his hands in his pockets trying to make it appear as a casual question.

Tess didn't fall for it though. She immediately knew what he was up doing. It was a tactic Morty had used in the past when he wanted to trick Tess into saying something she didn't want to. Unknown to him, this was old hat to Tess Logan, nothing she couldn't handle with ease. She swallowed the mouthful of pasta. It went down in a hard bulbous lump. She set her face to read denial yet still showing genuine curiosity, "How would I know that?"

"When you were standing in the window, you must have seen my partner return him to his mother." His brows frowned deeply and his eyes slightly narrowed with an unsaid allegation.

So, it was true. He had indeed seen her in the window the previous evening. Instead of becoming unnerved, she kept her head and persisted in denying that she had been there. "I think you're mistaken, officer. I went to bed right after you left my place. I was probably sound asleep by then." Then she promptly stuffed another fork full in her mouth, silencing her half of the conversation.

He stepped closer to her table, his voice somewhat accusatory, "By when? How did you know you were asleep before the lad was brought home?"

From across the room, Nina decided that the nice lady needed protecting from the forceful man that was disturbing her dinner. She was there in three long strides, "Jesus Kevin, leave the gal alone!" She walked as she scolded, "She says she was asleep, so what's the problem?" She placed the full glass of wine down, taking the empty one. She forced herself in between Tess and the cop, her fist hard on her rounded hip, "Now, don't you think it's time you were leaving for work?" Nose to nose, her squinting eyes leveled with his, making sure he got the message that she didn't like her female customers to be hassled, especially on her shift.

Mr. Lo was taking in every bit of the scene, sipping on his cold ice tea. His face held an expression of piqued curiosity as he realized that there was more to the situation than met the eye.

"Christ Nina, relax." With that she let her hipped hand drop to her side. Still, she didn't budge an inch, telling him to be on his way. He looked past Nina's stubbornness, "Sorry Mrs. Logan, I didn't mean to intrude on your dinner. You have a nice evening." Straightening up he gave Nina a 'good enough for ya' look. In spite of his retreat, she stood her ground waiting there until he was out the door.

Nina turned back to Tess, "Sorry about that. He can be such a jerk sometimes."

"No, it's me that should be sorry. I didn't mean to put you in the middle of it — especially with an officer of the law."

"Officer of the law? You mean my dumb brother? Nah, he was just his usual jerk self." She shrugged her shoulders, excusing her sibling. "Anyway, you all set here? Anything else you need?"

"Nope, I'm good." She smiled sweetly at Nina, thanking her silently once again for protecting her. The woman seemed to understand and nodded hard only once, before turning away to answer the cook's bell. Old man Lo was still staring at them which sent Nina into another quiet outburst, "And what are you looking at?" Mr. Lo's eyes grew wide at her. "She ain't got horns growing out of her head, so leave her alone." Instantly he swung around the stool and touched the glass to his lips. Although he didn't drink, he made it appear as though he had. He knew what would happen if he didn't do what he was told. The name of the pizzeria was Rosa's, but it was Nina that owned and ran the place with a firm yet loving hand. What she said, went — no questions asked. He did what he was told and did his best to ignore Tess, while still keeping an eye on her at the same time.

Tess stuffed in another mouthful of the rich pasta while she contemplated what she had just heard. Officer Adams was Nina's brother. What significance that had, she wasn't sure, but the knots in her stomach tightened again. *Jesus, I'm gonna need more wine,* she thought and took another deep drink.

As soon as Mr. Lo's glass was empty, Nina whisked it away, telling him without the use of words to leave. Slowly the senior swung about, placing his feet flat on the floor. His wooden cane he planted solidly in front of him, using it for support in pulling himself off the stool. Step by careful step, he made his way to the entrance, shuffling his feet as older people often did when their balance wasn't as skilled as it once was. As he passed her, he nodded and quietly offered, "You have a nice meal, Miss. And don't be drinking too much of that wine. It's unladylike to be drunk in public."

From the other side of the counter, Nina bellowed, "Don! It's time for you to go. And I mean now!" He nodded to Tess again, his eyes apologizing for Nina's rude behavior and started shuffling his brown leather slippers again. As he reached the door, she yelled after him, "And don't be hanging around my door. Or I'll call the cops ... charging you with loitering. Again."

Nina came around to Tess's table, her face screwed up tight with exasperation, "That old goat's nothing but a nuisance. All he does is sit outside commenting to everyone that passes by him. About what they're doing or what they're carrying — whether they want his opinion or not. Then the bugger tells the next passer-by what he just saw or said to the previous person. Just a gossip, that's all he is. To me, he's nothing but a ruddy nuisance."

Tess inhaled slowly. Nina's other blurry image was shifting above Nina's head. Not being a regular drinker, the wine was beginning to affect her vision, along with her mind. "He can't really be that bad? Maybe he's just trying to be nice, but it comes across wrong. I mean, how old is he ... sixty-five ... maybe seventy tops?"

She forced her eyebrows high, trying to convince Tess to be suspicious, "But remember, he's Asian, they hide their age very well." Then her face scrunched up tight with condemnation, "Lord knows what else is inside that man's mind."

Inside, Tess giggled at the rapid changes in Nina's expressions but stifled any sound or smile of her own. However, since Nina was still standing there staring down at her, she realized the conversation was not done. A little tipsy, her curiosity got the better of her, "Sounds like you and he, have a history? And maybe with your brother too."

Nina firmly crossed her arms, her tone turning harsh, "I'll say. Been battling that little bugger for months. He's ruining my business." Her voice became boisterous, "Loitering around out front and sleeping on the benches and uttering comments at everybody. Plain annoying to most of my customers and me. Some said they didn't want to come eat here, just to avoid his stupid, rude remarks." She puffed out a heavy sigh, "That's how he met Kevin. When I called the cops to get rid of him; the guys at the station sent my brother to handle it. My God damned brother! Can you believe it?" her voice hit a disgusted high pitch, "A courtesy, they called it. Courtesy my big fat ass. All he did was get suckered in by the old man's loneliness. Kevin basically did nothing." Her voice got louder while her arms flew into the air, "Oh yah, he can't stand out front of my place anymore, but he's still out there irritating the crap out of innocent people. And he's foreign ... I can't trust a foreigner."

It was with that narrow-minded statement that the cook hammered the bell, drawing her attention. However, there were no plates waiting on the ledge in front of him. She shrugged, "What?" to him. He didn't use words. Instead, the cook pointed toward the customers in the restaurant with the tip of his nose. To Nina's embarrassment, they were all staring at her, and a quiet hush had fallen over the entire restaurant. Apparently, she had said too much, too loud. A baby began to fuss, persuading the mother to pick her up, cradling the young one in her lap as though she needed protecting. The kindness of her mothering highlighted the uncomfortable tension that hung in the air. Nina's face flushed pink at being caught bad-mouthing a senior and no matter how annoying he'd become; her cruel words were still not acceptable to the disapproving cluster before her.

Tess felt Nina's mortification and quickly changed the subject to ease the crowd's judgment of Nina. She lifted a fork full of sauce and commented loudly to her, and in a way, to everyone else, "I have to tell you this is an excellent sauce you have — full-bodied, rich and meaty."

"Just the way I like my men!" roared the other waitress from across the room, adding to Tess's efforts to appease the others. One of the two ladies sitting at the back table snorted her agreement into her coffee and was quickly followed by her friend's 'Amen,' apparently in praise of a fine man she had enjoyed recently. The others laughed as well, breaking the heavily hanging discomfort. Soon everyone began to mill about as before. The sound of knives cutting on plates, cups clanging on saucers and idle chatter slowly returned to fill the room, wiping away the suffocating silence.

Relieved, Tess went back to eating, twirling another enormous fork full, stuffing the wad into her bulging cheek. Nina bent over, "Thank you for that. I didn't know they could hear me. I guess my blood pressure's high, stuffin' up my hearing again. You want another wine? On the house, shall we say? My treat."

"You don't need to ..." she managed to mumble through her mouth full.

"I know I don't. I want to." The kitchen bell rang as plates were hoisted into place. "Let's face it. You just saved my tips and more than likely the loyalty of a few customers. I screwed up, and you helped smooth it over. It's just my way of saying thanks."

Tess nodded, her heartfelt eyes showing her appreciation for Nina's kind words, "Then yes, I would like another."

Her acceptance brought a smile to Nina's face. She nodded over her shoulder, "Great. I'll be right back after I serve that miserable lot" Without another word she spun about and went straight to work, serving the meals with timid smiles and offhand jovial apologies.

The wine floated through her mind as she watched Nina work each table, making small talk as she did. Tess wondered if she could do that type of work, serving people she didn't know — or like — and enjoy it. She hadn't worked since she married Morty. He made sure of that as well, making it impossible to meet other people — mostly men who'd steal her away — so he accused. She vigorously twisted her fork through the now tepid tomato sauce. In doing so, she flicked speckles of it across her wrist from the whipping pasta ends. The clotted sensation immediately brought back memories of Morty's flesh hitting her skin just the day before. A memory she had almost forgotten for the moment.

She quickly scoured the red dots away with her napkin, trying to wash away the gruesomeness of the memory. Her hands strained taut to the point of shaking; her fingers gnarled blue and bony white. She frantically scrubbed at each spot until the red smears were gone completely. Suddenly she stopped, regaining control over her distraught emotions, and calmly placing the napkin beside her plate. The bloody reminder was gone. Inhaling deeply through her nostrils, she calmed her crazed actions, reminding herself where she was and how she might look to the others there. Her heart rate quickened as her perception of the world grew paranoid all over again.

She drank from her glass to wet her dry mouth. Had anyone seen her frantically scrub at her arms and hands? Over the edge of the glass, she scanned the restaurant, going from person to person, table to table, hyperventilating in its tiny bowl. It seemed as though no one witnessed her bizarre outburst. They were all eating and talking as before. Heavy anxiety overwhelmed her; she had to leave — to run away and protect herself. But how? Nina was on her way with her gift of wine, and she still had to get the bill. From the edge of her eye, a red-lettered sign gave her the way out if only for a few moments. She wiped her mouth placing the napkin on top of her plate, signaling to Nina that she was finished with her meal. Hopefully, she would bring the bill straight away, relieving her of the task of having to ask for it.

Inside the bathroom stall, Tess took a brief minute or two to gather herself, to steady her nerves and collect her thoughts. Mentally, she prayed for the check and wine to arrive while she was indisposed. Out at the sink she washed and rewashed her hands and arms, making sure all the red remains were completely obliterated. The mirror showed her face was stressed and frowning. Quickly, she relaxed the tension in her face, bringing back the friendly twinkle she had held there no more than twenty minutes before. Holding the door handle, she pulled on it as she inhaled a breath of courage.

To her happiness, Nina was at that moment walking away with her plate, the new glass of wine placed next to the nearly consumed one. And there beside it, was what she eagerly wanted to see, her bill. Sitting down she glanced at the total, $16.78 was a total she could work around. In the time she had been in the ladies room, the restaurant had thinned out. The baby's family had left as well as the two ladies in the back. She needed to leave, or there was a great chance she would get cornered by Nina again, a scene she couldn't endure in her state of mind.

Paying the bill without having to connect with Nina was trouble-free. All she had to do was leave a twenty-dollar bill on the table. It would not only cover her bill; it would leave a reasonable tip for Nina as well. But what was she to do about the full glass of wine? Drink it, was the first answer in her head and that is exactly what she did. She hoisted the glass to her lips and gradually swallowed down its entire contents, all in one long head tilting guzzle. Over the rim, she made sure Nina was busy before rising from the table. In one smooth move, she slid off her chair, strode straight for the door and was breathing fresh air within seconds.

She sped up her pace, her feet nearly stumbling along but not at a run, in fear of drawing attention. She quickly retraced the way she had come, the street blurred and the colors intensified as the last glass of alcohol were affected her wits and vision. Up ahead was the garbage can where she had deposited her first blue baggie. Her own morbid curiosity pulled her to it; she had to revisit the scene of her crime. Passing the trash can, she halted for a brief moment glancing inside its mouth until the little blue square registered in her drunken mind. Pleased to see that the baggie was still there, nonchalantly sitting on top disguised as just another disposed piece of debris. Her vision swirled telling Tess she had drunk more than she originally thought. Straightening herself upright, she aimed her body for home and her awaiting bed.

But she was not the only one in the street.

On the far side of the hot asphalt, Mr. Lo sat in the shadow of his favorite tree, resting in its cool shade. Leaning on his cane still as a stump, he squinted watching Tess depart Rosa's restaurant. His old eyes noted that she was in quite a hurry when she left, her feet traveling faster than they should, causing her to falter every now and then with a miss placed step. He was sure that she had consumed too much wine, a fact that infuriated the old man since he had warned her of that exact consequence. To him, she was an odd creature; naturally beautiful in her looks, but somehow still not as innocent as she seemed to appear. He felt it in his bones. She was one to watch, one to be concerned about. With her out of view, he closed his strained elderly eyes and ran their encounter through his head — maybe there was something he had missed, a single detail that would explain his uneasiness about the overly composed stranger even Officer Adams was intrigued with. There had to be a reason, an explanation for her odd behavior.

# Part 5

Tess prepared herself for the second half of the day ahead. Shorts and a thin T-shirt along with flip flops were all she intended to wear. With the temperature already in the high 80's, she needed to wear as little as possible to stay cool. During the morning's trip, she had heated up rather quickly in her jeans and long-sleeved shirt. Even Mr. Lo stayed hidden in the deep shade with the morning's withering heat. She hoped the dry spell would end soon. Before long she would have to burn the tarp to stop any further attractions from her furry friend, Lil' Bastard, her new nickname for the dog that scratched at the garage door.

Her tote lay on the kitchen table ready for the day's routine outing.

Tess's body jolted stiff with the startling BBRRING. She stood and watched it ring, before she curiously answered, "Hello?" It was the first call since Morty's death, and she was sure it was someone informing her that they knew everything and she was now going to prison for the demise of Morty Logan.

"Mrs. Logan?" A computer keyboard ticked in the background.

Tess recognized the shrilling nasal voice even before she announced who she was. "Yes."

"This is Libby from Healer's Physiotherapy. Ma'am, it looks like we're going to have to cancel Morty's session on Monday."

Although Tess's heart leaped for joy, she did her best to keep her tone calm, as to not raise suspicion, "Oh?" The woman on the other end of the phone had no inkling how those words had turned Tess's mood from dismal to ecstatic.

Libby's voice pierced Tess's eardrum, "Well it turns out that his therapist Connie, was rushed to the hospital this morning. Her appendix ruptured during the night, and it looks like she'll be in there for awhile. And with the rescheduled appointments, we're now booked solid for the next two weeks. And it looks like it may be three weeks before we can continue his therapy."

Holding in a delighted squeal, she calmed herself, squashing the excitement in her voice and replaced it with pity, "Oh no. That's terrible." She punched her thigh with her fist, trying to stop herself from laughing out loud. That was the best news she could have possibly received. Right from the beginning, Tess had been trying to figure out how to elude that exact situation. "Libby, can you hold for just a moment." She held the receiver over her chest, pretending to explain the phone call to Morty. She actually spoke the words out loud so they would resonate from her chest into the phone's receiver. Again, if Libby thought Tess was talking directly to Morty, it gave the impression that Morty was still alive. It thrilled Tess to add Libby to her list of involuntary alibis. She forced concern into her tone, "Morty hopes Connie's all right. Nothing too serious he hopes?" She did her best to give the impression that Morty was right there with her, still alive and concerned about the continuance of his therapy.

"Oh no, she's fine now. It's just that she will be laid up for awhile and we'll need to find a replacement for her while she's recuperating. Unfortunately, that will take some time. Good therapists are hard to find. We're really sorry for the inconvenience Mrs. Logan, but let me reassure you that we're doing the best we can to find a replacement. As soon as we find someone, I'll call you to reschedule Mr. Logan's appointments."

Tess swallowed down the swell of glee that was forming at the base of her throat and set her voice to be serious yet kind, "That will be fine. And Libby, please give Connie our best wishes for a speedy recovery."

"Can do. Again, thank you for understanding, and I'll call you as soon as I can reschedule Mr. Logan. Bye now."

"Bye." She hung up the receiver and stared at the phone for a long second. Then as if possessed by Lucifer himself, she ran through the house giggling and twirling at the relief the phone call brought her. From the living room, through to the kitchen and then back again, her arms arched as ballerinas would, she celebrated. Finally, drained of elated energy, she flopped herself onto the couch, limp and relaxed. But before long, her smile turned to a scowl. Although the news was good, it was also an unpleasant reminder — a horrible reminder — that Tess would soon have to cover up Morty's murder in a more permanent fashion. What was she to say when Libby called back to arrange the next appointment? Her mind raced for answers as it had before and tense knots settled between her shoulder blades. But then she shrugged them loose with a pleased grin after she had realized she had three whole weeks to come up with a proper lie, one that would hold them off until she could dispose of the evidence.

The evidence.

She had come to call it that, referring to her late husband's body as nothing more than a problem she needed to discard. Tess had finally convinced her conscience that since Morty was an evil abusive man, it was Fate's bidding that he was dead. She was not truly responsible. His bloody death was his penalty for the mean-spirited life he inflicted on others. The living Morty was dead, and she no longer deemed him a human, but merely a bothersome item to discard. Morty was gone — and good riddance!

Gone were the days of him holding her back, holding her up to his mean hearted self-indulgent standards. He was gone — gone forever.

She now focused her energy and time on the act of removing the evidence from her home, eliminating the possibility of being found out and arrested for the accident.

Tess's head swung to the front door. The gentle tapping on her front door was a familiar knock, the rhythm of Jenny's knuckles.

"Just a minute," she hollered at the door. Panic swept through her. Knowing Jenny, she would want to see the handy-man work Morty had done for her bookshelf. She smoothed out her hair thinking of a possible ruse she could use to distract her neighbor from the observable truth. Then it occurred to her that she had not talked to Jenny since she borrowed the extension cord. Jenny had no knowledge of any actual work Morty would have supposedly done. A simple little white lie would squash any suspicious questions Jenny might have. She opened the door with a huge, welcoming smile, "Jenny? Come on in." She stepped aside letting her neighbor through the doorway.

"Oh, pretty good. And you and Morty?" she talked as her eyes scanned the room, that same nervous involuntary habit of most people when visiting a neighbor's home.

"We're fine." At that instant, a single simple idea popped into her head. "Except right now Morty's at his sister's. I'm kinda taking a break from ... well, you know ... the work of taking care of him." She rubbed her forehead showing the weariness of her stress, "It kinda gets to me after awhile, and well, I need a holiday. With all this twenty-four-seven work, I need a bit of time for me to ... to recuperate." She let out a heavy sigh again conveying her weary stress. "Anyhow come on in and grab a chair. You want a cold drink?"

"Oh no, I can't stay. The kids ... you know." Her eyes darted around the room once more making her forehead furrow. "I thought Morty was building you that cubby you wanted?"

Before she could ask the next question, Tess answered it for her. "Oh yah, well as it turned out he bit off more than he was able to do. Poor thing managed to saw the shelves but didn't have the strength to cut the wall out, let alone do the drywalling and wiring. It kinda depressed him, so I made him stop. That's kinda the other reason he's at his sister's." It was time to change the subject back to Jenny's life so she would talk about herself and not the topic of Morty. "So, if you can't stay, what can I do for you then?" she blinked blankly into Jenny's eyes demanding an immediate reply.

The stare worked. Jenny felt compelled to answer straight away, "Oh ... ah ... I was wondering if you had a paint tray I could borrow? I can't seem to find mine." Her face flushed pink, telling Tess that the boys had probably destroyed it by some unholy means. Jenny's three boys would destroy a rock if they were told not to, it was just their way.

"Sure. No problem. Morty's got one in his workshop. I'll be right back." She turned quickly and strode directly to the garage, her flip flops slapping with each step. She grabbed the tray off its hook and brought it straight to awaiting Jenny. Setting her face with an overly friendly smile, "There you are. So, what are you painting this time?"

"The kitchen needs freshening up. And this time I'm using enamel paint so I can wash it as often as I want." Again, her face reddened, her expression was almost an admission of guilt that her boys were the reason her house was always a mess. Fingerprints, grime, spattered food and unwanted wall art were familiar sights in her home. "Well, I better get back before they tear the place apart." She said it as a joke but in truth, it wasn't funny, her boys were capable of such a monstrous act. She turned to the door and waved the tray from the front walk, "Thanks, I'll bring it back tomorrow."

"No hurry." Tess's mouth formed a self-indulgent grin, "Trust me, Morty won't even know it's gone." Her heart quickened at her own private witticism. "Bring it back whenever." She slowly closed the door, blocking out the afternoon sun and its accompanying heat.

Tess was dreading the day's humidity. Then again, she had no other option but to carry on with her mission. After all, the tiny blue bags were not going to scatter themselves. It had turned into her daily job to dispose of batches of three or more several times each day — a laborious task in the August heat.

But like her mother, Tess had her rules as well. Never in the same neighborhood within the same day, just in case someone noticed her being there too often and began to piece the incidents together. Today she would venture onto the town's bus system which would transport her to the furthest part of town. She had studied the bus routes, and her plan would bring her close to a public park. There were always garbage cans near playgrounds or shopping malls.

She counted the 'blue bag total' in her head. Another eight pieces and she would be free of them forever. And when she returned, she would carry out the next deed on her list - the burning of the tarp. At the refrigerator, she stuffed another five baggies into a plastic bag stashed inside her new tote. The plastic bag stopped the sweating frozen bags from bleeding into the lining of her new tan tote, an incident that ruined her regular tote. She checked for proper coinage before leaving the house. Opening her front door, the heat hit her face, nearly taking away her breath as she headed for the bus stop around the corner.

To her irritation, the old man was there again, sitting on the bench leaning on his hand-carved cane. Nina was right. Mr. Lo was a bloody nuisance, one that just seemed to be in Tess's way every time she went out. Yet, she had no choice in the matter. She had to pass his way each and every time she left her house, for the old goat had positioned himself directly in her path. As with each prior trip, she kept her head down avoiding any chance of eye contact with the old man's stare.

His wooden cane waved in the air, "Excuse me, Miss. Can you help me?" He watched as Tess nearly tripped over her own flip-flop. With a pitiful tone, he called again, "Please? A little help for an old man!" He didn't actually need help; it was a maneuver to get her closer to him.

Feeling that she had to obey her elder, she walked to where he sat, yet still refusing to make eye contact. "Good afternoon. How can I help you?" she reluctantly asked, pushing the tan straps of her tote over her shoulder, her thumb hooked at the straps base holding it tight in place.

He held up his elbow, "Could you help me to my door. I'm suddenly feeling rather light headed." He squinted up at her face, "I believe I've had too much heat."

Tess was curiously surprised. Although Mr. Lo was visibly of Asian descent, he had a barely audible British accent. The faraway country of Hong Kong popped into her mind. She didn't recall him having an accent at the restaurant, but then again, she barely remembered anything from that day, her rattled nerves taking over every portion of her senses with her unwanted conversation with Officer Adams.

In her youth, Tess's mother had imposed with a heavy hand, her own old fashion values of dutifully attending to the elderly. As a result of that heavy guilt, Tess took his arm and cautiously helped him to his feet. Together they leisurely strode down the street, Tess being careful not to rush him.

"You know, I haven't seen you about before. And I know everyone who lives around these parts." His face spoke of the pride he held in knowing the business of the entire neighborhood. "Are you new to our little community?" His question was friendly, yet he had worded it so that she would have to answer.

She considered fibbing, telling him a lie to quiet his questioning. But after what Nina had said regarding his nosiness, she decided that might be an error in judgment of the old man's intelligence. "No, I've lived here for several years. I just tend to keep to myself."

The use of the singular terms 'I' and 'myself' made him curious. He looked at her sideways, his face inquisitive, "That's a beautiful wedding band you're wearing. But I don't recall ever seeing your husband either."

Tess's stomach tightened. It was not a question she was prepared to hear ... or answer. She chose her reply carefully, weighing several answers before responding. "Well to be truthful, he recently had a work-related accident and has been in a wheelchair. It makes it difficult to get around, so mostly we stay home." Her answer was vague, offering very few details to the nosey senior.

"I see." Suddenly the old man stopped dead in his tracks, pulling on hers with his interlocked arm. Her tote slipped off her shoulder stopping at her elbow. The old man's eyes narrowed slightly. A kindly frown flipped across his brow, "But lately you've been out several times each day. What do you do about him?" The expression was not condemnation, but more concern for a poor sick man bound to his wheelchair, but his tone didn't quite reflect

She couldn't believe her ears. How dare he, a stranger, accuse her of neglecting her husband? She had always been there for Morty, day and night, every waking hour and beyond. Resentment rose in her chest making her heart race with the insult. He had crossed the line, and it was time to defend her actions. She turned to confront him but stopped herself with a caught breath. For the first time, she looked into his round creased face, years of laughter and worry etched into his leathery golden skin. How on earth could she be annoyed at someone with such serene eyes? It was then she understood why Officer Adams was so kind to Mr. Lo. Those grey-blue eyes seemed to hold the skies above and water below, ancient and youthful at the same time. She returned his gentle smile, "Oh, not to worry, I wouldn't dare leave him alone. Although, he would be all right on his own for a few hours. Morty's not really sick. He just can't walk anymore." Her shoulders tightened, she had let Morty's name slip out. She warned herself again to watch her words around the meddlesome old man. Once more the little white lie weaved its way through her thoughts. Without batting an eye, she pulled him into her deception, "And besides he's visiting his sister right now. She's taken him for a couple of weeks ... kinda giving me a short sabbatical."

His face lit up, "Oh dear, how wonderful for you." He patted her forearm with a supple shaky hand. His skin had lost its youthful elasticity, and even with the day's heat, his circulation left his touch slightly cool. "It's hard on a body, caring for someone constantly. I know this first hand. My wife was also bedridden, and I was the one who took care of her. Yes, yes, it is hard on a body." He stretched the cane's tip forward, declaring he was ready to continue the walk home. She fell in step, holding him steady as they took each step leisurely. Tess snuck a peek at her wrist, but the old man's eyes didn't miss the fact that she was actually checking her watch. Again, he cut short yanking on her elbow, "Are you late for something?"

"Um ... yes, I am. I was on my way to the bus stop." Again, it was more information than she wanted to give him, but it was too late to take the words back.

"Oh dear, I'm sorry. You go on. My head has cleared up. And that's my door right there." He pointed to the one door on the entire street painted an exquisite deep red, aged and adorned with a long thin carved dragon. An Eastern style dragon as Tess recalled. He released her arm and scolded her, "Now away you go. Hurry along. You don't want to miss the bus." He scooped his cane behind her and gently shoved her forward along the sidewalk, "Go on."

Uncertain why she said it, she thanked him for letting her go. As she strode off faster, her flip-flops kept time with her racing mind. Tess became aware that the old man had somehow overshadowed her cautious thoughts and had managed to manipulate her into talking about details she hadn't meant to confess. Maybe that was the true reason Officer Adams had befriended the senior. Maybe he too was drawn in by Mr. Lo's serene manner and mysterious influence.

At his door, he stared after her, making sure she was indeed boarding the bus. As her flip-flop disappeared up the steps, the old man noted the bus route, #460, the

Thompson Street run. The reason he bothered to note her action was due to what he saw during their walk. When her tote slipped off her shoulder, it gaped open — barely enough for him to see inside. A quick glance allowed him to spot a clear plastic bag that held several blue bags — blue bags that he had seen recently. It had been hard work holding his composure, trying not to let his face react to the sight of them. He racked his memory as to where he had seen them before and in no time, he recalled the small blue square in the trash can on the corner. As if by lightening, an additional memory flashed into place. Tess had stopped at that garbage can on her way back from Rosa's that night. What the significance of her and the blue bags were, he wasn't sure. But his instincts told him there must be a stronger connection than met the eye. He would talk to her again, ask more questions to get more answers — he'd make sure of that.

Closing his door behind him, he decided that the next time he saw Officer Kevin, he would have a chat with him about the travels of his new female friend.

# Part 6

Up the steel steps she bound, dropping the change into the glass and chrome coin box with the familiar clatter to the bottom. The air inside the bus was thick and hot with the scent of overheated bodies and bus fumes. The seats were full, crowded elbow to elbow. It seemed no one wanted to walk any measurable distance in the midday heat. The only vacant seat was next to a rather overweight man who, much to Tess's repulsion, was mopping beads of sweat from his forehead using a once white, now stained, hanky. The decision to not sit beside him was easily made, and as an alternative, she shuffled her way to a nearby pole. Her hand gripped the cool stainless steel as she stared out the window at the passing street, avoiding the scrutinizing eyes of the other passengers. The cheap knock-off fragrance of an overly perfumed female congested her lungs. She must have bathed in it for the scent to be that pungent.

The bus driver jerked the bus to a slow stop and lowered its hydraulics. The overweight man pulled himself upright and waddled his way out the rear door and down the low steps. Others left too. The man with the fluorescent lime green t-shirt followed the man in the baseball cap, both talking of cold beer at someplace called

O'Malley's. Tess quickly slid into their abandoned seat, hugging her tote close to her body. Her mind retraced the real purpose of her trip — to find garbage cans and deposit the five bags without a soul noticing. Legs crossed, she jiggled her foot nervously, nearly shaking off her flip-flop. The ride seemed to be taking an eternity. After eleven more stops, she was relieved to escape the vehicle's perfume tainted space and step off into the fresh yet heated air.

She slipped her tote on her shoulder and headed directly to the nearby park. She made her way to the far side of the green grassy opening. Children ran about chasing a soccer ball, no one caring who was winning or losing, merely enjoying the fun it provided. The sight filled Tess with sadness. Why did adults lose that carefree feeling? That innocent childhood freedom that allowed all children to simply have fun for the sake of fun itself. It was then she decided that once this was over, she would let herself live a more laid-back life, one that embraced their youthful exuberance.

In the far corner, she casually stood beside a garbage can, scanning for anyone who maybe studying her. The other adults were too busy watching their offspring to be concerned with what a strange woman was about to undertake in the shade. To make it look legitimate, she opened her tote and gently searched through it, pretending to be looking for something. In one smooth move, she yanked out one of the blue bags and dropped it into the oversized can as though it was an ordinary piece of trash. She returned to her purse searching and again tossed another bit of blue beside the first one. That was all— only two — never three. That number looked as though it might cause someone to investigate, but two simply appeared as discarded junk. As casually as she walked to it, she walked away from it strolling to the next can.

As she walked, she watched the children, their running and screaming. And as much as she enjoyed their youthful energy, she detested the boisterous ruckus they created. The shriek of one particular girl, made her head throb. How on earth could her parents stand it? All that noise and commotion, all the time? Again, she was glad she and Morty never had children. She reached the rubbish bin. That one, nearly full to the top. Tess leaned against the chain link fence and pretended to watch them play. A small dog lay in the deep shade watching them, his tongue panting in relief from the heat. In reality, she was intently scrutinizing the parents, one in particular.

He was her height with a nicely built body, his pale blue T-shirt clung to each muscle with the humidity. His short cropped dark hair and tanned skin made him an enticing sight for someone so lonely as Tess.

She let her mind wander to a place she rarely went. Letting her sexual thoughts paint a picture of him with his shirt off, revealing a naked taut torso. Then she mentally removed his navy shorts. Heat pooled above her thighs as she indulged in the fantasy of her and him lying on her bed, him pleasuring her in all sorts of passionate positions. She imagined his hands on her breasts, his lips and tongue tasting forbidden places on her body. She inhaled deeply as she envisioned her hands stroking every part of his body, exploring each hard muscle, caressing his smooth hot flesh. Her breath fought fiercely against her held chest, and she flapped her T-shirt front, waving away the accumulating body heat those thoughts brought her. From nowhere a woman appeared, kissing him quickly on the cheek before turning to call their children.

Married — he was married. And by the meager peck she bestowed on him, married to a woman who obviously had no idea how physically delicious her husband was in the eyes of other females. She watched as they gathered their things and made their way to the SUV. He leaned over the edge of the trunk, his round ass teasing Tess's eyes. Morty had never had a rear-end that luscious. Not one that made her want to grab hold and squeeze the handful tight. Morty had never made her feel that impassioned, it was always about him and never about her. Then Morty's angry accusations of her infidelity echoed through her memory. The guilt of her thoughts for a stranger flushed through her body, making the heat from the stranger disappear as quickly as it came.

Morty robbed her of that sensation too. Even after death he still manipulated her. 'Bastard!' she snapped. Instead of letting Morty control her current life any further, she turned her focus back to her blue baggie and let her lust for the stranger's body fade. She slid her hand inside her tote, retrieving a packet of gum and another baggie. The baggie she tossed in the can as though it was mere rubbish. She carefully stuck the smooth white square into her mouth and inhaled the cool fresh mint through her nose as she nervously pulverized it with her tense jaw. Casually, she dug out another bag and tossed it beside the first deposit. She strode away again watching the children and parents gathering equipment and retreating to their family size vehicles now that the soccer game was over.

One more to go she told herself. And the obvious choice was the garbage can nearest the side gate. From there, she could simply place it in and scurry to the adjacent bus stop no more than a half block away. She had planned it thoroughly, not wanting to draw attention to herself or her actions.

Approaching the can, she noticed it was nearly full to the rim yet enough space for the thin blue bag. She stopped at it, took the gum from her mouth and dropped it in the can. She then retrieved another piece as before and dropped the wrapper along with the last blue baggie beside the well-chewed gum. Her heart jumped as the bag left her fingertips. She had done it! The last bag of the day had been delivered to its final resting place. Her success felt triumphant, and a wide smile replaced her purposeful frown. As per her plan, Tess turned and escaped through the gaping gate in the fence line and quickly strode down the sidewalk.

On the edge of her eye, a tiny tan movement caught her interest. It was the dog that had been resting in the shade. A flurry of short legs raced to the trash can. Tess stopped to stare at the sight of his paws climbing the side of the mesh container, his nose sniffing and snorting at the rubbish it held. Before she got four steps in, the dog snagged the bag in his mouth and scurried away. Tess sped up her steps and chased after him her flip flops slapping wildly. But it was no use. He was too fast for her. Also, not wanting to draw attention to herself, she simply watched the little pooch disappear down the street the blue square dangling from his mouth.

Tess surveyed the people around her, wondering if anyone had seen her chasing after the dog. To her relief, the park was nearly empty, only a few mothers talking with their hands, none too interested in Tess's actions. She considered following the dog, but according to her wristwatch she didn't have time, the bus would be there within minutes. She would have to let it go, forget about the dog and the possibility that he might betray her hard work. After all, once she was gone and the dog was far away from the park, no one would be able to connect her to the thin blue baggie. Hearing the bus arriving she ran to board it. As before, it was jam packed with hot odorous passengers. Yet to Tess, this had still been a successful trip. Five bags had been disposed of, leaving only another thirteen to go. The ominous number thirteen concerned her, but instead, she merely chuckled about the recent events in her life. An accidental murder, a borrowed extension cord, two meddling dogs along with a stubborn police officer and a nosey old man ... what more could possibly go wrong?

Tess entered her house, enjoying the coolness of her living room. "Finally, a chance to relax," she told herself out loud as she plopped on her couch, sliding off her sweaty, gritty flip-flops. But that smell still hung in the air, faint yet detectable. The acidic stench of death was more difficult to suppress than she had thought. She sniffed the air, following the wafting odor which led her directly to the garage. She sniffed at the freezer's sealed lid. She shook her head that it wasn't coming from that location. And she sniffed once more. A strong scent invaded her nostrils nearly making her stomach climb into her mouth. Another fast sniff and she found the stinky source. The garbage bags no longer confined the decaying blood still lodged in the tarp's woven texture. Even the scent of bleach and cedar had completely dissipated leaving only the reek of rotting flesh. Her shoulder slumped as she closed her tired eyes. All she really wanted to do was to rest. It had already been a long trying day, and now she was faced with the task of burning the tarp whether she wanted to or not.

With a heavy sigh, she set herself to work. First, she gathered the tools needed to dissect the tarp into pieces small enough to burn without being noticed. Carpet knife and a large metal box lined with another garbage bag were placed in the center of the workshop floor. She pulled the wheeled tin box alongside, opening its lid wide. Donning her yellow kitchen gloves, she pried opened the tied garbage bags, holding her breath as long as possible, between deep gasps. Inside the tarp had solidified into a solid mass. She peeled the outer bloody bags off and dropped them into the black metal box; shards of dried, blackened blood flew upward. Nearly inhaling them, she spat out the few that touched her tongue. Those she would burn along with the tarp, newspapers and cereal boxes.

With her utility knife, she sliced along the outer folded edges, cutting through to the center layer, turning the square and repeating the process on all four sides. But getting the layers apart was challenging work. Her fingers burned with pain as they pulled the blood sealed layers away from each other. Her hands and shoulder blades ached. Eventually, she left two or three layers stuck together purely out of exhaustion. As each layer was peeled away she placed them within the fold of a newspaper's section — firstly, so they wouldn't re-stick together in the humidity and secondly, so she could place a piece of tarp on the fire disguised as a simple newspaper. Each section was laid in flat, the tarp tucked out of sight. This she had planned out in her head, every step and every action intended to minimize the chance of discovery.

With all the prepped segments of tarp encased in the metal box, she changed clothes and cleaned her hands thoroughly. Back in the garage, she took the long-snouted BBQ lighter from Morty's work bench and wedged it in the back of her shorts, like a hit man hiding his gun. Tess pulled on the rope handle, its tiny wheels squeaking all the way out of the garage and to the brick fire pit at the back edge of her property. She parked the metal container next to the blackened bricks and promptly returned to the house for the garden hose, dragging it next to the box. Because of recent arid weather, she decided it was better safe than sorry, in case a spark strayed, igniting the nearby dried grass. She sat upon the concrete block and whipped out Morty's lighter like a pistol, feeling the excitement of the criminal act she was about to commit.

As she had done every week that summer, she started the fire in the same manner; crumbled newspaper and twigs for the initial tiny blaze, then she slowly added cardboard and more newspapers as needed. Healthy flames made it easy for her to burn away the pieces of tarp that she added one by one from the metal box. The flames were hypnotic, even in the daylight. They danced as they burned through the paper covered tarp, emitting a thin black tendril of smoke into the air. Tess sat quietly on the concrete block watching the flames, the tension easing in her back and neck as she became lost in their beauty. Tired and hungry, it was easy for her to be pulled into the fire's spell, ignoring the world around her. She didn't hear the footsteps that approached her from behind.

He stopped two feet behind her, "Mrs. Logan. You do know that there's a city fire ban in place?"

The growl deep in his voice made her jump, shocking her out of her trance. Turning her head about, she saw the one man she did not want to see, Officer Adams in full uniform, his gun hanging from his hip. As dumbstruck as she was, she calmly stood up and proceeded to push the lid of the metal container closed and sit gracefully on its top, her legs crossed along with her arms. "No, I'm sorry, I didn't know that." She made her cheeks flush red with embarrassment. "I'll stop then." But she didn't move off the box. Instead, she stayed seated and squinted up at the officer. "Can I ask you a question?"

"Sure." That particular type of question was always a concern. It usually meant it was an awkward and insidious question difficult to answer.

"Is that gun really loaded? I mean, with real bullets and everything?" Her eyes never left the black iron revolver resting in his holster.

He chuckled softly before he answered, "Um ... yes. It would be kinda pointless to carry a gun that was not fully loaded at all times. Especially if I'm chasing a criminal, don't you think?" His tone was more mocking than clarifying. He witnessed her facial reaction. She winced somewhat with the unintended insult. He hurried to save the situation, smiling widely for effect, "I mean, it's only logical when you think about it." The wrong choice of words again by the way she recoiled from him. "It's not like I could stop and load bullets in my gun while chasing a perp? I've got to be ready at all times. Seconds count. Two seconds could mean the difference between life or death." Her face eased slightly, and so did his tone. "I'm sorry, I didn't mean to be so grumpy. It's been one of those long days. It's the heat. People can't cope with it. And we haven't had a break in the weather for some time now." He rubbed his forehead with the heel of his hand, "In the last two weeks we've stopped seven cases of spousal abuse. Between the boozing and the heat, it's been hell." He noted the minor change in her face when he said the words 'spousal abuse'. She blinked wildly then lowered her eyes disconnecting them from his. Her face paled within seconds. That, to his disappointment, was the evidence he was afraid to find. Mrs. Tess Logan was an abused woman. Instantly, his eyes searched for physical evidence — bruises, cuts, abrasions and the like — but there were none. She felt his eyes upon her, scrutinizing every inch of her flesh. Indignant, she lifted her head high looking at him, her jaw clenched to show her strength.

All he noticed was her vulnerable blue eyes and soft, smooth skin. She was so delicate how could any man bring himself to hurt her? Memories of other victims paraded through his mind. Bruises, blood, and broken bones. It tugged at him to know she too endured the evil of another human's hands. He tried his best not to think of her that way, as a helpless victim. Lowering his eyes in shame for the human race, he shifted his hat from one hand to the other, "How much you got left to burn?"

She slipped on a soft smile, "Not much really ... maybe ten more pieces."

He turned slightly scanning the ground. "Well, you do have the hose here. I guess you can finish up them few. But for God sakes, soak that pit down before you go inside. With this dry grass, hell, it would travel fast."

She couldn't believe her ears, "Oh, that's no problem. I'll make sure I drown it thoroughly."

Before Tess stood the very man she had been worried about, and he was breaking the rules by giving her permission to burn the evidence she literally was sitting on. It was all she could do to not burst out laughing at the enormous blunder he was unknowingly committing.

She flashed her twinkling eyes up at him, "Besides I wouldn't want to be hurting anyone by breaking the law. Only a few more pieces then I'll be done 'til next week. I just wanna burn them before they start smelling too bad." Then she caught her breath and her words. She had gone too far, almost revealing too much. Now she had to think fast to recover from her mistake. "Silly me, I spilled milk all over the newspaper pile. And in this heat, it'll stink sour by midnight."

The radio at his hip hissed, and a garbled female voice called out numbers and then an address Tess couldn't comprehend.

"Well, gotta go." He turned down the hissing, "Like I said, soak it completely." He was already walking to the cruiser when the police radio distorted more instructions.

"Consider it done," she yelled out after him.

Tess dug her hands under her outer thighs, holding them in place until Officer Adams was gone. Patience, she told herself, No point in tipping him off. She fought the urge to look until she heard the cruiser door slam.

As he pulled out of the driveway, Tess waved at him. Not a big friendly wave, but a weak, timid one. A forlorn wave a youngster would give when they were left behind with relatives for summer vacation. That too tugged at him. She was frail as a child. Vulnerable was more the word he wanted to use.

Yet there was something else about her he couldn't pin down. A gut feeling that ate at him. Was she as innocent as he thought she was? The radio blasted again, this time, he flipped on the siren and floored it. As he raced down the road slowing for intersections, it came to him — what had bothered him about Tess when he left.

She wasn't burning papers.

In fact, he recalled that she had remained sitting on top of the metal box, sitting very stiff and remarkably still. Why hadn't she added more newspaper to the fire pit while they were talking? It was hot, and he believed she would have wanted to be finished as quickly as possible in order to escape to the cool of the house. Why hadn't she started again?

A blue pickup truck blasted its horn, waking Officer Adams from his deep thoughts. He scolded himself, 'Yeah that's it, get yourself killed going to a beating that's already over with. Stupid! Pay attention!' He slowed the cruiser and pushed the thoughts of Tess Logan out of his head. He had real work to do — police work.

Tess had started burning again.

After the cruiser disappeared out of sight and the siren wailed, she continued her mission. Standing from the metal box, she slowly lifted the lid while visually scanning for possible witnesses. There were none. As before, she carefully retrieved one-fold of newspaper and placed it on the fire.

She enjoyed watching it burn. At first, it curled upward at the edges then began to smolder at the ends. The paper caught, next, the plastic tarp would melt before wisps of black smoke tendrils rose from it. Then flames. Tiny blue flames that slowly burned out to a pale orange. Finally, it was gone, mere ashes and gobs of black remained.

Tess added another newspaper to the pit.

One by one they ignited and disappeared until there was nothing left. Ashes to ashes, she thought to herself as the hose streamed water into the pit. Washing away her sin.

With the pit turned into a puddle, she turned the hose on the metal box, washing it thoroughly inside and out, just in case any blood or tissue had found its way on it. The task was complete. The tarp was gone. One less piece of evidence that could send her to prison.

But there was still so much more work to be done.

# Part 7

*Pop! Bang! Bang! Bang! Bang! Pop! Bang!*

Tess sat straight up in the air. Her heart pounding with what she thought was the sound of gunshots. Her frayed nerves were getting to her. Another round of firecrackers went off, popping and splitting the air outside her window. She inhaled deeply, releasing the knot in her stomach as her sleepy brain recognized the voice of her neighbor Jenny, once again, screaming at one of her children.

"You little bastard! Give me those." The sound of thundering footsteps running along the house told Tess that they were in a foot chase as she hollered after him, "You get back here with those." The footsteps came to a sudden stop and were immediately replaced by squeals of a struggle.

"No, they're mine. I paid for them myself." It was Jenny's oldest boy Billy, his whining protested while his mother confiscated his loud summer fun. "Nooo! They're mine!" His bellyaching echoed between Jenny's garage and Tess's house, bouncing from the old wooden structure to her house's brick exterior. It was a wonder the garage hadn't fallen down in the last wind storm, its walls having thin spaces in between its ancient dry, shrunken boards.

"Oh no, you don't!" She grabbed at the wrist being held out behind his back, pulling it forward and prying open his tightly clenched fist.

"Ouch! Stop it. You're hurting me!" he wailed in protest to her twisting his fingers, forcing him to release what he held in his rigidly knotted hand.

Finally prying open his hand, she took what he held and examined them closer. One round red cherry bomb and a square of tiny firecrackers, their wicks braided down the center for rapidly repeated detonation and maximum noise production. "I've told you a million times, no firecrackers. Now get in the house, you're grounded. For a week ... no, make that until school starts."

Even from her bed, Tess thought that punishment a little extreme. There was still another two weeks until summer vacation ended. In Tess's mind, she knew the true punishment would be put on Jenny. A 13-year-old boy trapped in a house for two weeks — last two weeks of summer vacation — would be pure hell on any mother, let alone a single mother in Jenny's situation. She climbed off the bed and went to the window to spy on the family skirmish first hand.

A group of kids had congregated at the back door, watching the struggle between him and his mother. "No God damned way!" he screamed back, shoving at her body in anger. "You can't make me." He wanted to call her names but held back the curse words in his head. No point in making it harder on himself than it was.

Within seconds, she grasped his wrist and twisted it, inflicting pain to stop him from any further physical threat. "That's enough. Now get in that house and straight to your room." Her finger pointed behind her back towards the house. He pulled away, but she held on tight. “I’m the mother here and you’ll do what I say.”

Tess stood in the window above, watching the strained moment between them with held breath. Surely, they weren’t going to hurt each other. She shook her head no, knowing full well that Jenny wouldn’t allow it. Although Jenny allowed roughhousing amongst the boys, violence was never permitted.

They stared at each other for the longest moment, testing to see who would give in first, surrendering their stronghold in this one of many mother-child clashes. She released his hand but held her stare into his defiant eyes. He blinked. Then in a sign of submission, he lowered his head, conceding to her motherly evil eye, knowing he couldn’t truly win when she was in that state of anger. He turned and did as he was told, his feet stomping out his objection at being treated like a child. The children at the door scattered out of his way, avoiding any confrontation with his frustration and possibly his fists.

Jenny watched her teenage son storm in the backdoor. Her heart went out to him. At thirteen he was neither a man nor a boy — an age of sexual confusion and torturous growing pains. And with no father around, he had it worse than most boys his age. But none the less, firecrackers were fundamentally dangerous. A simple toy that when not respected, caused fire and injury. He knew full well that they were forbidden in their home. They were only to be used under supervision and only during night time holiday celebrations. Looking at the tiny bombs she held in her palm, she decided to hide them in the garage, saving them for the Labour Day weekend coming in two weeks. They’d be her bribe of forgiveness when she relinquished his house arrest that weekend.

Tess watched through the tiny window on the side of her neighbor's garage as Jenny placed the handful of explosives on the top of the wooden utility shelf, pushing them towards the back.

Jenny then leaned against the workbench and lowered her chin to her chest. Her head bobbed slightly under the shield of hanging hair, telling Tess that she was once again crying quietly. Tess had seen it many times before. The garage was Jenny's sanctuary from her children. A place where she could go to let it all out. All her frustrations, all the uncertainties in her life, and the loneliness of being a single mother. She wiped the tears from her cheeks and did what she always did when she was emotional. She began to tidy the workbench behind her. A cleanup job she meant to do before then, but fatigue got in her way and she left it for whenever she could get to it. She hung up the old nylon blanket she used as a drop cloth, using the empty dowel of the wooden rake rack.

Through the cracked window pane, Tess noted the yellow extension cord on the hook beside it. The garage was truly on its last leg, as old as the house Jenny lived in, but with no upkeep. She squinted her eyes tightly, trying to see it more thoroughly. That's when she saw it. A long stain of rusty brown running down the fine lines of the cord from its plug end.

Blood — dried blood.

Tess held her breath, waiting to see if Jenny noticed the new streak brought on by last night's humidity. To her relief, Jenny was busy pouring in more paint thinner in a small container that held three paint brushes ready for cleaning.

She swished them about in the clear liquid, thinking about the fight she had with Billy. How she was going to find a male influence for him in his teenage years?

Someone he could confide in when a mother wouldn't do. She contemplated deeply as she swished the bristles back and forth.

"Mum!" a tiny voice barked from the doorway.

The word startled her with a jolt, her hand jerked, splashing thinner on her hands and the work top. "Christ Derek! Are you trying to give me a heart attack?" The four-year-old just stared at her, not understanding what she meant by the question. "What is it Derek?" she wiped her hands dry, then mopped up the puddle she had spilled.

"The baby's awake and is crying." He rolled his eyes at the rafters, "A lot! And she smells like poop again." He pinched his nose in disgust.

She smiled at his honesty, "Okay, I'll be right in after I clean this up." Tossing the damp cloth into a white plastic bag, she twisted the top tight and put it at the back of the work bench. "Just give her the bottle of cold water from the fridge until I get there."

He shrugged his shoulders, "I'll do anything as long as it shuts her up." He spun on his heels and ran for the house, full blast, his arms like an airplane.

Another pang of guilt tugged at her heart. She let out a long-straggled sigh and continued her cleaning binge to ease the tension in between her shoulders.

Knowing that the thinner would probably evaporate before she had a chance to come back and clean the brushes, she attempted to slow down the process by covering it with a plastic grocery bag, tightly wrapped and secured by tying its handles together. She shoved it to the back of the bench, unaware that she had toppled the rag bag over; its handles dangling over the wooden edge. That's when she saw what Tess had already seen — that the rust color was embedded in the electrical cord. She twisted the yellow plastic in her fingers examining it closer.

Tess's breath caught, her muscles tensed tight as she watched Jenny study the extension cord. Did she understand what she was looking at? That she was holding the only remaining piece of external evidence of Tess's brutal crime. What would she do next? Call the police? Officer Adams' face flashed in her mind, forcing the knot in her stomach to return.

Unsure what the substance was, Jenny simply let it hang in place while she pushed the lawn mower into its designated spot, tight against the wall below the dowelled rack and tight to the work bench. In doing so, she bumped the utility shelf, which in turn bumped the lawn mowers' gas line, easing it slightly from its normal taut position.

A tiny drop of gas collected at the minuscule gap and fell silently onto the floor. But no one was there to smell its fumes, for by the time it finally hit the concrete floor Jenny had already returned to the house and the miserable wailing baby.

In the window above, Tess's mind raced, first with thought crushing fear, then with possible strategies. She had to make that extension cord disappear. It could be the one piece of proof that could bring the police knocking at her door. Except for the frozen body, tarp, and carpet, it was the only other item that could connect her to Morty's death.

Fire — it destroyed everything in its path, erasing the sins of many a mankind.

She would burn it, just as she had burned the other blood tainted items involved in the dismemberment.

But how? She couldn't just throw Jenny's extension cord in the burn barrel. That would be too obvious, drawing too much attention to her increasingly odd behavior. She paced back and forth beside her bed, peering down at the garage each time she passed the open window. "Fire, fire," she muttered to herself. After twenty minutes of consideration, she came to one final conclusion — she would have to burn down Jenny's garage in order to destroy the yellow extension cord. She hated to do it to Jenny, but she had no choice. In her mind, she concluded it was either she set the garage on fire or end up in prison. And she was not going to prison for the death of her miserable husband.

But also in her mind, she knew that she would have to give the fire an appearance of being an accident, drawing any suspicions away from herself. She began to pace again. Another ten minutes slowly crawled by as she thought and rethought, yet nothing formed a logical plan.

Outside, she heard the voices of Jenny's twins, yelling up to the teen's window. She sat on the bed eavesdropping on their conversation.

"We're outside, and you can't come out and play." Derek teased from the ground.

Billy flew to the window, "Shut up you little shit!"

Dwayne laughed hardest, "Mum's really pissed at ya, and she's got your crackers."

"Not all of them," He smugly growled back, crossing his arms pompously.

The two twins glanced at each other, reading each other's thoughts as twins do. It was Derek who asked the question they were both thinking, "What do you mean, not all of them?"

His face went superior, "I hid some."

Once more the twins looked at each other, both realizing their older brother had brilliantly outwitted their mother. Dwayne was the one to start the taunting, eager to make their brother confess. "No, you didn't. You're lying."

"Am not," he protested back.

The other twin accused saucily, "Are too."

He stuck his head out past the window sill, "I did so hide them."

"Yah, so where are they?" Derek teased next.

Dwayne jumped in immediately, "No, he hid them in his room."

"In this house? Are you nuts? No way! If I did, Mum would find them for sure." Billy rushed to defend himself and his intelligence, "Christ, I'm not that stupid. I hid them outside." The instant the last words left his lips, Billy knew he had betrayed himself.

That was exactly what the Twins wanted to hear. As if their butts were on fire, they both turned and ran to the backside of the garage, nearest to Tess's house.

Up in the window, Billy's mouth fell open. He couldn't believe he had said it. He had been tricked by his much younger brothers. They knew exactly where he had hidden them and were on their way to pilfer his precious crackers. But worse, there was nothing he could do about it. If he went after them, he would be in trouble with his Mother for leaving his room. Nor could he snitch on them for stealing his stash of firecrackers, he would be in even greater trouble for hiding them from his mother. Either way, he was doomed. All he could do was watch his brothers scurry around the corner of the garage, straight to his hiding spot, where they would raid his secret hoard of naked girly pictures, matches and of course, his beloved firecrackers. He angrily slammed his window shut, declaring his frustration with his entire life.

Hearing the multiple footsteps, she scooted to her window and spied on the boys below her. They both ran directly to a single spot, both kneeling at a tiny crack in the garage's wooden boards. Head alongside head, they carefully pulled out a dirty paper bag. Opening it as though it were Christmas morning, Dwayne took out each item, laying them on the grass for further inspection. It was the pictures of naked women that intrigued Derek more than his brother. At four years old, he had never seen exposed breasts before. He looked at his own chest for comparison. *How come she doesn't have a thingy like mine?* he thought to himself. Unable to explain it and being more interested in firecrackers than their nakedness, he simply placed the pictures back into the bag.

As if by lightning, a plan blasted into Tess's mind — the firecrackers. She couldn't believe her luck. Those two brats had given her the solution she needed. As easily as breathing, her plan fell nicely into place all on its own. She would set the garage on fire using the firecrackers that Jenny had stored on the shelf. She would destroy the extension cord and Jenny's boys would take the blame for it. With the boys being so young, they'd be punished, yet not left with a criminal record. It was perfect.

"Let's leave some for later?" Dwayne stuck half the stack of firecrackers back in the bag, "Man, these are the best kind. Wanna go get the frogs down by the bridge?" Derek was halfway to his feet when Dwayne stuffed the bag back into its cubby hole.

Derek spun in spot and yelled over his shoulder, "Last one there's gotta kiss Stinky Winslow!" That set a fire under Dwayne's butt again. Becky Winslow was overweight and smelled of old stinky cheese, even worse with the summer's heat. And there was no way he was kissing her! Tess watched as the two disappeared out of sight, one chasing after the other as little boys and brothers do.

Tess dressed quickly, making her way down to the cubby hole as fast as possible. Scanning the neighborhood for others, she stooped down retrieving the paper bag. She ignored the pornography and took only one book of matches, immediately tucking them along with the firecrackers into her pocket. As she stood up from squatting, a familiar odor in the air caught the attention of her nostrils — it was the smell of spilled gasoline. Gasoline — a highly flammable fluid and the possible answer to her dilemma. She repeatedly sniffed the air following the acidic trail to its source. Reaching the window, she sniffed the thin crack that cut across it. The fumes were coming from inside the garage. She peered through the window and to her delight, she saw the most heavenly sight she could have wished for. A wet pool of gas had formed around the base of the lawn mowers wheels.

It was too good to be true. She looked twice just to make sure her eyes weren't deceiving her. There it was again, a shiny puddle of gas tainting the interior of the garage with its vapors. She almost squealed with excitement at her luck but covered her mouth to stifle the sound, dancing lightly instead. Instantly, she knew what she had to do. She had to find a way into the garage, light a firecracker, and toss it into the gasoline. *WHOOSH!* Up in flames it would go. No more extension cord - no more worries.

She placed her hands on the window pane, pushing upward, hoping to open the glass. It didn't budge. Next to it was the side door, but she was sure Jenny always locked it — more to keep her kids out than to protect against thieves. With a prayer, she tried the knob. As smooth as butter it turned, opening its solid wood to the interior of the garage. She peeked passed the doorframe's edge, making sure no one was around to witness her dirty deed. With the neighborhood empty she stepped just inside, her chest heaving with the stress of what she was about to do, her heart stuck at the base of her throat. She inhaled deep, trying to ease her tension but the gas fumes choked any oxygen she took in. It was then that Tess realized it was not safe to light a match inside the garage, being best if the firecracker was thrown from a distance. Outside was a better choice to ignite their sulphuric tips. Remembering the cracked window, she went to it, prying open the poorly made flip-lock and pushed it upward. Conveniently, Jenny had left a stick for her to jam in the opening, creating a place for her to ignite the crackers. She closed the door tightly behind her while she scanned her surroundings one more time, making sure there were no witnesses lurking about.

At the window, she carefully pulled the flat of firecrackers from her pocket and at hidden waist height, detached a solitary firecracker from the pack's end. Wisely, she returned the rest back into her pocket before fetching the book of penny matches. Her hands shook as Tess pulled off a single match, holding it in her fingers to strike against the grey strip.

For the longest moment, she hesitated, staring back and forth between the match and the tiny explosive. That was the final moment that she could change her mind. The final moment where she could still walk away and find another way to destroy the evidence, instead of burning down Jenny's garage. Gasoline fumes drifted under her nose, waking her from her contemplative trance. She took the vaporous invasion as a Divine sign that she should continue. With the cracker wedged between her first and second finger, she held the match pack with her thumb. In her head, she said another little prayer, asking that no one be injured and that only the inside of the garage itself be destroyed by the destructive power she was about to unleash. She held her breath, not wanting to blow out the match, but in reality, she was stopping the contents of her stomach from leaping out onto the ground.

'Now! Do ... It ... Now!' she spat out, ordering herself to stop being a coward and get on with it.

In one sharp strike, she lit the match and in turn, lit the firecracker. Tiny sparks flew in all directions from its wick. Almost shocked by its brilliance, she gawked at it for a long moment, only to remind herself she was actually holding a tiny volatile tube of gunpowder. Without further hesitation, she threw it through the window before it exploded, possibly injuring her fingers. Her heart raced as she watched it fly, in what seemed like slow motion to her racing mind. Through the air it flew, landing directly in the puddle of gasoline. A perfect shot.

She crouched down behind the window sill, peaking above the wooden edge to watch the resulting explosion. But to her astonishment, nothing happened. Gap mouthed, she watched as the firecracker's hissing wick was drowned by the gasoline, extinguishing its firepower. The lifeless firecracker sat in the flammable liquid soaking up, even more gas, its paper wrapper turning darker and darker with its absorption.

Her heart sank. How could gasoline put out a firecracker? Where was the logic in that? She stood up, looking back into the opening. It was going to be more difficult than she had first thought. She ran through her head what she had done and quickly came to the conclusion that she would have to toss the firecracker beside the gasoline pool, allowing it to explode before it drowned, hopefully igniting the gas from there.

She began to undo another firecracker when it occurred to her that the more she let off at once, the greater the chance of the gas catching on fire. She split the last third off and returned those to her pocket. If that toss didn't work, she had those in reserve for one last attempt.

As before, she balanced the matches and firecracker in her fingers and lit the main wick. She didn't wait like last time. She aimed with her eyes and repeatedly swung the flat until she was sure it was lined up just right and released the grip of her fingertips. Ducking down behind the sill, she watched as the firecrackers flew across the garage landing two inches from the thin flood of fuel. For what seemed like forever, the wick hissed.

She held her breath, mentally willing it to explode, igniting the gas.

The wait was agony as she stared at the tiny mesmerizing wick.

Then it hit.

*Pop! Bang! Bang! Bang! Bang! Pop! Bang!*

Each of the firecrackers ignited, one after the other along its braided strip. She covered her face with her arm, trying to protect her face from what would come next. To her surprise, it wasn't what she thought might happen. The explosion from the firecrackers did not light the gas, but ignited the cloud of fumes into barrelling billows, a fiery nebula cloud of electric blue. It rolled and roared with each second the fumes fuelled its heat until finally, the gasoline itself rippled with amber expanding flames to the gasoline's outer edges.

Tess watched as the golden flames grew higher, reaching above the lawnmower and up towards the rafters. The flames lapped at the tip of the old nylon blanket taunting it with the threat of fire. Then it caught, the flame smoldered until a tiny flame made a dark red-rimmed hole. Within seconds, the flames raced up the entire length, trailing fire from the floor to the wall and then up to the rafters. There the flames licked along the dry wood wall, setting it on fire as globs of molten nylon dripped from the blanket to below. Black soot danced along the outer edges of the amber fireball that was intensifying, its heat sending thick inky smoke across the rafters. Below the flames leaped at the handles of the white plastic rag bag, setting them ablaze and the contents of the bag exploded with a rush of fire. The plastic bag that sealed the brushes in the paint thinner melted, burning with a thin blue flame. A half second elapsed before the fumes of the paint thinner combusted into a fireball, spouting flames in all directions, each torching the old wooden work bench.

The black smoke had reached the traumatized Tess, suffocating her lungs of oxygen. To her amazement, the entire act took less than two minutes to engulf the interior of Jenny's garage. Choking hard, she pulled herself away from the window and retreated to her own house.

Upstairs in her bedroom window, she watched as the flames broke through the crumbling tarpaper shingle roof. The occasional flame would lick through the black smoke escaping from the open window. *BOOM!* Her body jerked with the unexpected explosion. Was it the gas tank on the lawnmower blowing up or the paint cans on the lower shelf of the workbench?

In the far-off distance, the sound of sirens rose above the roar of the fire. Sparks danced up through the sky, telling them exactly where the fire was located. She watched as the neighbors gathered at the curb, talking, and pointing at the soaring flames sending a stream of smoke that streaked across the sky. They began to wave and yell, calling out to Jenny who was carrying the baby on her hip, herding Billy, and the kids down the driveway away from the burning garage. Reaching the waiting crowd, they were hugged and comforted by those around them. Billy blushed as he betrayed his brothers, telling his mother that the younger twins were down at the pond blowing up frogs with his hidden treasure of firecrackers.

A pickup truck wildly pulled up over the curb, the green light flashing on the dash. Dwayne and Derek came chasing after it, only to be funneled directly to their mother's side by their neighbors. The volunteer firefighter rushed to the crowd asking questions Tess couldn't hear over the snapping, roaring fire. Heads shook, and children were pointed to, meaning that all were accounted for. At the end of the block, red lights flashed, and sirens blasted through the air announcing that the fire department was there, and help was on its way. Within seconds, people scattered, the truck parked where they had stood, and firemen raced with hoses, dragging them into place. White water spewed high in the air aiming at the hot spots in the roof, some now open flaming holes. Various vehicles arrived, delivering additional fireman, each immediately running to their pre-assigned jobs.

Wisps of thick smoke began to drift into Tess's window forcing her to close it tight. A thundering knock was heard from her front door. She raced down the stairs and flung open the door. She caught her breath at the sight before her.

Officer Adams was about to pound on her door again, his fist angrily hung in mid-air, "Ma'am, you need to evacuate the premises immediately. Chances are the fire's gonna spread this way. It's not safe for you to stay here." He looked past her, "Where's your husband? He'll have to come too. You get his chair, and I'll carry him."

Tess died inside. Not only was Officer Adams standing in her doorway but now he was demanding the appearance of her husband — the dead Morty Logan. Would this man ever go away? Her brain raced for an answer — the same little lie blurted out of her mouth, "He's not here. He's at his sister's." As fast as her feet could take her, she turned away, grabbed her tote and slipped between him and the doorframe. She didn't wait for him to follow her, she ran to the accumulated crowd, hiding amongst her neighbors, shielding herself from the Officer.

Although the burning garage was their main target, another hose was pumping gallons of water on Tess's house, wetting down the roof and walls so that the sparks wouldn't ignite her shingles.

Her heart sank. She had forgotten to take into account the direction of the wind, and now her own home could be in jeopardy of becoming engulfed by the very fire she created.

Initially, she began to consider the burning down of her own home a blessing in disguise. Then after more thought, she realized that the body of Morty would probably stay intact within its metal cocoon. Her thoughts and emotions whirled in her head. Her chest tightened, strangling what little oxygen it still held. Her knees let go, releasing the rigidness of her spine. Downward she slid; she was passing out from the strain. Then hands caught her, slowly pulling her upright.

A pair of strong arms enveloped her from behind, holding her steady on her feet. They felt warm and wonderful as they pulled her against his body. She twisted her head, peeking to see who belonged to those caring arms. It was a man she recognized as one of the tenants in the high-rise two blocks over. What surprised her was how delightful it felt to be held so tenderly by a complete stranger. Instead of pushing him away as she thought she should, she leaned into him, enjoying his taller stature and taut muscles. It seemed like years since anyone had touched her that way. Soft, yet strong. Stress and sexual tension built up in her chest, strangling her breathing, making her more light headed than before. Sparks from the garage danced above Jenny's house. Each one threatening to ignite the wet shingles, while long tangerine flames lashing high in the air.

A segment of blackened roof crashed inward, making her body jump. Again, his arms held her tight and upright. As if reading her mind, he leaned in and kissed her hair, rocking her gently from side to side for comfort. But it was that same comfort that triggered her pent-up emotions, all of them rising to the surface at once. She couldn't fight it anymore —didn't want to fight it any longer — letting it all flow out. Streams of tears rolled down her cheeks with each hard sob she sputtered out. He held her closer, pressing his face against her hair calming her with quiet hushes of shush. Others turned their heads to see who was crying. Once they saw it was Tess, they disregarded it as sadness for her neighbor and returned to watch the fiery entertainment. The wind shifted again, pushing the flames away from Tess's house and towards the backyards instead.

In contrast to the crowd, Officer Adams stood off to one side, scrutinizing the couple with great interest. As before, his intuition alerted him to the peculiar behavior of Mrs. Tess Logan. If her husband was at his sister's, why was she being held by another man? And a good-looking man at that. He could fully understand why the man wanted to hold her. Her tiny frame and delicate pale skin made her a very tempting target to embrace. How could he blame the man for wanting to kiss her silky-smooth hair? Hair that streamed honey blonde in the breeze?

But who was this man to her? Maybe a close friend? Or perhaps a lover? It wasn't uncommon for the spouses of wheelchair-bound persons to take a lover, especially if there were difficulties in the bedroom. Some even condoned their loved one fulfilling their sexual needs elsewhere, in hopes of not losing their love one completely.

Furious flames ruptured through the roof, eating away at the remaining wood timbers distracting him from his thoughts. Molten gobs of shingle tar dripped off the edge of the roof, telling all of the unfathomable temperatures the fire harnessed. The winds eased allowing the grey-black clouds to twist vertically up into the sky. The crowd slowly backed away from the fire's heat retreating onto a neighbor's front yard. When he turned back to spy on Tess further, she was nowhere to be seen. He craned his neck over the tops of people's heads to see where she had gone. The man stood alone gawking at the burning building with the others. Officer Adams ventured into the crowd, making his way to where he stood, casually positioning himself beside the unknown man.

"Shame, ain't it?" He kept his voice casual as possible, as though it was a question of a civilian rather than a police office.

"Yah," was all the man replied. His face stayed focussed on the fire, and the scurry of the men who were trying to control it.

"Do you know the people?" He flapped the front of his thick police shirt releasing body heat.

"Sorta. I talked to her once in a while at the park. Nice lady, great kids." Again, much to the officer's disappointment, his answer was short and to the point.

This was going to be harder than he had anticipated. He switched tactic by pulling a pack of gum from his uniform pocket and offered him one, "Do you know the neighbor?"

The man stuck the stick in his mouth and chewed, answering between chomps, "The blonde? Not really."

"Just thought you might, the way you were comforting her?" He kept his face calm, hiding his jealousy, but his voice didn't come across as tempered as he wanted.

The man raised his eyebrows at his question, "No, I don't. But I wasn't going to let her hit the ground. It happens to some people in situations like this. They get upset. Get all woozy and lose their strength." He chuckled, "My sister's a good one for fainting at the sight of blood. I swear, I've caught her a few hundred times."

He grinned along with him, "Yah, got me a deputy like that. Needles are not his friend." He glanced around, "Do you know where she went?"

"Down there ... I think." The tall man pointed towards the alleyway that ran along the row of attached townhouses. "Don't know for sure." Another hunk of roof fell in, causing everyone to scatter in all directions. Most returned to their homes, while others moved cars further down the street to avoid the possibility of their own insurance claims. Officer Adams fell into his position of authority, directing the citizens away from the fire zone and in the opposite direction.

Down on her knees, Tess peered around the edge of the shed looking for the cop. Relieved that he wasn't anywhere to be seen, she twisted down onto her behind and exhaled deeply. He was the last person she wanted following her. Knowing she would be there for awhile, she shifted herself into a more comfortable position. She rested her head back against the shed wall and closed her eyes. Gradually a satisfied grin grew upon her lips. The bloody extension cord was gone — gone for good, burned into an unrecognizable blob.

Or at least she hoped so? Her eyes popped open. Had it actually been destroyed to the point of non-detection? Her stomach lurched. She swallowed hard, forcing the bile back down. With eyes closed, she prayed that the fire had not been for nothing. Her thoughts quickly turned to her own house. Was it still in peril of being burnt by her fire? Her heart sank. As much as she wanted the answer, she dared not show herself at the fire scene. Officer Adams was surely there, still watching her from a distance. Would that man ever go away? Knowing that there was nothing she could do but wait, she closed her eyes and rested her head against her curled up knees. In her mind, she replayed what she had witnessed through Jenny's garage window. The flames were so close to the cord, it must have burnt along with the rest of the garage's contents. Tess let out a long slow breath and relieved the band-like tension around her chest. Yes, the cord is gone, she told herself. With that reassurance, she wriggled into a comfortable position. After all, she would be there for a long time, waiting until the fire department and police were completely gone. That she knew, would take hours. Unaware, she hummed in her head, a song she didn't know — but it came naturally, soothing her confused troubled mind.

# Part 8

Tess woke with a jolt. Her body ached from sitting so long on the hard ground, her heart raced violently in her chest, and she was covered in a chilling sweat, her reaction to her horrible nightmare. She dreamt that the heat from the fire she set, warped the top of the freezer Morty was encased in. It's two ends bent up yet still held down in the middle by the lock. Officer Adams was standing beside one end, peering inside with his long cop flashlight. As she walked closer, he shone the light in her face, accusing her of killing Morty for his pension cheques. She tried to defend herself, telling him the truth, but he wouldn't listen. She shook her head wildly, yelling, "No! No! You have it wrong! He was beating me. He was mean and hurting me. I was only protecting myself." But Officer Adams didn't care — he was holding his handcuffs to put on her wrists —

That's when Tess woke up, scared, cold and trembling with fear. She jumped to her feet and ran towards her house, taking back alleys and shortcuts so no one would see her.

Under cover of darkness, she returned to her house, able to slip by the few remaining firefighters. The interior of the house smelled of dense smoke, but she didn't care about that. All she cared about was what the heat from the fire had done to her garage. Had the freezer actually been effected? She had a mental image of the lid being warped, its ends exposing what was locked inside, just as in her nightmare. She ran straight for the garage and flung the interior door open.

Nothing.

As far as she could see by what little light there was, the freezer had been untouched by the heat. The lid was still flat, and Officer Adams wasn't peeking in the end. Tess grabbed the door frame to stop her body from weaving, her knees threatened to give way. Stumbling to the couch, she curled up on one end and quietly cried with relief until she finally fell asleep again.

When morning had come, Tess went upstairs to her window since it had the best view of Jenny's yard. From behind her curtain, she spied at the destruction below. Jenny's garage was completely gone, reduced to a pile of black rubble and ashes. Her house had fire damage as well. The vinyl siding had melted along with the tar shingles of her roof.

Tess was grateful that her house and garage was built of brick. She was also grateful that the fireman had started to soak down her buildings before any of the sparks could ignite her house and garage. She would check the exterior of her place once all the fireman and gawking neighbors had left. She made her way downstairs with the sole purpose of examining damage inside the garage — the freezer to be exact. Tess vaguely remembered looking inside it the night before but didn't trust what she had seen with her fatigued, stressed mind. At the door, she pushed it forward, saying a prayer to herself, *Dear God, if you make everything undamaged, I promise to never harm another human being*. She touched her head, her heart then both shoulders, sealing the deal she made with her Lord.

Taking the steps slowly, she stared at the white metal box. It was true. The freezer had remained intact. No bent lid, no bulging walls. She released her held breath then glanced upward, "Thank you!" she praised out loud. Next, she examined the interior of the wall beside Morty's workbench — no damage there as well. She frowned at the damage to the garage door. The large bulge in the upper left-hand corner was a problem. Her initial reaction was to open it up to see if it still worked. Half bent over and her hand on the lever, she stopped, realizing that if the door wouldn't close tight again, she would have a huge problem hiding her freezer and her actions normally done behind that closed door.

She stared at the bulge for a few moments, then stepping forward, she shoved the bulge with her palm. *POING!* The metal snapped back into place. With her hand, she rubbed it across the spot, "There. That'll do it." Satisfied that no other damage was done, she headed for the kitchen. Her stomach growled with the lack of food. Tea and toast could be quickly made before she started her day. Another day of getting rid of the evidence.

However, Tess decided against toast and tea, opting for scrambled eggs with her toast. On her toast, she slathered a liberal amount of homemade strawberry jam, another of Morty's favorites. Although making the jam was tedious and Morty was gone, she decided she would still make the strawberry jam, merely because she enjoyed it too. While she finished her last slice, she wrote out a long list for her shopping trip later today.

Putting the dishes in the kitchen sink, she heard a knock on the front door. Tess peeked through the window to see a short bald man in a suit scanning the neighborhood behind him, his briefcase heavily dangling from his left arm. She wondered who he was. Was he friendly or some nut coming to hurt her? Through her locked door, she called, "Who is it?" in a natural voice, hiding her panic.

"It's Paul McPratt. I'm from your neighbor's insurance company. When I called Jenny, she said you'd be home so I could inspect your home for damage from the fire on her property at the same time I do hers. Are you available now?"

Tess was silent as she ran through her mind her current situation. She tried to recall what state the garage was in at this point. Were there any clues in the garage that would give her away? She slowly unlocked the door and allowed him inside, "Please, come inside Mr. Mc Pratt."

Once inside, he placed his briefcase on the floor and held out his hand to shake hers, "Sorry for the inconvenience, but the sooner we get this done, the sooner the claim can go in." He clapped his hands and pointed back outside, "Shall we start out there first?"

Relieved, Tess nodded her head rapidly and followed him out the door, both walking around to the side of the house facing Jenny's place. "I haven't had a chance to look at the outside myself, but I know the inside is just fine. I have found no damage in the garage or anywhere else. So, we can skip that if you want."

The man stood facing the wall, looking up at the eaves troughs, "Looks like we got some damage there in the fascia. I'll make sure that gets replaced pronto." He scribbled something on the notepad he was carrying. As they walked towards the front of the house, he chuckled, "You know, in a manner of speaking, you're really lucky. Her garage was so old it burned down quickly, saving your place from more damage."

Tess followed behind him, hoping he would skip the interior examination. But she knew he wasn't going to when he stood by her front door, waiting for her to lead the way inside.

He nodded towards the interior door, "Does that lead to the garage?"

Tess simply nodded her head. She was afraid if she spoke, her fear would show up in her voice. He made his way to the door, and slowly opened it, with Tess right on his heels. She reached past him and flipped on the light. He began his examination in the corner opposite of the garage door. He looked along the top of the wall, all along the base of the wall until he reached the garage door itself. Tess held her breath while he examined the door itself. If he saw where the bulge was, he may be inclined to replace the whole thing. This was something she could not let happen. She did not want strangers milling about in her garage. Not to mention, all the time that would be wasted being unable to cut up the pieces she needed to dispose of.

He squinted to the upper corner of the metal door, "You know there's a dent in this door, right?" he turned to look at her, an inquisitive smile plastered across his face.

Her mind worked fast, pulling a lie out of mid-air, "Oh, that's been there forever. It happened the year after we moved in here. As I recall, I banged it with a long board. Doesn't matter, the door's nailed shut now anyway." She hoped the dismissive attitude would satisfy his question.

"That tends to happen more than you think. As long as you agree that the damage was there before the fire, we're good." He leaned against the freezer and scribbled in his notepad. "Okay, that's really all I need to do today. I'll have this typed up and sent to the head office. Should have someone here the beginning of next week to fix your fascia." Out by the front door, he stuck out his hand to shake hers, "Sorry to have bothered you. Enjoy the rest of your day." He grabbed his briefcase and gently close the door behind himself as he left.

Behind the closed door, Tess let out a huge held sigh. She walked to the kitchen table and sat down, releasing all her fears and strain. A slight smile slid across her face. The man had leaned against the freezer and had no idea what was inside. *If only he knew*, she laughingly thought. But Tess also knew that this had been a close call, and the sooner she got rid of the evidence, the less likely she was to go to prison.

As before, she went about preparing herself for the task ahead. The last eight blue bags were placed in her tote bag. She was going for the whole lot — all at once. Disposing of them had become too time-consuming, and she wanted that job completely out of the way before she moved forward with the next step. She checked for correct change before leaving the house. Reaching the end of the walkway, she noticed a huge box at the end of her neighbor's driveway. Apparently, they had a new dishwasher. But Tess didn't see it as a mere box, she saw a set of tiny walls perfect for stopping splatter. She walked across the street as casually as possible and began to pull the box towards her house.

She got half way across, when she heard the insurance agent yell, "Just a minute, I'll help you with that." He came to where she was and lifted one side, while she took the other. He placed the big box on the front step, while she unlocked the front door. Together they pulled it through the front door. Tess thanked him, as he walked away, back to Jenny's work site. After locking the door again, she headed for the nearest bus stop, but this time going the other direction.

Today's mission was not only to dispose of the blue bags but to also to carry out the other important duty Tess had to accomplish before she could move forward. She had to purchase her very own extension cord. No more borrowing from others. One fire in the neighborhood was enough.

Like always, the bus was crowded with sweaty people trying their best to avoid eye contact with each other. Except for one. The man sitting at the very back of the bus was fixated on Tess. So much so, she could feel his eyes roaming over her entire body even though she was sitting at the front of the bus. She dared to peek his way, wondering what he truly looked like. To her surprise, he was a rather handsome man —her age, with brilliant green eyes. Eyes that smiled back at her. Tess quickly turned her head away, pretending to not have noticed him at all.

Instead, she took the list from the pocket of her shorts and studied it, making sure she would have everything she needed for the next task.

- extension cord - 25 Foot
- vapour barrier
- duct tape - 3 rolls
- heavy duty garbage bags
- extra blade for Sawzall #1222-661

Those items she would pick up after doing groceries as to not draw attention to her hardware purchases at the grocery store. She was out of bread for toast, and her lettuce had gone to mush sometime during the last two days. She even decided to splurge on new shampoo and maybe a lavender scented soap. She was tired of smelling like Morty's manly soap. Tess wanted to smell like the woman she was, not the man he used to be.

Still feeling the stranger's eyes on her, she pondered just how she felt about him ogling her from afar. Was she enjoying the attention or was he making her feel uncomfortable? She decided it felt good. In fact, she did something she hadn't done in years — Tess Logan flirted back. It started with a simple smile in his direction, past an old woman and the rather large man in a Hawaiian shirt sitting on her other side. He smiled back, along with a fluttering wave. At the next stop, the man stood, walked her way, and slid into the seat beside her, his twinkling eyes flirting back with hers.

"Hi, I'm Eric." He held out his hand for her to shake, "You do know how beautiful you are, right?"

She blushed deep red. "I'm ... I'm ... Elizabeth." She lied to him, avoiding her real name, just in case. Taking his hand, she felt a spark of high energy attraction between them, a sensation that confused Tess. In all the years with Morty, she never felt an energy rush like she had felt with the dark-haired stranger. To hide her shock from Eric, she tilted her head downward, her hair creating a curtain for her to hide behind.

"So, what's a pretty lady like you doing on a sunny day like today?" he leaned sideways, so his muscular shoulder touched hers.

It was then she snuck a sideways peek at his body, thick thighs, and strong arms. She felt a rush of heat settle in between her legs. Why a good-looking man like him, was flirting with her, she had no idea. She shyly looked up at him, through her eyelashes, "Nothing exciting. Groceries and a quick stop at the hardware store." She cursed herself — why did she tell him the last part? That was leaked information that might come back to haunt her later on. She looked around to see if anyone else had heard her say it. To her horror, she saw a tiny head peering from behind the round gut of the Hawaiian shirt. It was the smiling face of Mr. Lo.

He waved his cane at Tess, "Hello Mrs. Logan. I thought I heard your voice. How are you today Tess?"

A heated blush burned at her cheeks again. She waved at him then quickly turned to the man beside her.

"Mrs.? Tess? But you said your name was Elizabeth?"

She held her chin high, "I did," was all she said.

Eric stared at her for a long moment. "Oh, I get it." He ducked his mouth level to her ear, "You're that kinda of girl." He gave her a quick peck on the cheek, "If that's the way you wanna play it, I'll play along ... Elizabeth."

His twinkling eyes and dirty smirk made her feel sleazy, "Um, no. You have it wrong. Tess is short for Elizabeth. And I *am* married, that's why I did nothing wrong. You are the one who assumed this was more than me being a friendly person."

She heard the chimes of the bus announcing the next stop. Tess stood quickly and made her way to the doors of the bus. Over her shoulder, she took a glance at the back with hopes Mr. Lo was still seated behind the Hawaiian shirt. Although she still couldn't see him, she could see his slipper-clad feet sticking out past the large man's boots. As the bus stopped, Tess darted out the door, escaping into the throng of pedestrians waiting to board. She walked away from the bus, fleeing by the fastest route available. From the corner of her eye, she watched Eric twist in his seat to look for her. Mr. Lo also looked for her, his tiny head barely visible over the window sill. As the bus pulled out of sight, Tess slowed her pace and turned back the other way, towards her first destination, the grocery store.

The trip for food would be the first since Morty's demise. She could, for the first time, buy whatever SHE wanted. With Morty gone, there were no more rules to shop by. Fresh vegetables were on the top of her list. She took her time, looking at everything through new eye — eyes that were adventurous, not restricted.

Leaving the grocery store, Tess carried two grocery bags filled to the brim. She didn't mean to buy so much. All the items in the store were so tempting. In truth, she had actually put back more items than she ended up buying. With all her new-found freedom, she found it difficult to narrow down her choices. Tess had already decided that she would have to take a taxi home from the hardware store since there was no possible way she could carry all her purchases on the bus.

Inside the hardware store was a world she had little exposure to. With her grocery bags tucked in her cart and list in hand, she meandered up and down the aisles. She found the duct tape, garbage bags and was deciding which length of extension cord she wanted, when an employee asked if she needed any assistance. She quickly grabbed a 50-foot cord, tossing it casually on top of the garbage bags. "Actually, you can. I'm looking for two other items." She pointed to the code number on her list, "I need that blade for my Sawzall."

He read the number, "Yep, right this way."

Following him with the cart, she asked for the other item she would need — heavy duty plastic. "I'm also looking for vapor barrier? Is that sold by the meter? I really don't need much."

As they turned the corner, there was another man looking at the blades as well. "It's sold by the roll — a 100-foot roll." The clerk reached up for the pack of blades she requested.

Her face showing her disappointment, "Oh. That's too bad. I only need about 5 meters."

A look the other man picked up on, "You know honey, I can help you with that. I have a partial roll on my truck. I'll sell it to you." His dark blue eyes begged a look at the clerk, "Sorry Teddy, but I don't need it anymore, and she does."

"Whatever Dom. Just charge her a fair price." He shot him a don't-be-a-greedy-jerk look.

Dom turned back to Tess, "When you're done here, meet me at my truck out back. I think a crisp ten-dollar bill should cover it." With that, he slid by her and headed for the checkouts.

The clerk leaned in to whisper, "Don't worry, he's a good guy. I'd trust him with my daughter." With a raised eyebrow, he added, "But not with my son ... if you get my drift."

Tess understood his message. Although she disliked his homophobia, she appreciated his advice, "Thanks for letting me know. A girl can't be too careful these days."

After paying for her merchandise, she hauled them, plus her groceries, out the back entrance. Dom was there, his elbow leaning against the cardboard tube the plastic was wrapped around. "Here you go." He looked her up and down, seeing her tiny frame and her hands full, "Um, where's your car? I'll stash it in the trunk for you."

She blushed slightly, "I don't have my car here. But I'll call a taxi from the pay phone on the corner." She pulled a ten-dollar bill out of her pocket and offered it to him.

He took the ten with pinched fingers, "No offense ma'am, but like hell, you will." He threw the roll into his truck bed, "I'll give you a ride to where you're going. And before you say no, understand that this is what true gentlemen do for nice ladies. And I, Dominic Catelli, am a gentleman. My Nona made damn sure of that." His smile was kind, filled with compassion, not pity. That helped make Tess's decision easier.

"That would be great ... but I'm way on the other side of town."

Before she could say more, he cut her off, "That's perfect! I'm heading that way too. Got a bathroom I need to finish up." He pointed at her bags, "Give me those." He took the bags and gently placed them in the truck bed. "Now hop in, and I'll get you home safe and sound.

On the way, they chit-chatted, keeping the conversation light. No personal questions, just commentary on the weather, the last big storm, and the addition to the shopping mall they drove by.

Tess pointed to her street entrance when Dominic got closer, "I'm the fourth house on the right."

But as soon as they turned the corner, they were confronted by the chaos that surrounded Jenny's property. A backhoe had finished scooping off the cement pad where Jenny's old burnt down garage had once lay in a blackened heap. The dump truck billowed out black smoke before it slowly crept forward, barely missing a parked truck.

Dominic made the sign of the cross, "Mother of Jesus. Was that your building?"

"No, no, my neighbor's place. And frankly, I was surprised it hadn't fallen down first."

"Well, she's going to get one hell of a nice one once these guys are done. They are what you say top-notch in this area. Best construction crew I've had the pleasure to work with. They call me, Dominic Catelli, when they need bathrooms created for the Gods." He maneuvered the truck around the other vehicles parked on the street. "Celebrity spas are my specialty." He put the truck in park. "There you are ... at home. Let me help you with your bags." He jumped from his side of the truck and ran to her side. He helped her down the steep step and closed the door behind her. He handed her the grocery bags but insisted that he carry the hardware bag and the roll of plastic to her front door.

Shyly, she accepted the roll and leaned it against the inner door frame. "Thank you so much for the ride. You saved me a ton of money." She began to dig through her tote in search of some money as payment for the ride. It was then she realized with defeat that with all that had happened, she had not had the opportunity to dispose of the blue baggies in her tote.

Seeing her expression of disappointment, he waved his hands in protest, "No, I will not take it. But I will take a hug instead."

Remembering what Teddy had said at the hardware store, she nodded her head in agreement.

With big open arms, Dominic enveloped Tess's tiny frame. Like an older brother, he squeezed her tight with a few pats on her back before releasing her. "And now, I must go make another woman very happy by finishing the tiling in her bathroom. A bathroom so big it has a pair of matching bathtubs and a walk-in shower." He held up two fingers, "Yes two! And no, I don't want to know why," he laughed out loud before turning to leave. "Enjoy your project, whatever you are doing."

Tess watched as he pulled away, again trying to avoid randomly parked vehicles. That's when she saw him. Officer Adams looked directly at her, across the back of a truck bed. There he was again. Would he never go away? Attempting to appear normal, she smiled widely and wiggled a wave in his direction. Before he had a chance to return the wave, she turned and disappeared inside with her bags.

It was the roll of plastic that caught the Officer's attention. What would she need with such a large roll of plastic? The more Officer Adams encountered Tess Logan, the more his cop gut talked to him. And who was the man with the truck? He made a mental note of the name on the side of his truck for further reference. He also noted the bag from the hardware store. He knew that particular store well and would stop by to visit his long-time friend, Teddy. He wanted to know what Mrs. Logan had in that bag. His gut spoke to him, telling him to do it pronto. Before she had a chance to hide it, whatever it was.

His gut was never wrong.

Behind her closed front door, Tess inhaled through flared nostrils. Not only was she infuriated that Officer Adams had again intruded on her life, she still had to dispose of the last eight blue baggies. And he was there, next door, smiling at her. How was she supposed to do that without him seeing her leave? Frustrated, she tossed her groceries in her fridge and cupboard. After crushing her cookies, she stopped herself, standing quietly over the sink to collect herself together. "Control ... focus," she muttered into the sink. "Get yourself under control."

*Knock! Knock! Knock!*

She carefully made her way to the window and peeked through the sheers. Seeing his head shift to the window, she knew he had seen the curtains move. Her stomach sank. She had no choice but to open the door to the nosey cop. With a huge smile and batting eyes, she spoke softly to him, "Nice to see you again." She lied, she was not happy to see him — not one damn bit.

"Afternoon Ma'am." He nodded politely. "I see you bought some plastic. Did your house receive damage from the fire too?" He stepped forward hoping to force his way over her threshold. But to his surprise, Tess didn't budge from her spot. Instead, she stepped sideways, her arm stretched out from the door, while she put her hand on her other hip, making herself wide enough to block the doorway. The wall she created with her rather slim body stopped him from entering her home. That stance sent a clear message to Officer Adams that he was not welcome to snoop around without it being an 'official police business' visit. She didn't know much about the law, but she did know he needed a judge signed warrant to get inside her home without her permission.

She looked him straight in the eye, "Nope, no damage. In fact, Jenny's insurance guy was here earlier today to check out everything. He said I was lucky that Jenny's garage was so old ... it burnt down super fast, meaning there was next to no damage to my place."

He picked up on the phrase 'next to no.' "So there was damage then?"

"Yes, one panel of the fascia is warped. He said he'd get it replaced as soon as possible."

Her answer forced him to come right out and say it, "But why the roll of plastic then?"

To this, she squinted up at him, narrowing her eyes to let him know she wasn't falling for it, "You know, that's kinda my own business." She paused for effect, lowering her voice to show her irritation, "But since you think you need to know, I'm setting up a little studio for me to paint in."

The cop's face fell. That was not the answer he was expecting to be given. But then again, he wasn't really sure what kind of answer he was expecting to get from her.

A horn in the distance blasted. They wanted the cop car out of the way.

Tess took the opportunity handed to her, "Well, looks like you need to go." With no additional niceties, Tess slowly closed the door, putting an end to their conversation.

Adams, faced with the closed door, swore under his breath at the blaring horn. Running back to the cop car, he made a vow to himself that the name Tess Logan would move up on his list of 'Persons of Interest.' Driving past Tess's house, he took a long look at her front window. He was sure she was standing behind the curtains, watching him. Nearly going up on the curb, he turned his focus back to driving, "Not sure what you've done Mrs. Logan, but whatever it is, I'll find out ... if it's the last thing I ever do."

Behind her sheers, Tess blew out her held breath. "Fuck!" She paced back and forth in her kitchen, wringing her hands. Had she made things worse by standing up to the annoying cop? Or would it be better now that she took a stand with him? She had watched him stare directly at her house from his car. The son of a bitch was watching her as though he knew she had done something wrong. As if an omen, the roll of plastic slid off the door frame, slammed to the floor, rolled across the hardwood, only to stop in the exact same spot where Morty had laid dead.

Tess stared at its resting place. She could not believe her eyes. Was it foretelling a future event or merely resting in the lowest part of the floor? Tess squatted down in place, and held her head with her palms, her fatigue finally catching up with her. Slowly, tears filled her eyes, only then did she allow her emotions to fully flow. Sliding onto the floor, she laid sobbing, large tears pooling on the wooden floor. There she lay, her body shuddered with each gut-wrenching sob.

Tess turned over on her back, her tears ceased to come any longer. Staring upward, she calmly asked what was going through her mind, "Why? Why are you doing this? Wasn't Morty's beatings enough? You have to stick a cop in my way?" Anger rose in her voice, "All I want to do is get rid of Morty and move ahead with my life." She jumped to her feet, angry and void of her spent sadness, she held up both middle fingers and aimed them in the cop's last direction. "Fuck you! Fuck you, you son of a bitch! No way, you'll get me. I'll make damn fuckin' sure of it!" She had to get rid of the body and fast. She picked up the roll of plastic and charged for the garage. The door opened so fiercely, it slammed into the wall, bouncing back at her. Again, she shoved it open, throwing the roll down the steps, where it landed beside the cardboard box.

Even more determined, Tess began the process of setting up what she mentally nicknamed 'the butcher shop.' Using Morty's utility knife to cut down one side and along two bottoms of the washer box swinging the freed sides open, she formed an extended corner wall to drape the plastic over. Positioning it near the freezer, she made sure there would be plenty of room to move about and have the table saw over the plastic sheeting. She stopped for a moment, calming herself before continuing. A tiny mistake at this point could become a huge problem later on. The cop had gotten under her skin, but she was determined not to let him win.

Unrolling one end, she attached the cut end edge to the back of the box. From there she pulled apart the folds expanding it to its full width and stretched it out to cover the box's base and the floor in front of the freezer. She taped the other edge to the floor, securing it in place. Pulling up her loose pants at the waist, she made her way to the table saw. It was at that moment, she was happy she had practiced cutting with it. She had even made herself a stick to wedge under the lid, so it opened even wider than normal, giving her more room. Carefully balancing the edge of the table saw, on her hip bones, she lifted it into place, careful not to rip the plastic below the metal legs. She pretended to saw, making sure that any bits or spray from the cuts would land on the plastic and not all over the garage. With a few tweaks, she was happy with where it was. Next, she placed the Sawzall beside the freezer and near the electrical outlet for easy access.

As before, she changed into her working clothes before she started. At the freezer, she braced herself for what she would see inside. It had been nearly ten days since she had placed the body inside and locked the lid.

Her hand shook so much it took three tries to get the tiny key inside the slot. She heard the click, but hesitated, gathering up her courage before lifting the lid. One sharp tug opened the lid wide. In her muffled mind, she heard herself gasp but was taken back that she did not feel anything at all. She was expecting to be overwhelmed with anguish, yet she wasn't. She slipped into her numb state, shutting down all her emotions of guilt, pain, and sorrow.

She propped up the lid with a stick she had cut in practice. Inside was the upper half of Morty's body, covered in sparkling ice crystals. Each strand of his hair was coated with frost, his face pale, laced with fine red and blue veins seen through nearly translucent skin. His eyes, open wide, stared blankly into space. Petrified for only a few seconds, she pushed past her numbness, forcing herself to not look at him but to get on with the job.

She made herself move quickly, avoiding any chance of her changing her mind. Grabbing the right arm, Tess yanked as hard as she could. It did not budge — Not even a centimeter. She tugged harder. Still, nothing moved. She began to panic. She tugged and pulled, but it was still frozen in the same wedged position she had left him in.

Furious, she placed one foot against the back lip of the freezer for leverage and pulled again, this time she gave it her all, grunting with the exertion she used.

It still did not budge.

Breathing heavy, she lowered her foot back to the floor and lowered her head to her chest in defeat. Accepting it would not be moved, she came to the only conclusion she could. She would have to let the body thaw enough to allow a bit of flexibility in his arms. Resigned to her decision, she lowered the lid, wedging the stick horizontally, creating a thin gap between the lid and the freezer's white metal casing. Tess stared at the gap, hoping it would do what she needed to do overnight. Although she wanted the body to thaw enough to move, she did not want the body to completely thaw, stinking up the garage and the house. But there was no way of knowing if the gap was wide enough for the day's heat to work. She would simply have to have faith, to walk away and wait for the hot temperatures to do its job.

In the meantime, she still had those bags to dispose of. Setting her mind on the task she could do, she left the garage to change her clothing. Grabbing her tote, she opened the door slightly and looked for Officer Adams. Not seeing any sign of him, she headed for the bus stop, clutching her tote close to her body. She thought to herself, *Only one more trip and all the carpet is gone ... for good!*

Tomorrow she would start the next part of the disposal of her husband.

Tomorrow.

# Part 9

It worked. The night's heat had thawed the limbs of Morty's body first, making them just flexible enough to wiggle the upper half free of the sides. Tess pulled and wiggled, using all her strength to get the heavy torso up and over the freezer's rim. Handling the frozen body, she had to stop several times to reheat her hands, jamming them between her thighs or ribs and underarms to thaw away the cold numbness. Twenty minutes later, and a lot of angry cursing, the top half thudded onto the concrete floor. Bent over, hands on her knees, she stopped to catch her breath, gulping air in her lungs. It was then she saw Morty's milky eyes staring in her direction — vacant of life yet they seemed to be staring directly at her. Tess froze before collapsing on her knees beside his face. She gently and lovingly touched his cheek, expecting to feel a warmth she was familiar with. Instead, her fingers felt cold and crystals on the surface. She instantly withdrew her hand out of shock. Her heart ached at the site before her. How could she have done this to him — her husband, the man she loved? Tears filled her eyes as she finally released all the sorrow she held inside. She lowered herself to lay across his chest, sobbing uncontrollably over his dead frozen torso. For the first time, Tess Logan allowed herself to mourn the death of her husband. A steady stream of tears rolled down her face, landing on his ice coated shirt, melting the crystals with their natural warmth. She could smell the scent of 'freezer' on his body, reminding her of the awful act she had performed on the man she had once loved so dearly.

But that was the point. She had once loved him in the beginning, but in the end, she despised him, hating every foul command and insult he aimed at her. In the end, she truly loathed him.

So why was she crying over his body?

Was she crying for him — or for herself?

She sat up straight and looked at Morty's face. A face that had become meaner and more tormenting as their marriage had matured. The Morty that lay before her was not the sweet, attentive Morty she dated and eventually married. Before her lay a man filled with jealousy, hate, and meanness ... a man she was glad was dead.

With trembling hands, she wiped away her tears and set her mind back to her original task. She inhaled deeply, blowing out all her sentimental emotion, clearing her mind of all feelings for the corpse at her feet. Mentally, she replaced those emotions with images of metal bars and bunk beds; and of a life more cruel and imprisoning than the one she had been currently living. She was not going to prison, she told herself as she reached for the Sawzall, "You bastard, you are not worth my freedom." She pulled the trigger, revving it above the body. She aimed the blade towards the right arm — but stopped instantly. His eyes were still staring at her. She lowered the stilled Sawzall and stared back at him.

She couldn't do it.

She just couldn't bring herself to cut off his arms with him watching her. Placing the Sawzall on the floor, she left the garage and walked to the kitchen. Numbly, she put on the kettle and washed the morning dishes while it came to a boil. Tess's place of refuge was her kitchen table with a cup of tea. Quietly sipping her tea, cupping her hands around the hot cup for further warmth, she slowly decided what her next step would be. After some deep thought, she came to the conclusion that what was truly bothering her was Morty's eyes — so she would remove them. Not his actual eyes, remove the upper torso altogether. Happy with her decision to switch the lower half for the upper half of the body, she finished her tea and went straight out to the garage.

First, she pulled the torso off the plastic, so it was out of her way. It moved so much easier frozen than when she brought it from the living room ... and no messy blood. Just smears that could easily be wiped away.

Next, she went after the lower half.

This was a problem for Tess's tiny frame. Not only was Tess short, she was also lightweight. This was definitely a disadvantage when trying to remove a heavy frozen half from inside the white metal box.

Her arms didn't reach all the way to the bottom. On tippy-toes, she leaned inward to pull out the lower half. Managing to grab the leg closest to her, she jerked hard in hopes of dislodging it. But to her horror, the body didn't budge. Instead, the force of her jerk pulled her forward, and she tipped head first into the freezer, her feet leaving the ground to dangle mid-air.

Panic set in. Tess frantically tried to push up and out of the freezer, but the downward force of her own body weight held her in place. She flailed her legs and feet trying to upright herself, but that didn't work either.

That's when she truly began to panic. She was stuck. Wouldn't that serve her right? To die stuck in the very freezer her dead husband's body was frozen in.

Since she had been panicking to the point of hysteria, she stopped herself for a moment, letting both her body and mind calm down. When she did that, her body naturally relaxed, shifting to the left, slowly sliding into the shell of the freezer itself. With some wiggling and shoving, she was finally able to stand up in the freezer. Relief swept over her in the form of laughter. Like a crazy woman, she stood on top of her husband's frozen lower half, laughing manically. As terrify as it had been, she also saw the strange humor in the whole situation. In fact, she laughed so hard, she nearly peed her pants. Exhausted by the intense laughter, she sat down on her haunches while she regained her self-control. After a few minutes, she focused on how to get the half she was standing on out of the freezer.

Luckily, there was enough room for her to wedge her shoes between the legs and the freezer floor. From that position, she could easily lift the legs up towards the other end and pull upward from outside the freezer. The first eighteen inches were the hardest, yet once past her knees, there was plenty of room to push up and past her body. With the legs sticking up in the air, Tess stopped to mentally take in the scene around her. How bizarre it would look to someone else if they had walked in at just that moment — feet sticking straight up, the plastic sheeting, cardboard walls, a plugged in Sawzall and a frozen torso off to one side. Once again, she hysterically laughed, mostly laughing at her own bizarre situation. No one would ever believe shy little Tess Logan was as diabolical as she was at that moment. No one.

One leg over the side, she crawled over the freezer's rim and planted her feet firmly on the plastic sheeting. "Safe at last," she chuckled to herself. She walked to the end, and with all her might, she pulled up and downward, pivoting the legs out of the freezer and onto the concrete floor with a frozen clatter. Tess did a little victory dance over them, "Gotcha!"

She pulled it to the plastic sheeting where she could start the cutting process. Behind her, she still felt Morty's eyes on her. Like an old oil painting in a haunted house, they watched every move she made. Unable to stand it any longer, she leaned the torso on the end of the freezer. Anticipating the struggle, she would have to get the torso out later on, she tied a rope under the arms, so she had something to hold on to. She was determined to not fall into the freezer once more. Then she carefully tipped the whole torso backward, so it slid back into the freezer. Even though Morty's head was facing downward, she slammed the lid, definitely blocking off any chance of contact with his eyes.

Returning to the lower half, Tess emptied her mind in preparation for the job ahead — the act of cutting it into smaller pieces. Pieces small enough to fit inside the little blue baggies. She stood above the frozen abdomen and legs, deciding exactly how to cut it up. Legs from abdomen; feet off legs; cut at the knees, so the half length of legs were easier to handle. Learning from the first time she cut Morty's body in half, she used the utility knife to cut away the clothing so it wouldn't bind up the blade. Off came the feet just above the ankles, the blade jerked and jittered, making it hard to hold in her tiny hands as it sawed through the larger tibia bone. To Tess's relief, the smaller fibula bone was much easier to saw through. She moved up to the legs, cutting just above the knees, the tool jerking wildly in her hands, almost pulling free midway through the thick femur bone. Those she threw on the pile next to the cardboard wall.

This brought her to the pelvic area. She racked her brain, going back to high school biology class. After some thought, she decided to cut right along the upper leg, missing the hipbones. She picked up the utility knife to cut away the material of his pants but froze in midair.

The penis.

She had forgotten about Morty's penis.

What was she supposed to do with that useless thing? To Tess, that's all it was — a thing that brought her no pleasure, a thing that she had to clean like any other part of Morty's body. It meant nothing to her. But somewhere in the back of her mind, she felt she needed to separate it from the rest of him.

As she cut through his pants, she decided to leave the hip and abdomen portion in one piece, focusing her efforts on the feet and legs first. Twenty minutes later, the two femurs were stacked with the other pieces. The remaining hip section was put back in the freezer to deal with later, once she had disposed of all the hunks she was about to create.

Tess was very happy to see that very little mess was made. With the body being frozen, only a pink slush had accumulated right at the Sawzall's blade. It was easily wiped up and deposited into her white bucket to be flushed away after she was completely done at the table saw.

Once again, she inhaled deeply, centering her thoughts and energy for the gruesome job ahead of her. She exhaled slowly while picking up the top femur off the pile. "It's just frozen meat and bones," she told herself out loud. "You have to do this, or it's prison for you. Just do it." She turned on the table saw, its blade scarily whirred a million-miles-an-hour. She remembered how the butcher had carefully pushed the meat past the big cutting blade at the grocery store and prepared herself mentally to do the same.

Tess slowly, carefully pushed the thigh into the revolving blade, keeping her hands — and more importantly her fingers — out of the way. The blade bit in, and to her surprise, it did not pull the thigh forward on its own. A one-inch thick piece of thigh was cut clean off. That piece she placed on the side of the table saw's top, ready for more pieces to be stacked on it. She quickly learned that just like the butcher, she too would have to make two passes of the blade in the thicker part of the thigh.

Once the first thigh was in pieces and stacked aside, she went back through them cutting them into smaller, more manageable pieces. With the day's heat confined in the garage, she used the back of her hand to wipe away sweat from her forehead and face. Tess continued cutting and stacking until she had sliced all of the leg pieces into baggie size. Turning off the saw, she unplugged it before meticulously cleaning both the saw blade and the table top itself, using her favorite toothbrush. She knew any fleshy bits left behind would begin to rot and smell within hours due to the relentless heat wave they were enduring. As for the pieces of flesh, those she bagged up and placed back into the freezer. Those she would deal with tomorrow. The long process of disposing of them one-by-one would take a week or more the way she had been doing it with the carpet squares. She needed to spend more time trying to figure out a faster method, one which would allow her to get rid of more than one or two pieces at a time.

But that was for tomorrow. Right then she needed to focus on the cleanup and dismantling of the plastic sheeting and cardboard wall. With all the saws' pink slush gathered in her bucket, she dumped it in her toilet and with one dainty finger, flushed away the evidence. Rinsing out the bucket, she refilled it with bleach, cedar chips, and steaming hot water before returning to the garage for a final cleaning. Forty-five minutes later the garage was spotless. Looking around, she was sure no one would ever suspect what had taken place there less than an hour before. Feeling her work was done, she made herself a cup of chamomile tea to help her relax.

Although it was late in the evening, she still had no appetite. All that gory flesh, blood, and bone had turned her stomach. Food, especially meat, made bile come to her mouth, making her want to vomit violently. She had done what she did because she had to, not because she wanted to. It was either do what she was doing or go to prison.

And Tess Logan was very determined to not go to prison for the rest of her life.

# Part 10

Another restless night left Tess totally exhausted even before she started her day. She let the hot water run over her body longer than she normally would. At the mirror, she pulled down her lower lid, exposing a very bloodshot eyeball. The rest of her face showed what the lack of sleep at night, along with days of overwhelming stress and relentless heat, could do to a human being.

She spent most of the previous night racking her brain with ways to dispose of the newly sawn chunks. She still could not call them by what they really were — pieces of Morty. She finally hit on a viable plan at two in the morning. She immediately went down to the kitchen, pulled out two large packages of ground beef and placed them, unwrapped in the sink. With the heat wave they were experiencing, the meat would be half-rotten and very smelly by morning. That spoiled meat would be the base for her disposal of the first batch of chunks.

Tess decided that she would press the ground meat around the frozen chunks, disguising them as meat from her freezer that had gone bad. She could easily put five, maybe ten bags, in her regular garbage without Hank, her garbage man, getting suspicious by the amount. She also thought of other smaller plans, ones that could be completed, here and there, without being noticed by anyone. At one point during the night, she began to wonder how much a meat grinder cost. Nothing fancy, just the hand crank kind that could handle small amounts at one time. But her own sickening thoughts had turned her stomach and later they had brought on brief guilt filled dreams during the night. Waking again at 5 am, for the fourth time, she promised herself that she would only buy a grinder if she needed to.

The pungent smell of overheated raw meat filled her nostrils by the time she reached the bottom of the stairs — a tainted odor that brought a pleased smile to her lips. The first part of her plan was ready and waiting for her, almost exciting her. Inside, she knew she could make this scheme work, taking care of the current batch of chunks waiting for her in the big freezer. "Coffee first," she casually told herself, "Then I can start."

Leaning against the sink, she sipped her coffee and pondered exactly how she would create the packages. The first rule was easily made. Not to use the same pale blue baggies for the next mass disposals, but to continue using them for the other smaller plans she had concocted during the night. The second seemed equally as simple. She would only do as much as she could without overtaxing herself. Last night's weariness had taught her one very valuable lesson; she was pushing herself too hard, and if she kept up that same hectic pace, she would eventually make herself very sick. Even though time was of the essence, becoming sick would put her plans back even more. Or worse, to draw attention to herself from others. And she did not need any extra attention in her life. From then on, she came first — not the frozen body in her garage. More sleep, less stress, and better meals were her top priority.

By the heavy stench of rotten meat in the air, she decided against eating first but went straight to work after her cup was emptied. From the garage freezer, she retrieved ten chunks and dropped them in the sink. Not wanting to touch the rotten meat with her hands, she pulled on her yellow rubber gloves to protect her hands from absorbing their putrid stench. With pre-opened freezer bags, the clear kind, at the ready, she began the disgusting job of sculpting the rotten burger around each chunk of frozen flesh. One by one, each chunk was transformed to a flatten lump of ground beef. She closed each freezer bag and placed it back into the refrigerator's freezer.

To her delight, there was still more ground meat left, meaning she could create more than the initial ten larger chunks she had planned on making. Back to the big freezer, she scurried, grabbing more bags of smaller pieces. To these she did the same as the first batch, creating more flat rotten lumps, putting them in her fridge freezer with the others. Happy with the resulting pile, she changed her clothing before making breakfast. A simple bowl of fresh fruit revived Tess's energy. And she would need it. Because today she had to play the most important role she had ever performed since Morty's death. She would have to convince her garbage man that her refrigerator stopped working, forcing her to throw out the contents of both her fridge and freezer compartment. Once the morning dishes were washed and left to air dry, she started to load up several grocery bags with the contents of her fridge freezer. Along with the chunks, she put in several bags of peas — Morty's disgusting peas. She was happy to see those go. It was ironic that his peas would help cover up the crime she was actually committing.

She kept an eye on the kitchen clock. Hank was always on time, so much so a person could set a watch by his arrival. She had another twenty minutes before he would grace the street outside her house. Quickly as she could, she found other items in her fridge that she had wanted to discard now that Morty wouldn't be using them any longer. Like his disgusting ketchup bottle. She couldn't remember how many meals he had smothered with a thick red layer, even before tasting what was on his plate. That bottle she shoved with gusto, "Here's your ketchup Morty. I hope you enjoy it in the back of Hank's truck." She smiled at the absurdity of it all. In another bag, she stuffed a loaf of freezer burnt bread and an almost empty salad dressing bottle. Truth be told, she was clearing out items that she no longer wanted or was past expiry date. Eventually, she tossed in bags of smaller chunks that contained no visible skin or bone. *Looks like stewing beef to me,* she thought with a crooked grin. With five minutes left, she hurried upstairs, changing into her low scooped summer dress and brushed her hair. A layer of pink lip gloss and a touch of blush finished off the look, making her appearance flirty. Finally, she gathered up the five bags of 'spoiled food' and headed out the front door.

At the curb, the bags laid at her feet, she waited for Hank's loud and stinky truck to come around the corner. As Tess had predicted, she heard the sound of the big white truck before she saw it. She was relieved to hear it grind to a stop at the first stack of black garbage bags. She wished he would hurry. The longer she stood with the bags at her feet, the greater the chance of someone discovering what she was doing. Two stops ahead of Tess's place, he nodded at her as he always did whenever someone was there on his route. She nodded back adding a huge flirty smile for effect.

When he finally reached her stop, he called over the noise of the truck, "Hey Mrs. Logan. What've you got there?"

She batted her blue eyes at him, hoping to distract him from what was really inside the bags. "You know what Hank, my fridge died on me last night." She bent down and picked up one of the bags and held it out in front of her, "And everything in my fridge is ruined." She gave him a wide smile, one that she hoped would dazzle him senseless, "Do you think you could take these even though I don't have any bag tags right now?" She made her face blush, putting on the appearance that she was helpless and needed to be saved by the big, brawny garbage man. She begged in a low soft tone, "Please, Hank? Just this once, okay?"

Her sultry voice won him over. He flashed his pearly whites at her, "It would be my pleasure, Mrs. Logan."

"Please, call me Tess. Mrs. Logan sounds so ... so ... stuffy."

He grinned at being allowed to call her by a friendly name, instead of the usual customer-employee relationship. He took the first two bags from her and snuck a peek as she bent over for the last three. He knew a good-looking woman when he saw one, and Tess Logan was so wholesome, it felt sinful the way he wanted to grab her ass right at that moment.

Tess knew he was looking at her ass. He always looked at her when she had happened to be outside on garbage day. In fact, she stood with her legs slightly apart and her back curved just so, making her ass rounder and sexier. "Here you go." With her arms outstretched, she pushed them against the sides of her boobs, forcing them rounder in the neckline of her top. Next, she touched her cleavage with her fingertips, pulling his eyes right to where she wanted him to look. As she predicted, his eyes focused only on her bulging tits and skipped past the contents of the bags. Men were so easy to fool. She had learned that all a woman had to do was flash a wee bit of ass or tit and a man was putty in her hands. She batted her eyes at him again; just to make sure he was only focusing on her and not the bags he was throwing in the back of the truck. Tess took three steps closer to him, "Thank you, Hank." She touched his arm, stroking with her fingertips. "I was so worried I'd have to schlep them all the way out to the dump myself."

As if he was showing off his prowess, Hank jammed the lever hard, impressing her with his big bad biceps. Behind him, the large inner scoop folded forward, crushing everything contained inside it. That included Tess's five bags of Morty.

She could feel the relief flow through her. They were gone, and no one was the wiser. She did a wee jump of joy, which made her boobs bounce. Hank's horny eyes nearly bulged out of his head. To put an end to her plan, she leaned in and planted a soft kiss on his cheek. "Thank you, Hank. You're a life saver." She gave him one more glimpse at her chest before turning away and running back into the house.

Behind the closed door, she jumped for joy again, happy to know she had pulled it off. That took care of nearly the entire batch of chunks in the metal freezer — along with many of reminders of Morty's existence.

But soon the thrill of her accomplishment waned with the reality of the cold hard truth. This was only the first phase of many more to come. She sighed heavily, letting her new resilient mood take hold. She switched her focus back to the remainder of the day and the jobs that lay ahead. She would have to set up 'the butcher shop' again and create another batch of chunks for the next project. It was at that point, she also decided she would have to design a set up that, to anyone else's concerning eyes, would not appear to be a place where she sawed her husband's limbs into bag size pieces. The words "a little art studio for me to paint" popped into her brain. She laughed at how she had previously uttered those very words to Officer Adams the very day before. "Tess Brown, you ... are ... a ... genius!" It had been years since she used her maiden name, but it somehow seemed appropriate since she had recently become a widow. She clapped her hands together, "So an art studio it is."

The whole scenario formed in her mind. She would leave the box in place, attach the plastic to it and push it up against its bottom as though it was there to catch splattered paint. In the future, all she would have to do is pull the plastic out to cover the floor. The table saw itself was easy enough to move when required so she would leave it in the same spot. It was the 'what' she would paint on that stumped her — and 'with' what? She looked around the garage for some type of art supplies, while she set up 'the butcher shop' for her next round of sawing.

On the top shelf sat several cans of house paint, two spray cans, some wood stain, and a large bucket of drywall compound. Definitely all the wrong colors, but they would have to do until she could buy some proper paints. Unfolding the plastic that was taped to the top of the box as before, her eyes searched into the darkest corners of the garage. Cardboard, thick sheets leaned between the shelving unit and the wall. She dashed to them, pulling them out into the light where she could examine their surfaces. The first three had globs of shiny hard glue on them, but the remaining nine were perfectly clean. On the same shelf, she found brushes of all sizes, tape and a scraper Morty had once used to apply the drywall compound to a hole he punched in the wall. All of her art supplies were neatly piled on top of Morty's workbench, waiting for the artist to begin her art projects.

Outside the sound of saws buzzed and hammers echoed through the neighborhood. Sounds Tess was pleased to hear. She could freely use the table saw without drawing any suspicion in the direction of her garage.

Unlocking the freezer, yet not opening it, Tess prepared herself for what was inside. Unlike the last time, she was finding it difficult to turn off her emotions as she had done the day before. Was it fatigue from the last few days — or was it what she had to face inside the white metal box. More the latter she concluded, after a flashed memory of Morty's frozen eyes staring at her from the floor. She remembered her collapse and subsequent tears. Inhaling deeply and bracing her parted feet, she talked to herself out loud, "Prison, Tess. You'll go to prison."

With one swift yank, she flipped the lid wide open exposing the contents inside. Her stomach knotted at what she was confronted with, all over again. She immediately lowered the lid, turned on her heels and began to pace in the remaining empty space in the garage, arguing with herself. "You have to do it. You have no choice. You know that fuckin' cop will be back again nosing around. The faster you get this done, the faster you will be free." She stopped directly in front of the freezer, "Focus ... focus ... focus." As if those tiny words held some sort of power, she let the tension release from her body and more importantly, from her mind. Falling into her mental state of numbness, she lifted the lid and stuck the stick under it. Her mind focused solely on the job at hand, allowing it to pretend the contents was nothing more than frozen meat. 'From the farm,' she told herself repeatedly, embedding the idea that the pieces were animal parts from a local farm, not the body parts of her dead husband.

First to come out were the feet, their ankles still attached. These she made quick work of once she had removed the shoes and socks, throwing them in a pile for later. She would wash the socks, returning them to his top drawer and the shoes would go back into the front closet, next to his work boots as if nothing had happened.

On the table saw she turned them into what looked like short ribs and soup bones. She cringed at the mental comparison she made to her husband's sawn feet to the meat found in the butcher's case. It was evil what she had done, and she knew it in her heart and her mind. But she had to disassociate her moral self with the actions of brutality she had committed. What truly scared her was how easily it had become. When she fully focused, she could switch off her personal ethics, flipping from 'Tess the Battered Wife' to 'Tess the Murderer - The Butcher.' Once in the state of disassociation, she felt nothing, numb from her emotions, numb from her Catholic upbringing. Seeing the newly created piles in front of her, she suddenly wished she hadn't lied to Hank as soon as she had. She should have held off longer, giving herself extra time to dispose more of Morty in one shot.

Sweat from her forehead dripped down her face. She wiped it away with the back of her hands, leaving red smears across her pale skin. The mounds in front of her, she quickly bagged into manageable sizes, enough for what would be needed for a meal-for-two. She placed those little blue bags into a larger bag and tossed it back into the freezer.

While there, she examined what was inside the open freezer, to decide what would be processed next. Mentally, she was not ready to deal with the hip section. She would have to forego that section and focus on the upper body — the upper torso that still had her husband's head attached to it. Her guts knotted at the thought of performing the decapitating she knew she would eventually have to do. That realization helped her decision process — she would switch halves and remove the arms to work on right then. The rest of the torso she would leave until later.

As before, she pulled out the hip section and placed it aside. Using the rope she had tied around the upper half, she easily pulled it over the rim and onto the floor with a frozen clatter. The lower half she returned to the freezer, leaning it in the corner, both putting it out of her way and so she could easily grab it without her falling in the freezer like before.

Although it was heavy, she managed to get the large piece onto the table saw — face down so she would not see those eyes staring at her. "Focus ... Focus ... Focus," she grunted to herself repeatedly all the while. With Morty's utility knife, she cut away his shirt so the blade would not get caught on the material, binding the blade. His muscles were frozen hard and glistened with a fine coating of ice crystals. The spots that were deep dark purple with settled blood had become paler, yet were still very visible. Was it from the freezing of the flesh? Tess was not sure, but it made no difference to what she was about to do. She whispered under her breath — more to convince herself than a spoken statement, "It all saws the same."

Even with being wheelchair bound from the accident, his frame became slender, but he was rounder in the stomach. This created a huge problem for Tess. Sizing up the height of the shoulders with the saw blade, it was obvious she would have to flip the torso onto his back — its back, she corrected in her thoughts. It was not an act Tess wanted to do. She did not want to see Morty's face — or more importantly, not his frozen eyes.

As if her mind shifted, she made a decision to do the one hideous action she was dreading to act upon in the future. Tess decided to sever the head completely from the body, removing those accusing eyes from the work she had to accomplish. Disposing of the head was a plan she was still forming in her mind. But most of the ideas she had, were gruesome, beyond what she was willing to do morally. Or at least at that point, but she admitted to herself that could easily change if she was threatened. Still, at the back of her conscious mind, she also accepted that she may have to resort to such psychotic measures if they became the last steps between going to prison, or keeping her freedom.

She stood silent for some time, concentrating on removing herself mentally — and emotionally — from what she had to do next. Words, defining words, slowly filled her thoughts completely, forcing out all others in her mind.

'No prison ... From the Farm ... Freedom ... Dead ... No Prison.'

Bits of the angry numb sentence she repeated over and over again in her head while she flipped the torso onto its back and slid it in place. This became difficult as the thawing ice crystals turned slippery against the rock-hard tissue. As before she was immediately drawn to the eyes, nearly white, pale blue eyes staring off into space. At first, it shocked her, turning her stomach into a tight painful knot, threatening to push acid up and out of her dry mouth. But after a few deep swallows, her shock abruptly switched to anger. With several huffs, her hands tight at her side, she decided what to do next. She stomped across the garage and dumped out the plastic bag from the hardware store onto the work bench. In two strides, she was standing beside Morty's head, and with one swift move, she forced the bag over his entire head. She tied the handles together, closing the opening tight — tight enough that she would no longer see any of his face. That simple act of concealing his face removed any possibility of guilt while she removed the head. Almost hysterical, she lifted the edge of the bag, tucked the handles out of the way of the saw blade and let the head drop with a thud on the table saw top.

Still rage fueled, she used that rush of emotion to her advantage. The increased adrenaline from her anger made her stronger, more powerful than ever before. She easily moved the torso around, holding the heavier end by the rope under its arms. She lined up the blade with the narrowest section of the neck. With one flick of the saw's switch, the blade spun to life, the whirring sound almost soothing to Tess's ears. Unfortunately, the table of the saw wasn't wide enough, and the heavier end of the torso hung over its edge. With her feet planted wide on the concrete floor, she balanced the heavier half and slowly shoved the entire torso forward. Feeling the teeth of the blade bite into the frozen flesh, she firmly pushed it forward. Bits of pink flesh flew up, landing on her cheeks and forehead. The torso slowed slightly as it severed the bones of the spine, but she continued to move it forward as the blade cut cleanly through. Concentrating hard on not allowing the torso to fall off the table edge, she failed to stop before the blade went all the way through. In a split second the saw broke through the final bit of skin and sliced it free from the main body. Encased in a slippery plastic bag, the frozen head twisted slightly, touching the spinning blade, its coarse teeth grabbing the frozen flesh of the neck and flung it forward, bouncing it off the cardboard wall, where it clattered to a stop against the metal garage door.

Tess stood, mouth wide open, watched the whole horrible event happen in front of her. It took her a few minutes to get over the shock and refocus on the rope in her hand. She slid the torso to the center of the saw where it rested safely.

She took her time walking to where the head rested, its exposed saw marks facing her direction. She could see the frozen pink tissue, the deep red veins against the blue-white bone, and their middles peachy pink in color. She kicked it lightly, turning the cut against the door, away from her view. Inhaling deeply for courage, she picked up the head, two-handed like a rock from a farmer's field and stomped to the freezer. Lifting the lid, she dropped the head inside with a loud clunk and immediately slammed the lid.

*Knock-knock ... Knock-knock ... Knock-knock*

Tess froze in place, her stomach leaped into her throat. *Who the fuck could that be?* she wondered. *That damned Cop again. Fuck!* She looked down at her blotchy bloody clothing, her hands streaked red, bits of pink flesh clinging to her fingernails. How could she answer the door looking like that?

She looked around her — she was covered in blood with a frozen torso balanced on her table saw. If anyone were to come into her garage at that moment, she would have been arrested on the spot. Her heart raced so fast with terror, she could barely breathe.

She heard the knock-knock again, this time softer and followed by a round of giggles.

Kids. Girls to be exact. She tip-toed into the living room to peek through the sheers. "Girl Guides ... selling God damned cookies," she muttered through clenched teeth. All her fears turned to anger. She went to the door and yelled through it, "Go away! Go away!"

A timid voice offered, "We're selling cookies. Five bucks a box. How many do you want?"

Tess screamed at them, "Go away you little fuckers ... and shove your disgusting cookies! Just go away!" She hammered on the back of the door with her flat palms, “Scram you fuckin’ brats! Get lost!” She stood with her palms spread wide, leaning on the back of the door, holding her breath while she listened. Her blood thudded through her ears so loud she could barely hear the words the two girls had said to each other before they ran away. Tess was happy to hear their shoes on the sidewalk and slowly fade away.

Her heart still pounded when her knees let go with relief. Twisting she leaned back against the door and slid to the floor in a heap of nerves and tears. How close had she come to getting caught? Not so close — this time. But what had happened was an important lesson for Tess. In truth, she would be vulnerable as long as Morty's body was still in her freezer. The faster she got rid of it, the safer she would become. Suddenly feeling exhausted, she pushed herself off the floor and forced herself to return to the garage — to the butcher shop.

Taking one step, she felt an envelope under her shoe. It had stuck to the sole of Tess's shoe with bloody bits from the plastic sheeting on the floor. She pulled it off and flipped it over in her hand — it was Morty's disability cheque. Another task to add to the long list she had compiled over the last few days. She tossed it on the kitchen counter and headed straight to the garage.

Having returned to her bloody work, she hastily slid the torso in place. She removed both of the arms from the top of the shoulders, down through and out the armpits. Those she then sliced in half, below the elbows, before removing the hands at the wrists. She fought off images of those same arms holding her at night when they first wed, and other images of him hitting her with those same hands — fists that broke her bones — hands that left scars, both on the outside and the inside. It was a constant struggle of emotions for her. She flipped between her love and her hate for Morty. Each time she felt sad for what she had been doing, she counterbalanced it with a larger, stronger anger. Her intense anger allowed her to stay in the disconnected state of mind she required.

She finished slicing the limbs into pieces that looked more like thick slices of pork leg, ready to be put in a smoker, rather than what they really were. Tess was happy that his hands had frozen in closed fists; that made it easier to saw them into thinner slabs, and then those slabs cut into smaller chunks. Every bit of the arms was bagged up to appear to be meat bought "from the farm." These she placed in a larger bag and slid them into the freezer with a satisfied smile.

All that was left was the hip section and upper torso. Those she needed to contemplate about further, due to their thickness. She was not sure if a double pass on the table saw would cut clean through the entire thickness. "Maybe a combination of the table saw and the Sawzall would do it? But no hurry ... that's for the next phase," she reminded herself. Lowering the limbless torso back into the freezer, she hummed a tune she could not name.

As she cleaned the pink slush from the table saw, she felt her stomach rumble. When was the last time she had eaten anything? According to her stomach, she hadn't eaten a decent meal in days — not since her last spaghetti dinner at Rosa's.

That thought brought her to her next mission in Tess's life — the forgery of Morty's signature on his disability cheque that had arrived in that morning's mail. Cashing the cheque was not a problem. She had done that many times in the past while Morty had been in the hospital. The tellers at the bank knew her by name and were very aware of Morty and Tess's financial arrangement. But she had never signed the cheques, Morty had, even from his hospital bed, he had insisted on it. This too, Tess had been thinking about, until her mind hurt. Finally, she decided to do her best at forging it and if there was any question about its authenticity, her calculating mind had a planned excuse to cover that as well.

After flushing the pink bits of tissue down the toilet, she rinsed out the bucket with bleach and hot water. She stored it away in the closet before returning to the bathroom to strip down and have a full hot shower, scrubbing away anything that would be deemed evidence by any onlookers.

In her favorite sundress, she added her work clothes and bloody rags to the washing machine. Warm water and bleach would do the trick. In the kitchen, she sat herself down at the table, a pen in one hand, in the other Morty's life insurance policy containing his signature, and the disability cheque laying on the table in front of her. Could she do it? Could she reproduce his handwriting properly enough as to fool the bank tellers? As anxiety crept in, she went to the kitchen drawer, took out a scribble pad to practice on before putting pen to cheque. After ten minutes and a hundred signatures later, Tess finally felt ready. With a held breath, she signed the cheque in one fluid movement. She held the newly signed cheque next to the policy — and was very impressed by her own handiwork. "That should do it. If I can't tell which is which, how is some cashier we see once a month supposed to know the difference?"

She would soon find out how good that signature really was. Her next stop was the bank and then onto a dining adventure as the reward for a day's work well done.

# Part 11

Into her tote, Tess stuffed the cheque, right beside the large bag containing five smaller blue baggies. She patted the side of her tote and joked under her breath, "Might as well make this trip worth my while." She locked the door behind her and on foot, headed straight for her bank.

The relentless heat wave had not broken yet and sweat quickly formed on her upper lip and behind her neck. She lifted her blonde hair to air out the building heat, her flip-flops slapping in rhythm with her steps. She lowered it after she turned the corner, her eyes immediately honing in on the bent over figure sitting in the shade.

Mr. Lo, the neighborhood busybody, was standing — or rather sitting — on guard, watching every move everyone made in his neighborhood. She saw him lift his head and focus his eyes on her from across the street. She had no choice but to continue in that direction, turning around would create more suspicion than to be helpful. She had taken no more than ten steps when she saw the cane wave in the air. Her heart sank. She would have to talk to him after all.

"Mrs. Logan! How are you today?" the old man yelled from his bench. He patted the space beside him, "Come sit with me and chat awhile." His grin was wide, yet his lonely eyes begged for her company.

Oh Shit! Tess cursed in her head. She waved his way and plastered a fake smile on her face. "Oh, I can't. I'm very busy today. Maybe another time. You have a great day now," she made her feet walk faster, hurrying away from him and his snooping.

"Busy, busy, busy. People are always so busy these days." He lowered his cane, "You have a great day too."

Tess pretended she did not hear him and kept walking down the sidewalk as fast as her feet could take her. Six more blocks, she told herself.

From the shaded bench, Mr. Lo watched Tess make her way down the sidewalk before she slipped into the bank seven blocks away. His body may have aged, but his eyes worked as if he was a twenty-year-old. Those eagle sharp eyes narrowed with suspicion. He never let his eyes wander off the front door of that bank, waiting for Tess to exit.

Tess, hot and tired, waited patiently in line but her nerves were starting to show by the time she finally reached the teller's wicket. She slid the cheque on to the counter, "I'd like to deposit this and take out fifty dollars." She was so nervous about getting caught, she forgot to say please.

"Well hey, Tess! Happy to see you." It was Bernice, the teller that had helped Morty and Tess set up their joint account so that Tess would have a debit card for grocery shopping and buying Morty's booze at the liquor store. "Where's the old ball and chain? Not with you today?" Although Bernice was joking, it added to Tess's nervousness.

"Oh, I left him at home. Too hot for him to go too far without getting sick. Best he stays home in the cool of the house." She could not tell her the same lie she had told the others. After all, if he was at his sister's, how did Morty sign his disability cheque? "Um, and can I have the fifty all in tens ... please." She added as not to be rude.

"Sure thing, Hun."

As Bernice's fingertips touched the end of the cheque, Tess held her breath. The teller looked over the cheque, checking for the amount and to make sure it was signed. Her fingers ticked across her keyboard, "Yah, that heat's been a real son of gun lately. And Lordy, don't we need a good long rain? My lawn looks like shredded wheat, brown and crunchy." Her cash drawer popped open with the rattle of coins. She counted out the bills for herself, then turned to Tess to do it all over again. On the counter in front of Tess, she counted out loud, "Ten, twenty, thirty, forty, and fifty." She slid them towards Tess. "Anything else I can do for you today?"

"Nope. This is great." Tess carefully scooped up the bills, "Thanks again." She made a point of not talking too much, mostly out of fear she would let something slip out, ruining the whole deception. She quickly turned to leave but Bernice stopped her in mid-stride.

"Wait a minute Mrs. Logan."

Tess's heart leaped into her mouth. She was caught. Of all the monstrous acts she had performed lately, this would be the one tiny thing she would get caught by. She turned to face Bernice, her timid voice shaky, "Yes, Bernice?"

"Signature."

Tess's knees went weak with fear. The teller had found the fraudulent signature on the cheque and had called her back to bust her for it. Drawing up her courage, she turned to take her punishment.

"You forgot to sign the slip saying you received your money." She held out the pen for Tess to use.

Tess's body immediately went limp with relief, "Oh, yah ... silly me. Must be the damned heat." She signed the slip and slid it back to her. Her nerves frazzled, she smiled politely, "Thanks again. Enjoy your day." She turned and headed for the front door again. A large sweaty man stood in her way, partially blocking the entrance to the bank. She had been so nervous, she had not noticed that the line behind her had become rather long. In that line, was the one man she did not want to see. Officer Adams. And it was obvious that he had been watching every move she had made. She pretended not to notice him and slipped around the sweaty man and out the front door, the fifty dollars clenched in her fist, hugged to her chest.

She walked as fast as her flip-flops could carry her — one block — two blocks — then she realized she had no real reason to run. Adams knew nothing. He had merely looked in her direction. When had she become so paranoid that just the sight of him sent her into a total panic? She slowed her pace and stopped along the sidewalk, under the cool shade of a maple tree. She unclenched her hand and counted the money in her palm. Fifty dollars — she had fifty dollars to do with what she wanted. Her stomach grumbled again, protesting its lack of food. Tess stowed away the bills and headed down the street, to the one place she wanted to visit again — Rosa's Italian Restaurant. She had been craving lasagna — meaty, saucy, spicy lasagna. With more cheesy garlic bread like she had before. And lots of wine, enough wine to forget her wretched life for awhile.

It was the last desire that hit Tess squarely in the gut. It was then that she understood why Morty drank so much. He drank to escape his meaningless life. She had always known that he drank to avoid thinking about his miserable situation, but up until that moment, she hadn't truly understood the need to escape completely from one's existence. She felt suddenly sad for Morty's misery, almost understanding why he was so mean in the end. From across the street, she heard his voice again, his cane waving in the air as before.

"Mrs. Logan. Do you have time now for a chit-chat? The breeze is very strong here ... like a big fan." His eyes pleaded with her to come join him, to be his friendly company for a wee while.

Tess, still melancholy about Morty's reason for drinking, almost caved into the old man's loneliness. She quickly came to her senses when from the corner of her eye, she noticed Officer Adams making his way down the opposite side of the street, heading straight for the old man and his shaded bench. She waved at Mr. Lo and yelled over the sound of kids on bicycles, "Sorry. Still busy. Another day maybe." She kept the words curt but smiled widely in hopes of making her rejection pleasant, rather than nasty. With that, she walked up the sidewalk as quickly as she could. She desperately wanted to turn around and see where the cop was headed but decided it was best to wait until she reached the next street. She was walking so fast, her left flip-flop flopped when it should have flipped, tripping her up. She managed to catch herself and straighten up just before she reached the corner. After that she walked slower, taking her time as she walked around the large brick building, stopping just out of sight from both the cop and the old man.

She peeked around the corner of the building, being careful to not be seen. What she saw not only alarmed her but warmed her heart as well. Officer Adams bent over to give Mr. Lo a man-hug before he sat down beside him on the bench. She watched as they began to talk; regarding the hot sticky weather most likely, since that is all everyone seemed to talk about these days. But when Mr. Lo pointed in her direction with his cane, Tess slipped out of sight behind the brick wall. "Shit!" she cursed out loud. They were talking about her. Why else would that nosey old man be pointing in her direction? Not wasting time, she dashed down the street and crossed at the next intersection on her way to Rosa's. She slowed her pace a half block from Rosa's, catching her breath before reaching the restaurant's front door. Even from outside, she smelled the rich aroma of tomato sauce and garlic. It made her stomach growl even louder than before.

Once inside, she was greeted by the same waitress that served her last time, Nina. It was then that her memory came back to her. *Nina — Kev's sister — Officer Adams's kid sister. Shit!* she cursed in her head. Had she made a mistake in coming to this particular restaurant? Why had she not remembered that? Wine. The amount of wine she had consumed that night; so many glasses it had clouded her memory until that moment. But it was too late, Nina was already there, standing in front of her. She couldn't just turn around and run. That would have drawn too much attention to her and the last thing she wanted was any attention at all.

With a huge smile, Nina showed her to a table in the back corner, the table where her brother had sat before, "Nice to see you again." She bent over and whispered, "Honestly, after what happened last time, I didn't think I'd ever see you again." She placed the menu on the table, "Red wine?"

Tess laughed at her recalling that she drank red wine, not white. She handed up the menu, "Yes. And I'd like your lasagna with gar ..."

Nina finished the sentence, "... garlic bread with cheese." She took the menu and suggested in a motherly tone, "You want a small salad to start? Helps with digesting all that cheese and pasta."

Tess nodded, "No thank you. I'll have a hard-enough time finishing the lasagna."

The cook rang the bell, ordering Nina to the kitchen for service. She stuck the slip in the carousel and loudly joked, "See, I told you she would come back." She gave him a wink, "They always come back for your cooking, baby." He lip smacked an air-kiss her way and turned back to the grill.

So, the cook was Nina's man, Tess wondered if that fact could be used to her advantage in the future. She watched as plates were placed in front of the other customers, ready with smiles and forks. Nina then served Tess her glass of wine.

"Bread will be here shortly, enjoy." She scurried away to refill coffee cups and take away dirty dishes to the kitchen. The place was packed with people of all ages - seniors, young families, and smiling couples holding hands, clearly on dinner dates.

It was obvious that Nina enjoyed her job, it showed in her smile and the way she treated her customers with motherly love. This saddened Tess. She began to wonder if she would ever be that happy in her own life. She had not really thought about what she would do after all of Morty had been disposed of. She had spent so much energy on getting rid of him, she forgot about herself — Again! Even in death, Morty had become the center of her world, consuming hour after hour of her precious time and energy. But she stopped thinking about Morty when she heard street sounds as the front door opened and two new customers entered.

Waiting to be seated was not only Nina's brother but Nina's annoying enemy, Mr. Lo.

Tess's stomach knotted tight. *Shit!* she swore in her head. She had made a huge mistake in coming to Rosa's, one she deeply regretted at that moment.

By the brief but bitter expression on her face, Nina was none too happy to see them either. With a pleasant smile, she filled the last cup of coffee, then headed straight for them. She stuck her face right in Officer Adams's face, her voice low but still audible to Tess and everyone else, "You got some nerve bringing him in here. What did we talk about? No more than two damned days ago!"

Big brother held out his hands to create a wall between them for protection, "Yes. I know what you said. But he's with me, not alone like you complained about." He saw the twitch at the corner of her eye and knew he was in for it.

"So, that makes it better?" her hand gripped the coffee pot handle so tight, her knuckles were white with anger, "What he did was wrong and you know it."

He leaned back into her face, "He said he was sorry. Ain't that good enough?"

From the kitchen, the cook slammed the bell several times to get their attention. He waved with his metal flipper at the customers, who all had their full attention on the trio arguing at the front door; one who was wearing a police uniform. Then, like a pointed sword, he aimed it directly at Officer Adams and mouthed the word 'behave,' his eyes tight with dominance, telling him which male was in charge in the restaurant.

All three looked around at the staring people. It was Nina that took control, "It's okay folks. Just my big dumb brother trying to treat me like a dumb little sister." She plastered a big happy smile on her face and turned back to the two men in front of her. "Happy now?" she growled under her breath. "Besides, I don't have any tables open. I have a full house." She said the latter as a reminder that she was running a business, not his personal coffee shop.

"Sure, you do." He squeezed by her, with Mr. Lo right behind him. "Right there, in my table." He walked straight to where Tess was sitting, calmly sipping her wine. In a pleasant voice, he asked her, "May we join you?"

She choked on her mouthful of wine. She had to swallow hard to stop herself from spitting it out all over the table. Again, being put on the spot, and feeling obliged, timid Tess nodded in agreement. As the old man took his chair, Officer Adams sat himself directly across from Tess Logan. "Thank you for allowing us to join you. The place is packed as always. My sister might be a bully, but she sure knows how to make people happy. And happy people come back. Just like you, I guess."

Tess braced herself before answering. If she answered any of his questions wrong, it could bring more scrutiny her way. And that was the last thing she needed was a cop nosing around in her life. Thankfully, before she could answer, Nina was standing right beside her, a hand on her hip, "You don't have to have them sit here you know. It's not his table, even though he thinks it is." She gave her brother a slap on the arm, "Ya big jerk!"

It was the frown on Mr. Lo's face that caught Tess's attention. He looked so sad, so needy it tugged at her heart strings. Or was it the strings her mother wrapped around her heart that was bothering her.

"Please let us stay," he begged her, "Kevin is going to buy me dinner ... a steak he said. And I haven't had a good steak in a very long time." He rubbed his hands together in anticipation of a meaty meal and even more, the good company.

*Shit! Shit! Shit!* she swore in her head. Her heart hammered so hard in her chest with the decision she had to make, she nearly fainted with the heated rush. But it was Mr. Lo's pleading eyes that made her change her mind, "Yes, they can stay." The old man's shoulders slouched with relief. "But only on one condition." Tess quickly added, "I get a free glass of wine and they don't pester me with too many questions. Like my husband, I like my privacy too."

Between pursed lips, Nina spat out, "Fine." Then she stabbed the end of her pen at Kevin, "But you brother, better be paying for that steak for real. Your 'police eat free policy' only applies to you. 'Cause you're my shit head brother ... and Mom would kill me if she found out." The latter part made her blush like she was a young girl who had been scolded by her mother already. She smoothed down her uniform and pointed the same pen at Mr. Lo, "You want a baked potato like last time?"

He nodded wildly, "With sour cream ... please." He folded his arms on the table top, "I'm starving. How about you Tess, what are you having?" Then he looked at her shyly, a little smirk on his lips, "If that's not too personal."

Another swat to her brother's arm, "See what I mean? He never stops."

"Jesus Nina, he's only joking around with her. Relax already."

"He wasn't joking two damned days ago!" She said it louder than she meant to, resulting in heads turning her way, once more. "Sorry folks. Won't happen again," she covered her mouth with her hand to prove her point. She leaned forward, down at ear level with her brother, "Jesus Christ Kev, make him behave. I can't lose any more customers because of him." Her furrowed brows told him she was genuinely angry but curbed it before she spoke to Mr. Lo directly, "Last chance old man, last chance." Being an intelligent man, he did not speak, only nodded that he understood and agreed with what she had threatened. She stabbed her pen at him, "Good! Keep it that way." She walked away, her hand still on her hip.

"Phew!" Officer Adams wiped his forehead with the back of his hand. He leaned over to the old man, "You're one lucky dog. I was sure she was going to boot you out."

"Yes, me too," Mr. Lo chuckled.

Tess being very curious, and wanting to focus the attention on anyone but herself, finally inquired, "What on earth did you do to make her that mad?"

The old man blushed dark red, yet remained silent.

Kevin spoke up for him, "He suggested to a customer ... a young lady ... that she would attract a better type of man if she dressed properly. With less ..." He motioned to his chest, referring to her cleavage, "... showing."

Tess gasped at what he said. She looked straight in the senior's blotchy red face, "Oh my God. You didn't actually say that, did you?"

The old man held out his cupped hands, indicating how large the girl's breasts truly were, "Like ripe melons," he grinned widely. Officer Adams sent him a behave scowl, so he toned it down. "But Kev, you saw her, the girl was that large." He crossed his arms over his chest, "And that boy she was with ... trash ... pure human garbage!"

The cop nodded deep in agreement, "That's no lie for sure. I've had him in my cruiser many times as a juvie." Nina arrived with the men's drinks, setting them down without her usual smile. Conversely, she slid Tess's garlic bread to her with raised eyebrows and a wink. "But I do have to admit, the last year or so he's straightened himself out. Stopped running with the East Hill Gang. Hell, he even got himself a part-time job at Timmy's over by the mall." He leaned into the old man and whispered under his breath, hoping Tess wouldn't hear him, "So, Miss Big Tits, as you called her, has done him a world of good. Been a good boy ever since that day you saw them arguing in the doorway of the drugstore.

Mr. Lo nodded he understood what the cop was saying, adding nothing more. He was not the type to admit to his error in judgment.

Tess pushed her plate of garlic bread towards the senior, "Mr. Lo, please help yourself. There's always more than I can eat anyway."

He reached for a cheesy slice. "It would make me very happy if you called me Don. Mr. Lo is so ..." he batted his eyes at her, "... stuffy."

Tess couldn't believe it. The old geezer was using her favorite flirt line, on her.

He made a point of looking directly into her pale blue eyes, "And please, call me Kevin. Unless I'm arresting you. Then it's definitely Officer Adams." The cheese from his piece of bread stretched long. He pinched it off with his thick fingers and stuffed it in his mouth. He sucked the garlic butter off his fingertips with a soft moan. Thick fingers and a moan Tess found somewhat erotic, making her inner thighs flush with heat.

"Officer Adams? Listen to this man's modesty," scoffed Don. "He's the Staff Sergeant and still wants to be treated like an ordinary cop, like the guys beneath him."

Bright red filled Kevin's cheeks at the old man's accolades.

Inside Tess became terror-stricken. The cop she had been worried about was not only nosey — he was the god damned Head of the City's Police Department! She stuffed a wad of bread in her mouth, disguising her inner groan as a food related moan.

Silence fell across the table. The two men munching on their oily cheesy bread, Tess, on the other hand, was trying her best not to show her new-found fear. She made a point of looking out over the restaurant, mostly to avoid eye contact with the two men at her table.

What she didn't see was the way Kevin was looking at her. He didn't make it obvious by staring, but he was studying her over his bread, taking in her beauty. The way her honey hair fell on her bare shoulders, the tips ending at her small breasts. Her skin looked soft and scented, like bone china, pale but warm to the touch. He was pulled out of his daydreaming when Nina arrived with all three meals. She served them accordingly, "You folks need anything else?"

Tess glanced at the men's plates. Bloody juices leaked from their rare steaks. The sight of the thin red pools made her stomach queasy. Her appetite for the lasagna in front of her wavered. She shook her head 'No' at Nina, but Kevin pointed to her wine glass and spoke up for her, "Her glass of free wine. She's empty."

Nina scowled at her brother, "Yah, yah, yah," she muttered as she walked away.

Kevin then turned his attention fully back to Tess, "So, when is your husband coming back? You said he was visiting his sister. Is he coming home soon?"

The bold in-your-face question was so unexpected, Tess nearly choked on her lasagna. She reached for her wine to take a sip, to wet her constricting throat — but more to prolong her answer — but it was empty.

"You okay?" Kevin jumped to his feet, ready to perform the Heimlich Procedure if needed. She waved him away while she caught her breath. "Jesus, I didn't scare you, did I? It was only a question."

At that exact moment, Nina showed up with Tess's wine. "What question? You two badgering this poor lady?" her hand went straight to her overly abundant hip, proving she meant business.

"Nothing. Just a simple question, that's all," griped Kevin.

*Simple?* thought Tess. It was one of the many questions she was hoping he would not ask. She could easily cover any other question; unfortunately, that particular one was trickier to answer than the others. If she said he was returning too soon, he would want to know when. If she gave a later date, she was positive he would be back to check up on her, to check if Morty had actually returned. Either way, she knew she was headed for trouble.

"I said to leave her alone or you two can take your meals to-go."

Kevin's back went up, "What? What did I do? I only wondered when her husband would be back." He lowered his voice so others wouldn't hear, "Look, she's alone. And you know how I feel about women being alone. With no one to protect them and all."

"Oh, for shit sakes. You still have it in your head that women are helpless. Get with it, bro. We women are doing it for ourselves," borrowing a powerful line from some famous song.

"Damn you. You know what I mean." He turned to face Tess, her eyes wide and very blue. "Look, I'm a cop, I see things in this city you don't. Robberies, rapes, and murders. And you being so damned pretty and slender makes you a perfect target for all the wackos and sick dirt bags this city has." He turned back to his sister, "I'm not being a jerk. I'm being a gentleman ... like Mom raised me to be."

Nina couldn't argue with that. Their mother did raise all of her children, to be honest, honorable, and a protector of those who needed it. It was the reason her brother had become a cop in the first place. She let her shoulders relax, "Fine. But like she said ... no personal stuff." The bell dinged in the kitchen forcing Nina to leave. *Behave*, she mouthed at the two men before she left.

The trio returned to their plates, Old Mr. Lo attacking his steak like he had not eaten in a month. It was then she looked from Kevin, then back to Mr. Lo. Slowly it dawned on her that the cop was, and probably had been, paying for the senior's meals. He wasn't a mean cop at all. He was kind and caring, the complete opposite of what she had pegged him to be. An impulse took her over. Her voice timid and barely audible, she lied. "We're playing it by ear."

Kevin only caught the last three words, "Pardon?"

She inhaled her courage and repeated it into her plate, "We're playing it by ear. With the construction next door, we decided Morty should stay at his sister's place until all the work is done." She lifted her gaze, making contact with the cop's eyes. "Since the accident, he can't handle the loud noises or the sound of machinery. You know ... things that beep when they back up."

Kevin was no idiot. After their first encounter, the cop listened to his gut and started to investigate the life of Tess Logan. He quickly learned that Morty Logan had been the casualty of an industrial accident. Some said it was no accident, but more an act of revenge by a disgruntled underling. "That makes sense," he nodded with understanding.

"Besides, I still need a break from him." She saw his expression question her statement and clarified it, "From taking care of all his needs, day and night."

"Exhausting that is." Don pointed with his fork, "You remember how tired I had been looking after my Suzie." He stuck the hunk of very pink steak in his mouth, then talked right through it, "There were days I was so tired, I couldn't think straight."

As the old man spoke, it finally registered in Tess's head that the cop understood what she had vaguely confided. He knew about Morty's accident at the plant. Meaning, he had been investigating their lives — and her. She decided to add some sympathy grabbing woes, in hopes of making the cop back off, leaving her alone. "Yah, some days it's non-stop. The daily baths, preparing special meals, extra laundry from accidents, and the daily physiotherapy. I'm only one person. I only have so much energy to give." She made the corners of her mouth sag and her eyes reflect a burdened wariness.

"No wonder you're worn out. You poor thing," Don sympathized in between forks full of potato.

Kevin watched her rose colored lips say the words; lips that were plump and soft — very tempting. He cleared his throat and tried his best to ignore the need to kiss her, "I had no idea you had to do all that, and every day. Probably best if he did stay where he is." Kevin shoved a very pink square of steak in his mouth and talked with his fork. "I'll just cruise by your house more than usual. Must protect all you folks living alone." After Nina's scolding, he used the term 'folks' instead of just women.

*Shit! Fuck! Shit!* she cursed in her head. That's just what she needed, a fuckin' staff sergeant driving past her house constantly. Tess began to eat faster, each mouthful larger, trying to clean her plate as quickly as she could. The sooner she was done eating, the faster she could escape the hell she was currently sitting in. Not wanting to discuss her life further, she switched the conversation back to the old Asian, "So Don, you didn't finish telling me about what happened after you gave the girl your advice about her choice in clothing ... and men."

He stopped mashing the second half of his potato, and with a twinkle in his eyes, he continued the tale, "For some reason, she became very upset with me. And that made her man mad as a bulldog. He stood up to threaten me and the back of his legs knocked his chair over backward."

Kevin cut in, "And of course Nina was walking by with her arms full of plates. She had to stop fast or trip over the chair. Yep, you got it. She ended up wearing all three plates of spaghetti, all down her chest and arms."

In his own defense, Don continued the story, "That's when she started yelling at me ... for no reason." He jabbed his fork in the air, "It wasn't my fault he tipped the chair over. And it wasn't my fault she didn't see where she was going."

From across the room, Nina bellowed, "But your suggestion to the young lady that caused it all, was your fault." That hand found her hips again, signaling not to bother arguing with her.

Kevin leaned into Don, "Shut up before she kicks us out."

With Nina looking their way, Tess took the opportunity to call her over. Tess pointed to her plate, "Can I have a doggy bag for this? And my bill, please."

"Sure thing, Hun. Just come down to the register when you're ready." She took away Tess's plate and sent Don another nasty look down her upturned nose.

Tess swallowed down the last bit of her wine and stood to go, "Well gentlemen, thank you for the lovely company." Without waiting for a reply, she spun on her heels and walked directly to the cash register. Nina was there waiting for her takeout container from the kitchen. She took it from her man, and with a huge grin, handed it to Tess.

"How much do I owe you?" Tess opened her tote to search for two of the ten dollar bills. Inside she saw the baggies, rather thawed but still not disposed. Shit!

Nina grinned smugly, "Nothing."

"But ..."

She waved her hands in a halt, "Nope. Big Brother is paying for yours too. After what Mr. Lo did the other day, you bet he's paying. Damn near caused a fist fight in my restaurant. I lost six customers because of that old man's mouth. Kev brought him in here, so he's gonna make up for my lost customers." She reached across the counter and patted her shoulder, "Don't worry, I'm making the big jerk pay for a lot of people's meals. It'll keep him honest."

She slid the white Styrofoam container her way, "But if I were you, I'd run like hell before those two idiots decide to follow you."

Tess didn't need to be told twice. She blinked her gratitude, "Good point. Thanks again." Within five long strides, she was out the door, her flip-flops slapping her hurried pace.

The two men ate quietly, knives cutting near bloody steak along with forks full of sour cream laden potato until the cop said what was on his mind. "So, what do you think she's hiding?"

"Don't know yet. I need to watch her some more. But I do know this ... she's not as innocent as she's pretending to be." Don stuffed another baby carrot in his mouth. "And if I were a cop, I'd be checking out where that sister lives. Making sure her husband is actually there."

"Funny, I was thinking the same damn thing."

# Part 12

Safe inside her home, Tess threw the used grocery bag on the counter with a loud *KLUNK*. She plopped down in her favorite chair, trying to catch her breath. The sprint she ran from the second-hand store to her house in the heat was exhausting. After she had left Rosa's, she made a point of disposing the blue baggies still in her tote. Two blocks away she knew there was a garbage can she had used before, right in front of the Sally Ann Store. When she slipped the big bag into the nearly empty trash can, her eye was drawn towards a bright orange object in the front window — a manual meat grinder.

She could not believe her luck. After spending a very intense half-hour with both the nosey old Asian and the city's head cop, she jumped at the opportunity to buy the one thing that could help her dispose of Morty faster. And in a less recognizable form. She made sure all the parts were there and promptly paid for it. She felt guilty handing the ten-dollar bill to the older lady dressed in her starched Salvation Army uniform. *If she only knew what I was going to do with it,* she thought to herself. She threw her change from the ten in the donation box, hoping to ease her guilt.

It didn't work.

She put on the kettle for tea. As she waited for it to boil, all the hours of work, walking, and worrying, finally took its toll on Tess. Her feet hurt from her cheap flip-flops. But her head hurt more from tirelessly thinking of ways to dispose of Morty. Ways to cut up the two remaining pieces in the freezer. Ways that weren't deprived, if not completely ghoulish. She winced when the kettle whistled. She reached up to get the box of tea bags, her hand hitting the bottle of brandy. Morty's cheap brandy.

She pulled it down and examined the label. With a one shoulder shrug, she joked out loud, "Why not? Probably a better high than wine." She pushed the tea bag in the hot water to steep. At first, she was going to simply drink her tea to relax, but after the day she had, the brandy seemed like a better idea. She unscrewed the lid and sniffed its open neck. Her head jerked back at the potency of the fumes, "Phew! How did he drink this shit?" She held it out, looking at the label, talking herself into it, "One big sip ... You can do it. Think how good you'll sleep." She held the bottle to her lips, squeezed her eyes tight, and chugged back a mouthful. It burned her throat as she swallowed it down. It made her choke, and her stomach lurched from the hot liquor. She slammed it on the table, "Christ that's awful." Deciding that brandy was not for her, she made her tea and sat down at the table to drink it. She calmed her nerves by watching the birds outside, flitting from one shrub to the other, wondering what it would be like to feel that small, that light, that free. She would feel that free some day soon. When she wasn't sure, but right then she simply wanted to enjoy her tea and relax in the coolness of the house.

Halfway through her tea, the brandy began to kick in. Feeling her muscles relax, she decided she liked the mild high so much; she added some to her cup of tea. She looked at the bottle in her hand, "What the hell." She took another big swig straight from the bottle, choking on its potent heat as before. She grabbed her tea and drank deep, thinking the tea would cool her burning throat. It was cooler than the straight liquor, but it too burned all the way down. With another shrug, she drank the cup empty. Enjoying the added sensation so much, she poured another half cup of pure brandy. The rest she slowly sipped, her feet up on another chair, her body unwinding as the brandy seeped further into her mind.

Once her drink was finished, she forced herself up from the chair and made her way upstairs for a desperately needed shower. The brandy made her head light and giggly. A feeling of elation she had not felt in years. She slipped out of her clothes, leaving them where they landed and stepped into the shower. The water ran over her body, her skin reacting to the liquid heat. She felt her nipples harden while she soaped her breasts clean. She smiled at the tingle, washing them over and over again, before moving on to her belly. Washing between her legs, she took her time, enjoying the sensation of her fingers in places she didn't normally touch. With the buzz of the brandy, she let herself go, uninhibited, free to enjoy herself without guilt. Rather drunk and self-absorbed in fondling herself, she nearly lost her balance. She clung to the white tiled walls, steadying her wobbly legs and equilibrium. Light headed and giggling; she decided she was too intoxicated to stay in the shower safely. Tess let the hot water wash over her body, rinsing the soap from her clean, slippery skin. Drying herself off, she let the towel fall to the floor in a heap. Why not? There was no longer anyone there to tell her she had to pick it up. She didn't even bother to brush her hair, letting it fall wet down her back, tickling her aroused flesh.

She stumbled to the bed and flopped out on her back, spread eagle on the covers. Drunk, she simply lay where she was, allowing sleep to take her over. She slipped into the darkness of her mind and felt her consciousness float free. Free of worry and exhaustion.

But the calm, tranquil darkness turned to a fitful nightmare ...

A lightning bolt flashed, but once, then the blackness swirled about her. Flames licked at the darkness, sparks rising upward, disappearing beyond the red blaze of the fire. The fire's faint roar grew louder with its intensity. The red glow illuminated a face in the distance, a face she could not fully see, half highlighted by the fire's radiance on the left brow and cheek. Yet, intuition told her it was that of a man. Gulping air, she tried to move, to get away, but her feet felt tied together. She struggled to get free with no avail. Each determined step he took, brought him closer to where she was, his body still half shadowed, half lit. Her heart thundered with fear at who the unknown man maybe behind the half-hidden face. From the edge of the darkness, a flame flared bright white, illuminating his entire face.

Eyes wide with shock, she screamed at the figure that had been revealed before her. The scream fell mute in her throat; no sound could be heard, terrifying her even further. It was the face of Officer Adams, his body void of his uniform, naked and very aroused. He appeared devilish in the glow of the red flames, sinister and sexual. Standing before her, his hands reached for her body, seizing her heaving breasts, brutally rubbing her nipples erect with his palms, grabbing at them with wide open fingers.

She wriggled on the bed, pulling her whole body away, trying to free herself from his forceful hands, but couldn't. She clawed at his thick arms, trying to pull them apart and away from her. She screamed at him to stop, this time her voice screeched high, echoing through the void. He merely laughed at her demands; at her struggles against his rough groping. Her dire struggle to escape from his molesting continued. She fought until she could fight no more, too weak to battle his powerful strength any further, she gave in, letting him do what he wanted. With her no longer fighting him, the brutality eased to gentle groping, his thumb softly sweeping across her nipples. Slowly her terror was replaced by arousal, a sensuality she allowed herself to experience.

He reluctantly released her breasts and stood before her, looking over her where she lay. She watched his eyes take in her body, from tangled hair to curled toes. His grin was wicked and wanting. Excited by her gentle beauty and the knowledge he could ravish her any way he wished, he greedily took what he wanted. He swept his hands down her belly, stopping between her legs, his fingertips digging into the soft flesh of her thighs. She closed her eyes to his face, not wanting to see it. In one quick motion, he spread her legs, opening her wide, vulnerable to his desires.

She gasped when his thumb found her engorged nub, it reacting instantly to his touch, sending waves of raw pleasure through her body. He rubbed in circles until her pleasure built, making her writhe with ecstasy. She held her breath. When she felt him lower his face to where his hand had been, using his tongue to bring her higher and higher. Without warning, he thrust in his finger, plunging it in deep, sending a rush of heat through her body. Her hands found their way to his hair, grabbing on, not wanting him to stop. She moaned out loud, letting him know his talents were bringing her higher still. Her deep throaty moan spurred him on. He increased the pressure and sped up the rhythm in order to bring her over the top.

She arched her back, every muscle in her body shuddered as she came to a full climax ...

*Beep! ... Beep! ... Beep! ... Beep!*

The sound of a truck backing up next door pulled her from her dream. Surprised, she found her hands tucked between her legs, her fingers damp and tense. She tried to stand, but her feet were tangled up in the sheets, holding her legs in place. She laid back, her mind spinning erratically and confused at what had happened. Had she actually dreamt of the cop? Him in her bed, pleasuring her. A smile slid across her lips. He was there in her dream, a dream that left her feeling sexually satisfied — more satisfied than Morty ever had. Her husband had never once touched her down below with his fingers, let alone his mouth. She had never reached such a high climax as she had in that night's sleep. With a lustful grin, she thought again of Kevin's thick fingers and snug fitting uniform.

*Beep! ... Beep! ... Beep! ... Beep! Swoosssh!*

The annoying sound pulled her back to reality. She kicked her feet wildly, untangling her blanket bound feet. She sat up, only to have her head pound at the temples. The Brandy. Not only did her head hurt, her stomach was not happy either. She immediately dashed to the bathroom and vomited into the bathtub.

She heaved until she emptied the entire contents of her stomach. She slid to the floor, the hard tiles cold on her sweat covered skin. She lay still until her breathing eased and her heart slowed to a regular beat. Morning had come whether she wanted it or not. The day ahead of her would be as stressful as the days before. Another day filled with more blue baggies and mind-bending plans to dispose of them.

She could not do it. She could not get up off the floor. Not only was she tired to the bone, she was depressed by what her world had come to, what her life would become in the future. She still hadn't figured out what she would do when all of Morty was completely disposed of — gone for good. What was she going to tell people when they ask where he was? The sister story would only work for so long; soon she would have to tell them another story — a story she had not thought of yet. It was all too much for her exhausted mind to handle. Tess simply closed her eyes and wept until she slipped back into the darkness of sleep.

It was noon when she finally woke again. Her body ached from the hard floor and the coldness that seeped into her bones. She took a hot shower to stave off the cold and wash away the sweat and vomit. Dressed, she stood in the kitchen, sipping hot tea, this time with no addition of brandy. In the shower, she had promised herself that she would take the day off from all of the madness in her life. Tess decided to set up her 'little art studio' and actually paint a picture. Although it was part of the whole 'butcher shop,' she was also looking forward to getting her hands dirty with paint instead of bloody pink slush. And maybe, just maybe, she could relax enough to have her throbbing headache disappear.

Once in the garage, she set up the art studio as she planned in her mind. The box created the walls that she lined with fresh plastic from the roll. Against it, she leaned a piece of the thick cardboard. She opened the cans of house paint and stirred them, their color palette bland. She lined them up on the plastic sheeting along with the paint brushes and scraper she found on the same shelf.

She stood for a moment, studying the cans of paint, deciding which would be the background for her new abstract piece. Beige was chosen, and she went straight to work, applying the first layer in an even coat. Next, she held the can of blue paint from the bathroom and dipped in a two-inch flat brush, soaking it until it held all it could. In one hard slash of the air, the paint exploded from the bristles onto the surface of her cardboard canvas. A long blue splash landed down the center, cutting the boring beige in two, like a bolt of lightning.

She loved it.

Tess laughed at the joy of it being so freeing to make a mess. An act she could never do with Morty around. She spotted the butter yellow of her kitchen and did the same with a larger brush. Two short thrusts of the brush and the yellow splattered across the blue. She dipped again and laid down another one, to balance the canvas. The hunter green was too dark and ugly for her taste, so she combined some of the beige with it to create a sage green. But the two paints mixed together, one oil and one water base, became thick and looked more like liquid putty. She scooped it up with the scraper and slapped it in the upper corner, laying it in layers, like scales on a lizard. To counter balance it, she did the same in the opposite lower corner. The last color she had open was black, from the railing by the front door. This she dipped the long-bristled brush in and tapped against her forearm, spraying tiny droplets here and there over the previous colors.

She stood back, her hands covered in smears of wet paint and her face covered with a wide smile. "Tess Brown ... you are a genius!" Still excited by the new hobby, she put that one aside to dry, leaning a glue globbed board in its place. This time she used Morty's drywall compound to layer on several patches. While they dried, she studied the other three cans she had not used yet — one red, one white and one brown. Blood colors she thought. She pushed the idea aside and reached for another brush. She slashed and splashed the white and the brown. With the compound not being completely dry, she smeared the paint into it, creating whirls and mounds, rough textures, and smooth plains. Just for fun she plunged into the red and dabbed it along the top of the board, allowing it to drip down, like drips of blood at Halloween. Happy with the gory effect, she put that painting aside as well. She continued to dip, splat, and slash until she had only one cardboard canvas left. That one she would leave blank as though she was about to create another masterpiece. In the end, she had not only had fun; she created her justification for having the 'butcher shop' set up permanently in her garage.

Her hand on her hip, she taunted out loud, "Take that you stupid cop." She still could not get Kevin Adams off her mind, but more for his interference in her life, than the sexual magic he had performed on her during her dream. Pushing the thoughts of him aside, she leaned the last painting against the freezer front, along with another one.

The freezer — the God damned white metal box that held her freedom inside. No matter what she did, it always came back to that freezer and its contents.

She sighed, knowing she needed to forget about the fun in her life and get back to the task ahead of her. The setting up of her mock art studio in case Officer Adams comes snooping around again had been important. If there was anything she had learned from yesterday's dinner with the old Asian man and the cop, it was that the cop was onto her. How much he knew, she was not sure of, but she did know he had been looking into her and Morty's past and that scared her plenty. She muttered to herself, "No rest for the wicked, they say," as she draped the older butcher plastic over the newer art plastic that remained on the box. She cleaned up her brushes, arms, and hands before moving onto the next phase.

Taking the key off the hook and unlocking the freezer, she pulled out the large bag of smaller bags and headed for the kitchen. She sorted through the bags and created two piles — one that had to be disposed of in the outside world and those that she could take care of with her newly purchased hand grinder. The first pile she stuffed in her fridge freezer in batches of five to seven, batches she would dispose of as she had previously. The second pile she lay out flat in the heat while she set up the orange plastic grinder. She batted away a fly, noticing that there were more and more of them in the house than the day before.

It took her some time to affix the suction cup bottom and metal clips to her kitchen table. She laid out a large cutting board beneath the grinder for easy cleanup. At the counter, she cut away any bones that the grinder could not crush in its spiral, unable to then force out the holes on the faceplate. She repeated in her mind *Fresh from the Farm*, refocusing her rational mind on the act of what she was doing, rather than what she was doing it to. It was easier to think she was cutting up meat from a beef farmer, than her husband's arms and hands. Disengaging her mind allowed her to work without guilt, making it easier to do the gruesome work quickly. After all the bones had been removed, she stuffed those in a blue bag she had labeled 'Soup Bones' and shoved them in the same freezer. She ran warm water over her hands to ease the cold from her numb burning fingers.

Back at the table, she started the long process of converting the newer chunks into ground meat. The first handful of flesh she stuffed in the grinders mouth, slowly worked its way through the spiral feeder but not much came out of the tiny holes on the face plate. She reversed the spiral, pulling the flesh back from the metal plate. She replaced the smaller holes for the largest plate she had and turned the handle, pushing the spiral forward again. That time the flesh oozed out of the holes and dropped onto the cutting board like long pink worms. Worms of flesh and freedom.

She had to stop several times to remove the sinew from the inside of the faceplate, so the flow of chunks could continue to be pushed through the holes. When she had hand-cranked all the chunks through, she examined the texture of it with fingers, "Nope, not fine enough." She put on the fine holed plate and ground it all again. Happy with the finest of the ground meat she had produced, she scooped it all up and placed it in a large glass bowl. The bowl went into the fridge, and Tess began the cleanup — the grinder, table, cutting board and counter top. As she rinsed them with warm water to not encourage staining, the fine bits of flesh whirled down the drain and disappeared from sight. It was the swirling motion that placed the idea in her head. After everything was completely washed, bleached, and hand dried, she retrieved the bowl from the fridge and raced up the stairs to the bathroom, taking two steps at a time.

Tess kneeled in front of the white toilet, the glass bowl of ground flesh on her right, the seat in the upright position. She scooped out a handful and shaped it to resemble a human turd. She carefully slipped it into the cold water. With one finger and a prayer, she pushed down on the chrome handle and stared into the white bowl. To her way of thinking, if a human turd could go down the toilet, why wouldn't ground flesh. She was careful to flush the empty toilet in between to clean anything that might have been left behind. The last thing she needed was to have the toilet clog up and have to bring in a plumber. She continued to make turd after turd, flushing each one separately until there was no more. She rinsed the bloody bowl and flushed away the pink water — forever.

Her heart sank with the thought of having to perform the next action — the sawing up of either the upper torso or the hip bones. She had no idea how she was going to cut through the thickness of the chest with her table saw. She imagined sawing across the front and then flipping it over to cut across the back. But what she could not figure out was, would both cuts meet in the middle, separating the two pieces. She knew the best thing to do was to measure the thickness of the chest and the depth of the saw's blade and compare them. A job she was truly dreading. Her stomach tightened with the thought of seeing his body, frozen solid and mutilated — mutilated by her own hands. But she had no choice in the matter; it was either dispose of Morty or life in prison.

While she washed the blood from under her fingernails, she glanced at herself in the mirror. It was the dark circles under her eyes that frightened her. Her skin was pale and her cheeks nearly gaunt. Even her hair was dull and lifeless. She looked like she had aged ten years from the stress and lack of proper food and rest. She immediately decided she would wait until tomorrow to start on the next phase. She would use the remainder of the day to drop off blue bags in trash bins. And maybe while she was doing the deed, she would take the time to enjoy the sunny day she saw outside her bedroom window. "Tomorrow ..." she told her reflection, "... tomorrow."

# Part 13

Tess had a very productive day, disposing the remaining blue bags in trash bins at the biggest mall in the city, committing crimes while people walked by her, unseen and dismissed as an ordinary woman. Once they were all disposed of, she took the time to have a Chinese combo at the food court, watching people going about their business. She rested her sore feet, weary body and overworked brain. She let her mind go numb, emptying it of all worries and schemes. With no immediate pressures, she even enjoyed the scenery on the sweaty bus ride home. That evening, she lay on her sway backed couch and watched her favorite TV show. Within no time at all, Tess slowly fell asleep on her couch. Purely out of exhaustion, she slept the entire night soundly, feeling refreshed when she woke in the morning.

Tess stretched out her aching back, preparing herself for the day ahead — the day she had been dreading, but could no longer be avoided. On her way to the bathroom, she glanced out the window to see what the weather would be for the day. She froze in her tracks. Her body fell limp with despair. Across the street was parked a police car and in the front seat sat Officer Adams, drinking a cardboard cup of coffee, and eating what looked like a Boston cream doughnut. Her anguish quickly turned to fury. "Shit!" she cursed out loud. She hid behind the curtain, watching him watch her house. "Fuckin' shit!" she stormed to the bathroom and with her pent-up frustrations, brushed her teeth so hard her gums bled. She spat out the blood into the sink and rinsed the red away. She calmed herself by brushing her long blonde hair a hundred times while contemplating her next move. A move she would have to perform with a nosey cop sitting at her doorstep.

After pulling on her jeans, she straightened her body up. To her smug reflection in the mirror, she laughed out loud. She could do whatever the hell she wanted to do. After all, she was inside her own home, and without a search warrant, the pain in the ass cop could not bother her. She laughed at the sight of the cop car as she made her way downstairs for breakfast. Once she finished her toast with jam and tea, she headed to the garage with a faded notepad and blunt pencil.

Along with the freezer key, she took Morty's measuring tape off the peg board with a heavy exhale. After gently placing the measuring tape beside the paper and pencil on the table saw top, she turned back to the freezer. She stood still before the white metal tomb, bracing herself for what she would see inside. She inhaled deeply, clearing her mind of all her morals and anxieties. The act of disassociation had become second nature to her now, like flipping a switch off in her head. Shut down and numb inside, she unlocked the lid and propped it up with her stick. She forced herself to look down inside, yet to not actually see what she was truly looking at, disassociating herself from the frozen body parts that remained within.

Without emotion, she hauled the upper torso out by the rope. Being covered in ice crystals, the heat of her hands quickly melted them, creating a thin slick layer on the exterior. With it liquid wet on frozen hard, the torso nearly slipped from her grip, causing her to hug the large bloody lump to her belly for stability. At the table saw, she stood on tippy-toes to lift it onto the flat metal surface. Immediately, she shook her stuck-on shirt free of her body with pinched fingers, her face cringing with the feel of cold, wet death next to her skin. Tucking her hands in her armpits, she took the time to catch her breath but more importantly, to warm her chilled hands.

She measured from front to back the thickest part, just below where the armpits used to be. She scribbled down the number and sighed at its width — eleven inches. Next, she measured from the base of the table to the height of the blade's teeth — only three inches.

"Damn it!" she cursed through clenched teeth.

The two cuts would not meet each other in the middle. Ignoring the torso, she stared at the blade; her mind focused on what else she could do to lessen the five-inch strip of frozen flesh and bone between the two cuts. "Cut into the sides," she muttered to herself. She examined the torso's sides, "That would take away an extra three inches on each end of the inside strip." She ignored the fact that she was talking to herself again; maybe a sign she was starting to lose it. A quick calculation in her head, "That leaves a strip of six inches by five inches right in the middle" But then she realized that Morty's body was not square. Like most humans, he was oval in shape. "Oh, that would make it much easier." Her eye keen, she measured the outer sides of the torso, scribbled the new dimensions. Through a quick sketch on the same paper, a fast algebra equation, she came to her final tally. After all her cuts on the table saw, she would be left with a strip measuring three inches by four inches. How she was going to cut through that last bit, she was not sure. But that would be a problem she would tackle after she created the initial cuts.

She braced herself both mentally and emotionally before she began. To avoid the blade binding in the material, she had to remove Morty's shirt. As fast as she could with the utility knife, she cut down the front of both his plaid shirt and white undershirt. Slipping them over the shoulders, and lifting the one side, she pulled hard to dislodge the clothing from underneath him. She let them drop to the floor, kicking them aside so they would not get in her way.

What shocked her was the small heart tattoo on his upper left chest. She had seen it every day, but the colors stood out bright against his frozen pale skin, colors that drew in her eyes. He had gotten it done just before they were married, still madly in love with a future filled with promises. Both their red initials stacked inside the black heart-shaped outline, the blue ribbon below it read *Forever Mine*. Tess was taken aback by those two foretelling words, at last recognizing the misogynistic meaning behind them. Even then he knew he would hide her from the world and control her every move. The possession of her by Morty turned her cold and angry inside. A hatred that made her even more determined to finish the job. She flipped him over on his stomach to both hide the vile tattoo and to start the sawing on the portion that had the least bones in it.

But her biggest fear was that the saw would not be able to cut through the solid frozen tissue and bone, jamming mid-way. But as with everything she had been doing, she would simply do it and hope for the best. Once she completed the first cut from one side of the chest to the other, she would switch to the back for the second cut. Lining up Morty's chest with the blade, she flipped on the switch and held her breath while slowly shoving the torso forward into the revolving teeth.

The teeth caught. The skin around the slit stayed taught as the pink sludge built up on the top edge of the cut. She shoved it forward again, gently and slowly as to not bind the blade. She felt the blade grab hold of the thicker portion, sending swelling curls of pink sludge to the cut's surface. She pushed with a steady pressure, keeping her eyes focused on the spot where the frozen flesh met the blade. Her hands pained from gripping the icy torso. The cold burning crept deep inside her fingers and palms. Yet, she held on, determined to get the first cut finished.

It was going well, the circular blade slicing through it smoothly, like it was a section of the thigh. Getting closer to the final edge, she braced her arms for the final release of the teeth. Because of the outer curve of the torso, the blade started to shudder, her hands nearly slipping free with their own frigid numbness. She clawed at the frozen lump, holding it steady until it came clean through the other side. She turned off the saw and balanced the torso on the table top.

Not being able to handle the stinging ache in her hands any further, she headed for the kitchen to run warm water over them. She stood with her hands under the faucet, looking at the sun shining down on the police car parked in the same spot as before. He was still there, waiting and watching her house. She chuckled to herself, "Having fun yet, Kev?" his name said with a mocking tone.

As if he heard her say his name, he straightened in his seat and looked her way. She automatically ducked behind her yellow gingham curtains. Although he could not bother her inside her home, she was not going to give him a reason to go get that search warrant either. She turned off the tap and dried her almost warmed hands. She quickly returned to the garage, to make the second cut in the thick part of the back.

Back at the table saw, she flipped the cut side up and carefully lined that slit with the blade. The last thing she needed was to have the two cuts misalign, creating an even bigger problem of dividing the torso cleanly in half. With a flick of the switch, the blade spun into action, the teeth biting into the flesh. The frozen tissue had started to thaw with the hot mid-morning temperatures, creating a greater mound of pink slush than earlier. Condensation on the frozen torso also made it harder to control. She grasped it as tight as she could with her undersized hands and guided the lump in a straight line, aligning it with the red bloody gash above it.

She gradually moved it forward, feeling the teeth slice in the thawed skin and the solid frozen flesh beneath it. She pushed steady, keeping it aligned. The blade sliced through — one inch — two — four — six. But all the while her eyes darted back to the heart tattoo, distracting her concentration. Mentally she tried to think of a way to cover it, to hide it out of her sight line. Duct tape would not stick to its sweaty surface and plastic or fabric might get caught in the blade, so they were off the list of possible solutions. Then her right hand slipped off the wet waxy skin. The pressure of her opposite hand twisted the lump on the damp metal surface of the table saw. It all happened in a split second. She felt it shift and catch on the blade's teeth at an angle. "Shit!" The entire lump shuddered under her left hand. Before Tess could grab it with her right hand again, it stopped shaking, jerking hard but only once. The blade stopped dead. "Noooo!" The motor below it whirred with the electrical power still trying to rotate the blade. "Shit! Shit! Shit!" she frantically flipped the power switch to the off position. She stood above it, panicked as to what she was to do next, her heart erratic in her chest.

Using both hands, she grabbed the lump and tried to dislodge it by pulling it towards herself, backing it off the blade. It did not budge. She tried wriggling the torso from side to side. Gently at first, but with no resulting movement, she wiggled it even harder, putting all of her muscle into it. It moved slightly when she shoved it towards the workbench and then the other way as well. She repeated the same action several times, but it still refused to budge any further. She stopped for a moment to catch her breath. Through gulps of air, she studied the angle of the torso and the angle of the blade. "The other side might work better," she muttered to herself.

She wiped down her sweaty face with a nearby rag before she walked around to the back of the table. The heat inside the garage was starting to climb with the outside temperatures. From there, she stood with her feet wide apart, braced for leverage. She seized it with wide spread fingers and shoved it hard with both hands. It did not move, so she shoved as hard as she could. *SNAP!* It immediately let go of its hold, the lump flying away from the blade — and from Tess. Her body jolted forward in that same direction, her hands landing palms down on the tabletop. Her right palm just missed the top teeth; landing so close beside the blade, she could feel the cold steel against the side of her thumb. The torso itself, shot across the table top, dropped onto the floor, skidded on the plastic, and slammed into the side of the freezer. *THUD!*

She stood looking downward, each hand on either side of the steel blade. It was her stiffened arms that braced her body above the sharp blade, stopping herself from landing on top of it. It was then she realized how close she had come to slicing her hand wide open on the teeth. An accident she could not afford to have happen. She lifted her head to see the torso on the floor beside the freezer, water drops and blood smears on the floor beside it. *More mess to clean,* she thought. She hung her head again, closing her eyes, striving to calm herself from the anger that was bubbling up inside.

In front of the freezer, she struggled to pick up the torso, hoisting in up to her chest with her knee. Her smallest finger became caught in the sawn slot, making her skin crawl at its gelatinous texture. She returned it to the table saw and withdrew from it, her face and body recoiled in disgust. She gagged, her stomach threatening to heave onto the floor. Over the freezer, she braced herself against its top with her arms, taking in more hot air, forcing her stomach to stay down and behave. Turning around and leaning against it, she decided that she needed some protection for her hands. Although warming them in her armpits worked, there had to be a faster way to revive them. A bucket of hot water in the garage would work wonders. She took one step to get the bucket and stopped dead. The bottoms of her shoes were covered with the bloody slime left on the floor by the torso. "Fuck!" she swore, wiping her feet on the clear part of the concrete floor. Still not wiped clean enough, she reluctantly slipped them off at the edge of the plastic and made her way to the kitchen for the bucket of water.

Her hands now thawed under running warm water and her red bucket filling with hot water, she watched through her window, spying on the cop still waiting on the other side of the street. With the cruiser parked in the full sun, he had to have been cooking in the days high heat. "Hot enough for ya, Kev? You can go away anytime you want. I won't mind one damn bit." She laughed in his direction, not caring whether he saw her or not. She was too tired and too hot to care anymore. Or was her mind beginning to slip into a state of irrationality? All she knew was that she was inside her home and he had no warrant. The bucket overflowed into the sink, pulling her away from him. She turned off the hot and turned on the cold water. Tess stuck a tall glass under the tap and drank down the entire glass of cold water in one long guzzle, smacking her mouth when she finished. She also wet a tea towel and wiped her sweaty face down with it. Pulling it away, she saw all the bits of pink flesh that landed on her cheeks and chin without her feeling them. Still indifferent, she wrapped it around her neck, enjoying the coolness against her heated skin. She took one last look out the window at the cop car before hauling the bucket into the garage.

To avoid having the torso slip out of her hands again, Tess wiped the lump down with a nearby rag, removing both the beads of condensation and slick thawed blood that was smearing from the cuts and opened ends. She also took the time to search through the drawers of Morty's workbench, finding what she wanted in the bottom drawer. Cotton gloves with tiny rubber dots on the face of the fingers and palms. Them being non-slip definitely help in gripping the frozen lump, giving her more control over its movements.

She examined the lump and decided to saw from the other side, hopefully meeting the two cuts in the middle. But before she continued with the cut along the back, she changed her mind and lined the torso up to slice down the side, removing a three-inch strip off the right side. Switch turned on, she moved the lump towards the blade, holding it as tightly as she could, as it came closer to the open-ended flesh, she braced her arms and slowly shoved it into the teeth. They caught, twisting it slightly downward. She counter-balanced by pushing down on the opposite side. Pushing it forward, the blade easily sliced through the flesh and rib bones alike. The blade hesitated when it met the first full cut of the chest.

It shuttered in her hands, making her grip the lump firmer in hopes it would go still. No such luck. She pulled it backward to ease the tension between the blade and body. That flung a fine mist of red droplets, spraying diagonally across her face, some landing in her mouth. She turned sideways and spat repeatedly, violently spitting out the taste of rotten flesh and blood. Her one hand still holding the torso in place, her stomach heaved, trying to empty itself onto the floor. She gulped in lungs full of air until the gag reflex in her throat stopped. When her stomach was nearly settled, she returned to the table saw. She pushed it back towards the blade and once again, it shook in place.

Tess twisted it slightly, releasing the pressure on the side, so it did not bind up as before. The lump stabilized, moving over the blade smoothly and effortlessly. The blade came out the other side, the slab flopping on the table top with a frozen clatter. Automatically, she turned off the saw and centered the torso on the table. What she saw before her, was shocking — yet, very intriguing. She held up the slab with both hands, examining it closer. She could see the ends of the ribs, white-blue bone that rimmed frozen pink marrow. Patches of red muscle were separated by fine lines of white sinew or pale yellow layers of fat. There was a large brownish grey spot; she determined to be the liver after poking her own body for organ location. The colors, the shapes, the way they meld together, gave Tess the urge to paint. She could see the finished artwork in her head, smiling at the final results, abstract and vibrant.

From the garage door came a familiar sound she had not heard in some time — the tiny paws scratching at the bottom. Lil' Bastard was back — a fact that worried her. The only reason the mangy mutt would return is if he could smell decaying flesh on the air. She sniffed the air but smelled nothing. She bent down to sniff the surface of the torso. No smell there as well. Either the pieces did not smell, or she had become accustomed to the odor and could no longer detect it.

The dog scratched again, whining with excitement. In four strides, Tess was at the door banging on its metal panel, "Go away! You Lil' Bastard! Get!" The scratching stopped, but only briefly, starting again with even more fury. This time she kicked the bottom of the door, rattling the entire door from the base upward to the top. She heard the yelp and waited for more scratching sounds. None came. She returned to the table to make the next slice.

Officer Adams had seen the little dog in his rear-view mirror. He watched it trot along the sidewalk, cross the roadway, and stop near the end of Tess's driveway. The dog sniffed the air, his nose held high until he caught the scent. He dropped his nose to the ground and raced up to Tess's garage door. He sniffed along the rubber gasket, scratching with his front paws. Then he jumped back at the sound of banging coming from inside. Seconds later, another louder bang scared him off, his feet scurrying away as fast as they could. What was it the dog sniffing for? And why had Tess Logan scared him away from inside the garage?

He knew she was there. He could hear her saw over the other construction noises of next door. Even that struck him as odd. Petite Tess did not seem the type of woman who could work a table saw. And for a very long period of time, at that. The more sounds he heard from that house, the more suspicious he became. Even as he watched the dog disappear out of sight, the whir of the table saw came to life again. He crushed his coffee cup and tossed it on the passenger floor. He would give anything to see what she was doing in there. Just a glimpse of what she was secretly doing behind that large metal door. But he knew damned well she would stop him at her front door just like before. He would have to find another way. He would have to sit and wait for a chance to talk to her or see some sort of inkling as to what she was sawing inside. And since it was technically his day off, as far as he was concerned, he had nothing to do and all day to do it in.

Back inside, Tess had dutifully cut the side piece into smaller chunks, stowing them away in the kitchen fridge to thaw. The grinder would make quick work of them later. She peeked out her window to see if the nosey cop was still there, and as she feared, he was, fanning himself with a magazine to keep cool. Oddly, this time the sight of him did not strike fear in her as it had in the past. At that moment, it felt like a challenge to have him sitting there, yards away, while she dismembered her husband's body. That fact worried her. Had her mental state disintegrated so far away from normal human behavior, that she no longer saw the danger in the situation? Although the cop could not ask to come in without a warrant, he could bust down the door if there was 'probable cause.' If he thought she was doing something illegal and witnessed even the smallest glimpse of a possible crime, he and his cop buddies had the legal right to storm the place, finding her elbow deep in mangled frozen flesh.

Somewhere in the back of her mind, she felt the urgent need to finish with the torso today. All she had to do was simply cut the lump up and be done with that horrible job. If she had the energy after the torso, she would tackle the hip section next, but only if she was feeling up to it. She had been pushing herself hard lately, and it was beginning to take its toll on both her physical and mental health. She returned to the garage and began the process of removing a strip from the other side, narrowing the torso even more.

She lined up the blade and inched the torso into it, holding it as steady as she could. The body had thawed more in the day's heat making it much easier to grip than before. The blade also cut through the softening tissue faster, allowing the lump to go through quicker than she thought it would. When the blade reached the spot where the first cut had been made, she felt it begin to twist again, but this time she was prepared for it and held it down so it would not leap off the blade. She twisted it back in place and pushed it forward, making the blade cut in further and faster. Within minutes the second left slab was cut clean off and ready to be cut into smaller pieces. In this slab, she could see the white ribs, the burgundy brown of the spleen and the fleshy pink of the intestines. She was also pick up on the foul odor that current came off the thawing lump. She brushed a fly off her cheek, leaving a thick streak of thickened blood behind. The smell and flies were a sign she needed to work faster before it could be noticed by those passing by the sidewalk — or someone sitting in a police car a dozen yards away.

Quickly, she chunked up the left slab and bagged it for the kitchen fridge. It took no time at all. Those she would take care of tomorrow. She needed to get through the torso today. It was priority number one on her list. Back at the saw, she lined up the second half of the back cut that sent the torso flying into the freezer. To her delight, the torso was much easier to handle with it cut almost square. It did not tilt like before, and it was easier to grip with her gloves, even though they were completely saturated with watered down blood and pink slush.

With a firm grip, she guided the lump forward, the blade slicing in the spot she lined up with the cut below, as well as the one on the upper side. The teeth caught the skin first, stretching it a bit before they cut into the flesh itself. She was amazed at how much smoother the sawing was compared to the previous cuts. She made a mental note to take out the hip section and allow it to thaw before she proceeded with it. She told herself to take it out of the freezer once she was completely done with the torso. Slowly the blade inched its way to meet the other cut. With less than three inches to go, she realized they would not line up exactly. She let off pushing it and put pressure on the right side of the lump, forcing it to cut in the direction she needed it to go. Deliberately aiming the lump in the direction she needed it to go, she felt the blade meet up with the first cut and release the tension on the blade. She flicked the saw off and let out a heavy sigh of relief.

She had done it.

Tess was pleased with her triumph, yet at the same time, unsure of what to do about that three by five-inch frozen square in the middle, holding both halves together.

She took another rag off Morty's shop cloth pile and wiped the sweat from her face. The garage was sweltering, the humidity in the high eighty percent. She was sure the weather would erupt into a thunderstorm by nightfall — more of a prayer than an actuality. The heat added to her exhaustion. All the lifting and holding onto the heavy torso seemed easy, but after doing the same motions repeatedly, her back, arms, and hands ached with strain. While wiping away sweat, she looked around the garage for something to cut the remaining center section.

Hand saw? But that would take too much effort with little yield, especially in the high heat. Axe? She chuckled at the thought of her actually hitting the cut so precisely that the tip would go inside the slot. What started as amusement, turned to a belly laugh, uncontrolled, agitated, nearly manic. She let the waves of elation take her over, allowing each one to release her pent-up emotions. Tess had no idea how long she had stood there beside the thawing lump, laughing to herself at the insanity of it all. Finally, calm and sedate, she looked again, spotting what she had been searching for all along. The hand saw Morty had used to cut tree branches. The red bow saw was tucked behind the one shelf stack, as though it had fallen there by mistake.

"Perfect!" She dashed to retrieve it from its hiding place. Smiling, she weighed the thirty inch saw in her hand for balance, talking to it, "Yes, yes. You will do nicely."

The problem she had to figure out next, was how to hold the lump while sawing at the same time. The lump was too large for Morty's little blue bench vice. And there was no possible way she could hold it between her knees and saw with the long bow saw. As she contemplated a solution, Tess examined the ends of the shelves.

The large X bracket on the shelf's end would work well. Using all the strength she had left, she lifted the torso to her chest and warily slugged it to the shelving unit. With a primeval grunt, she heaved it onto the shelf, wedging the lower, narrower end in the X bracket, like it was a log in a saw horse. "Tess Brown ... you ... are ... a genius." With renewed hope, she picked up the bow saw and slipped the narrow blade into the cut and began to saw by hand. She quickly discovered that the center had not thawed, the teeth making minimal damage with each passing of the blade. Her heart sank. At that rate, it would take forever to saw all the way through. But what choice did she have? None and she knew it. Instead of allowing herself to feel defeated, she turned those emotions into angry determination, putting all her muscle power into each stroke of the blade.

It took some time — and a lot of wiping away of sweat, stopping it from running in her eyes. Eventually, the lump gave way. The side not wedged in the X, fell free on the shelf with a soft thud.

The first thing that traumatized Tess was the exposed organs inside Morty's body. She could clearly see his severed spine and the tips of the ribs. Half his heart, his lungs, and more of the liver were visible, vibrant colors that this time, didn't look either artistic or inspiring. This time the shapes and bloody hues repulsed her, revolting her emotionally.

How could she have done that to another human being? Had her soul given way to such wickedness that she had gone beyond the point of merely protecting herself against going to prison? Overheated and appalled by her sickening actions, her stomach heaved, wanting to empty its contents. She inhaled deeply, hoping to swallow down the searing bile that was rushing upward in her throat.

It did not work.

Hand over her mouth, she ran for the kitchen sink, repeatedly purging until nothing more came up. Slumped over the tap, she ran the water, washing away her yellow-green vomit. Holding her breath so she would not vomit again, she soon felt light headed, enough that she saw stars dancing across her vision. Stars like she used to see when Morty would hit her hard in the head. She stumbled to her chair and laid her cheek on the coolness of the table top. Memories of Morty's abuse flooded her thoughts. Each image followed by another; each one filled with mean, hateful words, followed by hard punches that made her fall to her knees in pain, only to plead in that same position for mercy for an action she had not done. As the images continued, so did her hatred towards Morty. The tiny stars faded away, but her anger remained. She sat up straight and waited for her stomach to settle. She braced herself for what she would return to. "Garbage bags," she muttered, "They will hold them while I figure out what to do next." Turning off the water, she retrieved the garbage bags from under the sink. Rising, she looked out the window, only to be annoyed by the sight of Officer Adams still parked across the street. A quick image from her erotic dream flashed in her memory, a tantalizing image that made her cheeks redden. Didn't that man have other police work to attend to? Was the city so safe that an important cop like him could spend hours watch her house? But too busy to actually give a damn, Tess ignored him and headed to the garage.

As she warily stepped towards the shelf, the grisly sight of the dissected organs hit her hard. She felt herself gag again but swallowed down the acidic bile. Opening a garbage bag, she quickly shoved the upper half of the torso inside it and tied the knot tight. She let it drop to the floor and spun around to the bracket. Opening the next black bag, she unhooked the second half and slid it into the opening. As soon as the knot was tied, she let out a held breath; her stomach continued to churn inside. She needed to get away from the horrible act she had done to another living being. She left the bags lying on the garage floor and walked back into the living room.

She lay fetal on the couch, her hands across her chest, eyes closed as tight as possible, hoping to block out what she had seen. In no time, she drifted off to sleep, her arms wrapped tight around her knees, hugging her broken soul for protection.

# Part 14

Hours had gone by while Tess slept. She woke feeling groggy and listless, yet having no other option; she made her way back to the garage, her feet unconsciously pulling her forward, her mind and body not truly willing to go with them. Dark inside the garage, she turned on the light before entering. As soon as she stepped down inside the garage, a powerful stench choked the air out of her lungs. She felt her stomach lurch again. She held her breath and ran to open the garage door for fresh air. But when she reached for the door latch to unlock it, she realized she could not open the door. Not with that damned cop sitting across the street.

"Son of a bitch!" she cursed him. Straightening up from the latch, she yelled, "Go the hell away!" as she slammed the door with her flattened palms. Her frustration about to turn to tears of hopelessness, she stopped herself from wasting her energy on such a useless emotion. Instead, she inhaled deeply through her clenched teeth, straightened her shoulders square, bolstering her inner strength.

She knew it was pointless to waste what little energy she had left on Officer Adams. She had to save it for the next task — to reduce the size of the two large lumps clad in black garbage bags. Finally, unable to stomach the stench any longer, she found her bleach jug and poured a large bowl of it with hopes that its strong odor would mask the smell. It worked somewhat enough she no longer wanted to vomit with each breath she inhaled.

She had no idea exactly how long she had been asleep on the couch, but with no sounds from the construction site next door, she knew it had to be night time. By the smell coming from the black bags, it had been long enough for them to thaw out further, beginning the process of rot.

She picked up the upper half of the torso and placed it on the table saw top. Her nose instantly told her that was where the stench was the worst. She had not cleaned the saw before retreating to her couch. All the bits of pink sludge had thawed with the day's heat, rotting right where they lay. The tiny piles were no longer pink but had turned dark reddish brown, the edges dried, looking like shiny pools. Worried that the blade would be stuck, unmovable by the dried hard blood and flesh, she viciously flipped the switch, "Come on! Come on! Work, damn it!"

It spun freely, flicking dried bits ticking on the plastic covered box. Relieved, she turned it off and focused back on the garbage bag. She pulled at the plastic, opening the top, exposing the chest's front. The damned tattoo stared up at her — *Forever Mine* — the two words filled her with rage. As if a switch flipped in her head, her mind emptied of all rational thought, numbness replaced it, allowing her to focus on the lump in front of her. She manically ripped off the remaining plastic, tossing it to the floor. Tiny white maggots wriggled out from the torn plastic, making their way onto the concrete floor next to her feet.

The texture of the thawed flesh felt warm and mushy compared to its previous rock-hard frozen state. It was malleable in her hands, able to be formed in any way she wanted, like a raw bloody roast of beef with its bones left in for extra flavor. She took full advantage of that flexibility. She pressed down on the front of the lump, trying to flatten it as much as possible. Her hope was to make only one pass of the blade on each side — leaving no connecting tissue in the center as before. A quick eyeballing told her it might just work. FINALLY, SOMETHING POSITIVE FOR A CHANGE, another voice spoke in her mind.

She turned on the saw and passed the lump over the blade four times, adding a slice every four inches or so. Done with one side, she flipped it over and repeated the same process. With each cut, that slice fell away, exposing what was hidden inside. She could see each organ, thawed, and oozing clear liquids that smelled of putrid, rotten meat. Her stomach raced for her throat each time a slice fell open. Those pieces, however, did not provoke the urge to paint, but made her ill, her thorough disgust overriding any artist notion she previously had. Determination forced her forward, made her swallow down her bile and continue working.

With a satisfied grin, she forced the blade to slice directly between the two words *Forever* and *Mine*. Feeling as though she had symbolically freed herself from his control, she laughed manically, almost as though she had finally lost her mind. She yelled at the two halves, "You're dead to me!" She mockingly poked the first word with her finger repeatedly, "Forever!" She laughed at the ceiling, her long blonde hair dancing to and fro behind her back, her arms tight to her jerky body, fists tightened.

As if a switch flipped in her mind again, she abruptly stopped laughing; her expression became serious and fully attentive. Those slices she cut again, bits of coagulated blood, flesh, and white bone chips, flying off the back of the blade. She took each chunk and piled it to one side with the others. After all the six slices were complete; she bagged them up and returned them to the freezer — maggots and all. To her way of thinking, there was no way she was ever going to use the freezer again, so why worry about a few maggots.

That was another problem she had been worrying about. Where would it all end? Eventually, people would notice that Morty was missing. Her excuse that he was at his sister's would not work for very much longer. People — mainly the damned cop — would want physical proof that Morty was still alive and well.

Not being able to solve that situation at that moment, she pushed the thought out of her mind and concentrated on chunking up the next lump.

Up onto the table, she slammed the lower torso; the black garbage bag sucked tight against the heated flesh. She grasped the plastic with both her hands and tore it apart. As it split, foul air rushed up into her face, making her gag once more. She swallowed hard, holding her breath until she had completely removed the bag and threw it on top of the other. It too had long white eggs and small wriggling maggots on the inside, trying their hardest to crawl away.

As before, she began sawing the top cuts. But on the third cut, the lump twisted slightly in her slippery hands. The ribs jammed the saw's blade, the lump jittering in her tight grip. Tess slammed off the switch and pulled the lump backward, off the teeth completely. Prying it open, she looked inside the cut, realizing if she put it back through, the rib bones would make it bind. She wiped the sweat from her forehead with the back of her hand, leaving behind a long streak of melted blood — and a maggot stuck in her hair. "Pruning shears!" she yelled before turning on her heels to retrieve them off the peg board and stomp back to the table. With three effortless snips, she had severed the ribs, clearing a path for the saw blade. The shears she tossed on top of the black bags on the floor, both crawling with white maggots, their milky bulks pulled along by their tiny brown heads.

Back at the saw, she finished the third cut and continued until she was done. With much struggle, her stomach still on the edge of vomiting, the six slabs were chunked up, bagged up and tossed in the freezer with the others.

Exhausted and hot, Tess sat down on the garage stairs. She hung her head, closed her eyes, and let her hands relax.

JUST ONE MORE PIECE, the voice in her head proclaimed.

But there was more than the remaining hip section. On the bottom of the freezer lay two items she was not sure how to dispose of — Morty's head — and his penis. It was the latter of the two that brought both amusement and misery to Tess's scheming mind.

Using her very vengeful mind, Tess had thought of many humorous ways to be rid of his dick. But in reality, she could not actually bring herself to act upon them. In her mind grinding it by hand seemed both despicable and barbaric. On the other hand, slicing it to pieces and tossing them in a blue baggy did not seem punishment enough for his selfish lovemaking. A crazy laugh erupted from her lips at her mental image of 'Lil Bastard' running down the street, Morty's dick dangling from his mouth, the dog happy like it was the biggest prize of his dog life.

That decision too, she pushed aside. Flicking a fly off her cheek, she stood again, her muscles protesting to the amount of abuse she was inflicting. Readying herself for the next section, she walked to the freezer to retrieve it. She could feel maggots squashing beneath her shoes. Ignoring the popping sensations, she went straight to work.

From the depth of the cold metal box, she removed the hip section, still frozen solid and heavy. She hugged it to her body, carrying it to the table saw. Enjoying the cold against her overheated skin, she hugged it closer to herself. Then she squatted down, enveloping it with her arms and vise-like legs. She smiled at the absurdity of the scene, her hugging the murdered remains for relief from the heat. She stayed still for a few moments, the cold slowly seeping through her hot blood stream. She held it as long as her hands would let her, then reluctantly stood to carry on.

Feeling refreshed, she placed it onto the saw and with her fingers, flicked off a few remaining maggots. She studied the frozen lump, determining where to cut, with the least amount of resistance from the dense hip bones. Deciding the first cut should be between the spine and the hip joints themselves, she threw the switch, bringing the saw to life. Speculating where the joint and spine would be she shoved the lump towards the teeth. But being frozen, it did not cut in as quickly as with the thawed torso. Releasing a frustrating sigh, she held it tight against the teeth, yet trying not to push so forcefully it might jam the saw.

Halfway through the first slice, she pulled the lump back off the blade and shut down the saw. She had changed her mind, deciding to let the lump thaw in the heat before continuing. She moved the lump from the saw to the top of the freezer. Knowing it would take several hours; Tess would kill time by cleaning up the garage. With the number of young maggots crawling all over everything, including her shoes, she needed to kill and dispose of them before her garage became overrun with flies, a tale-tell sign of rotting flesh. A sign Officer Adams did not need to witness, giving him 'probable cause' to search her residence.

In the kitchen, she first put the kettle on to boil. Then from her pantry, Tess pulled out a full jug of white vinegar. It combined with boiling water created a solution that would thoroughly kill masses of the white larva and any unhatched eggs — all in one swift application. She tucked the jug of vinegar in her bucket and carried her kettle filled with boiling water; she headed back to the garage to start a task she was truly dreading. Even in a disassociated state of mind, the little white creatures made her skin crawl, sending shivers up her spine. The bucket she placed centrally between the freezer and the saw, still over the plastic sheeting to protect the floor.

Putting the hot kettle on the freezer top, she filled the bucket half full with vinegar. To the vinegar, she added an equal amount of boiling water, the acidic steam burned at Tess's eyes. She blinked rapidly before squeezing them tight, keeping her eyes from searing. A quick wipe of her fingers took away the tears that weld up. She stood back from the bucket opening, giving the harsh fumes time to dissipate.

With the rag she had used to wipe her face in so many days' past, she began to wipe down the table saw, making sure she captured the squiggly white beasts in the folds of the rag. Those she shook over the bucket, so they dropped directly in the vinegar solution. She smiled while she watched them wriggle frantically, only to cease moving within a few seconds — Dead.

It seemed silly to clean the saw since she had more cutting to do, but she was not actually cleaning, her aim was to destroy the eggs and larva. Unplugging the saw, she saturated her rag with the hot vinegar solution and squeezed it out over the blade area, quickly using it to scrub both the table top and the blade itself. White eggs smeared across the surface with each vigorous scrub. After a bit, she began to enjoy the popping sensation —

similar to a teenager popping a pus-filled pimple. With the saw surface free of eggs and maggots, she turned her attention to the floor. Shockingly, she witnessed an odd event; the maggots were wriggling along the floor in a sparse line, heading towards the bottom of the garage door. Why they were doing such a thing she had no idea, nor did she care. She was simply happy they were making it easy for her to clean them all up with very little effort. She walked on top of them, popping many of them under the heels of her runners. Using Morty's nylon push broom, she swept them in a tidy pile ready to be picked up with the dustpan. She shook the dustpan over the bucket, once again enjoying the vision of them wriggling to their deaths.

The last job was to drop both black garbage bags inside the bucket and push them under the hot water, the vinegar poised to kill them on contact. And they did exactly that. The white maggots crawled from the folds of the plastic, instantly writhing in agony, pinching up tight, and then flinging themselves open again, until they no longer moved. The dead ones floated on the surface, un-hatched eggs sticking to the sides of the red bucket. Using a long-handled screwdriver, Tess poked the bags several times to make sure all of the maggots were out; to be drowned and burned by the vinegar's acid.

Happy with the results, she carefully pulled the bags out with the screwdriver, allowing the water to drain away and then flopping them in another gaping garbage bag. She tied the new bag tightly before placing it in another bag. That one too she tied tightly, mostly in the hopes of keeping any live maggots inside and maybe asphyxiating them to death. She placed that bag by the garage door, thinking that if any did escape, they would vanish through the thin gap along the bottom of the door.

The bucket itself she took to her bathroom, poured its contents into the white toilet bowl and flushed it — three times to be sure the larva and un-hatched eggs were completely gone forever. Just to make sure, she rinsed the bucket with bleach and flushed that away as well. Dawn was visible in the small bathroom window, and soon the men would arrive next door to start up the construction of Jenny's garage.

To the joy of Tess's heart, the insurance company had come through for Jenny, giving her an even larger garage than before. Or perhaps Jenny's Dad had added to the kitty without Jenny knowing. It had been such a blessing that Jenny and her kids were still away at her father's, giving Tess lots of opportunity to saw without being questioned about what she was doing. But Tess knew she would need to contrive a story for Officer Adams. The cop would be back, asking questions and sticking his nose where it did not belong.

Another flashback feeling of his strong hands between her legs made Tess's lips twitch. She shook her head in attempts to remove the memory. How could she have had such a sensual dream about a man she both feared and detested? She shook her head again, chastising herself out loud, "Snap out of it." She forced her brain and body, to shut down any desires she felt for the police officer. The voice inside her mind encouraged, YOU'LL COME UP WITH A GOOD STORY. JUST GIVE YOURSELF TIME.

Back at the freezer, she poked the hip section with her finger, testing for mushiness. The heat held in the garage had done its job, thawing the outer few inches of the lump. PERFECT, the voice in her head said, SAWING WILL BE MUCH EASIER NOW. She slapped it with the flat of her hand, the SMACK! sound reviving her need to be finished with the chunking up of Morty's body. After the hips were severed, she would no longer need the table saw set up over the plastic. She was looking forward to not dealing with flesh and blood, endless cleaning, and daily laundry. Instead, she envisioned herself painting more crazy abstracts, colorful and flowing with energy. Her mind flashed back to the first slice off Morty's side, the colors and shapes she so desired to paint on canvas.

Tess no longer needed to force her mind to be numb, detached from reality. Her mind easily slipped into a mental state where she did not acknowledge the depraved acts she was carrying out but concentrated only on the technique she was performing on the remains of her husband's body. They no longer seemed despicable, just a necessity to survive — to avoid prison.

Lining up the previous cut with the blade, she flipped the switch and shoved the partially thawed lump towards it. As she had hoped, the saw sliced straight through smoothly. The left side was next, it too cutting completely through. Flipped over, she made two more passes over the blade, connecting to the previous cuts. With the lump in three sections, she bagged them in a single garbage bag and took them to the fridge. Those three pieces she would process first. Between the grinder and Hank's garbage truck, she would be rid of them — along with a few other bags — the very next day.

The voice questioned her, OR WAS IT TODAY? Her erratic sleeping pattern had turned her world upside down. She counted on her fingers and then checked the calendar to be doubly sure. Releasing a heavy sigh, she was grateful she had not completely lost her mind. YOU'RE FINE, reassured the voice, TIME TO CLEAN, THEN YOU CAN RELAX.

With the end in sight, she felt reenergized, felt as though she might actually get away with hiding the murder. Turning on Morty's radio, she started the cleaning of the garage — the entire garage. To her way of thinking, it would seem very odd to only clean a specific area of the garage and not the rest. No point in giving the cop more clues than she needed to.

The red bucket filled with hot water, dish soap and bleach, she went to work, her toothbrush scrubbing away tiny bits of leathery tissue and flakes of dry blood. She continued cleaning, wiping down the freezer, the work bench, and the shelving units. By the time she had finished, the garage gleamed, everything back in its place, orderly just as Morty had always had it.

But what she was truly proud of was her new "little art studio." She had added fresh plastic to the box walls and floor, bagging up the original plastic sheet after washing them clean. They too were heading for Hank's garbage truck. The sooner she disposed of the evidence the better. And with a shorter dress and no bra, Hank would be so focused on her sexy body he would not even notice the odd collection of items in the back of his truck. After a refreshing cool shower, she hummed a song she did not know the name of, while she added the dirty rags to the same washer containing her blood smeared clothes. Closing the lid had a sense of finality to it. No more sawing — no more body parts to haul about — no more flies and maggots. She made herself some tea and toast, slathered thick with homemade red strawberry jam. Again, she watched the birds outside, her feet up on the opposite chair. A weight had lifted from her, allowing her to breathe easier. Even the smile on her face was one of serenity. She was very close to being completely rid of the body. So, so close.

Inside the garage, Tess did one last thing — she leaned two of her paintings against the end of the freezer, facing towards the garage door. Then with a light spring in her step, she walked to the large metal panel, unlocked it and flung it open wide. Fresh air rushed in, replacing the caustic air the hot garage had held for so long. She inhaled deeply, a large sun worshipping smile on her face. The smile was for the sunny day, but more importantly for the absence of a police cruiser sitting across the street. In a way, she was oddly disappointed that he was not there. Tess was proud of her paintings, and deep down she was hoping Kevin Adams would be there to see them, even if it had only been from a distance.

Walking down the driveway, she looked around the corner of her house to see the progress of Jenny's new garage. Shocked by the advancements the construction crew had made in the last few days, she was glad her sawing was finished in her garage. The sound of her saw would be noticeable once they were gone from the neighborhood. Judging by the stack of vinyl siding lying on the ground alongside Jenny's new building, they would be done tomorrow, if not the next day. Tomorrow — garbage day. Those two words reminding her she still had lots of work to do before Hank showed up in the morning. Returning to the garage, she locked the door from the inside, the space replenished with fresh cool air. She brushed her fingers along the top of two paintings, promising herself that she would create more — as soon as she bought some real acrylic paints in bright colors and a few actual artist canvases. "But only after I've prepped the hip for tomorrow morning." she reminded herself.

AND MAYBE A QUICK NAP, added the voice.

# Part 15

The buzzer on Tess's alarm jolted her out of a dead sleep. She groaned at the thought of having to get up so early. But there was no choice, it was either get up and wait with her garbage bags for Hank to show up or risk being caught and going to prison.

MOVE YOUR LAZY ASS, ordered the voice.

She automatically did what it commanded and began dressing in the flimsy flowered sundress she had laid out the night before. She took the time to curl her hair in long soft curls, brushing it into a style reminiscent of Hank's high school years. THAT'S RIGHT, TEASE HIS INNER TEENAGER. MAKE HIM HOT FOR YOUR SEXY BODY. MAKE HIM LOOK ONLY AT YOU. Tess did not answer the voice in her head; she simply added a thick layer of bubble-gum pink lipstick to complete her naughty look, an act that, to her surprise, aroused her. Her eyelashes heavy with black mascara and pale blue eyeliner smoky smudged, she looked so sleazy, so slutty, that inside she yearned to become her new whorish look. A whore who'd spread her legs for any man she wanted.

With no bra under her gossamer thin halter dress, she pulled back her hair to admire her rosy nipples through it in the mirror. She pushed her breasts forward, feeling the rough fabric chafe against the two buds, making them react. The sight of them beneath the sheer white material turned her on, transforming them into hard, swollen knobs. She twisted sideways to see how far they stuck out. She pinched them into excited points between her fingertips, making them hurt just a bit. That too added to her arousal. A dirty smile slipped across her glossy pink lips. She had never enjoyed her own body that way — touching, feeling, exploring. She wanted more.

She closed her eyes and let her head fall back. Cupping her engorged tits in each hand, she squeezed them full handed, her palms rubbing over her nipples like the unclad cop had done in her dream. The sensation of her silky hair sweeping along her naked back added to the heat that was building between her thighs.

The image of Officer Adams thick hands flashed through her thoughts. Doing as he did in her dream, she let go of one breast and slid her hand down her trembling belly, then up under her dress. Her eager fingers crept inside her panties, searching for her excited nub. Rubbing gently at first, she brought herself higher, her heaving breath turning erratic. Within seconds she could no longer hold back, and with one quick thrust, she buried two fingers deep inside her wetness. She opened her eyes to watch herself in the mirror, her face flushed with heated excitement, her eyes sleepy with pleasure, she closed them again, concentrating on the intense sensation made by her fingers. Her mind drifted to the dream of the much aroused Kevin. She fantasized about her hands holding his head down as he pleased her with his tongue. Her fingers strained with each deep plunge. Over and over again she thrust deep until she screamed out, "Yes! Make me ... Come!" bringing herself to full climax, her body shuddering with its sexual release. Catching her breath, she let her body relax while she readjusted her dress. She sinfully smiled at her reflection. She had satisfied herself in front of a mirror, an action she had never done before. The air in the bathroom filled with the scent of her sex. A scent that would drive Hank crazy, distracting him completely. At least, she hoped so.

The night before, she had spent the entire evening de-boning the hip chunks, removing larger tissue with her big chief's knife. Her paring knife worked better for the detailed cutting away of finer flesh between bones. Eventually, she ended up with several bags roughly marked Soup Bones using a big black marker. The cut away flesh was ground in her grinder, her hands hurting with each crank of the handle, her shoulder tired of going around and around in its socket. The resulting piles of thin pink worms she flushed down her toilet. She no longer bothered to make turd shapes or flush several times in between. Instead, she merely dropped in small handfuls of ground meat shreds and watched them float in the still swirling water before pushing down the handle. The voice egged her on, YOU SHOULD ADD MORE AT A TIME. IT WOULD GO FASTER THAT WAY. Annoyed, she inhaled deep before answering, "No, that's not a good idea. Too much might clog it up. And we don't want a plumber nosing around here, now do we?" The voice did not answer her in return, which seemed to be of no consequence to Tess.

Her toilet had been her saving grace, allowing her to dispose of so much ground flesh she wondered what she would have done with all of it otherwise. Knowing there was a possibility the blue opaque bags might bust open, she mixed the newer bones with the other Soup Bones already bagged in the fridge freezer, hoping no one would recognize the bones as human, rather than calf bones. A full-grown cow's bones were larger than a human adult, so she would tell anyone who asked that they were calf bones. From a farmer friend who had known Morty had taken ill and thought she could use them for soup. 'To stretch out your budget,' she would quote the imaginary farmer as saying. More lies. Her head hurt with all the lies she had to remember. But it was still better than going to prison. She had bagged up the garbage the night before, leaving them by the front door. That way they would be ready to go in the morning.

With her dressed to seduce, and the bags waiting, she slapped on the bag-tags and began bringing them to the curb. There were five in all. They held all the remaining bags of Morty, the plastic from 'the butcher shop' and mixed with other simple household garbage. She was not sure why she bothered mixing them, Hank would be so preoccupied with her tits, he would not even notice or care what was inside them. She knew she looked sexy since the construction workers stopped their hammering when she first came out, looking at her like she was a whore in heat.

At the curb, she waited, watching for Hank's truck to come around the corner. The heat of the day was already setting in, creating a dewy layer of sweat on Tess's skin. She lifted her hair to let the heat out, exposing her neck to the breeze. Then she heard it, the grunt and grind of his truck coming down her street. She quickly rubbed her forearm across her breasts, making her nipples harden up, peaked and ready to impress. As it came closer, Tess stuck out her chest and rounded her ass. A wide sexy smile slipped across her mouth, her pink lips glossy wet from a quick lick of her tongue. Her smile fell as the truck came even nearer — Hank was not driving the truck. Instead, it was a very large man, all muscles, and tattoos. His thick beard was carefully trimmed, and his clothes fit him tight as though they had been tailored to fit.

Tess's stomach twisted. The voice immediately questioned, NOW WHAT ARE YOU GOING TO DO? To Tess the answer was simple. He was a man, and like any other man, her nearly naked tits would distract him just the same.

Reaching Tess, the truck stopped, and the giant of a man jumped down from the cab, "Mornin' Ma'am," he nodded politely.

Tess coyly swung her body side to side in attempts at appearing shy and cute, "Good morning yourself." She dipped her ass a bit while raising her one shoulder, "Um, where's Hank?"

"He's on sick leave. Broke an arm water skiing." He squinted down at her and pointed to the bags, "Ma'am we have a problem here."

Her heart crawled up her throat and stuck there. "Oh? Why's that? I've got bag-tags on all them." She held her breath, the voice in her head giving her orders. STAY CALM. DON'T LOSE IT NOW. SHOW HIM YOUR TITS!

He eyed her from head to toe and held up three well-manicured fingers, "You're only allowed three bags per week."

Her mind raced for a reason why he should take them right there and then. Thanks to the voice in her head, she had her answer. "Oh. I didn't know that." She placed her hand across her bosom, directing his eyes to her tits. "But that's a big problem for me." She smiled up at him, batting her eyes to persuade him. "You see ..." She flipped her hair over her shoulder, showing him her full front, basically shoving her tits in his face. "... my freezer broke down yesterday, and this is all the stuff that was inside it. If you don't take it, my house will smell awful by next week." She intertwined her fingers and pleaded with him, "Please take them all? I have no other way of disposing them."

He looked in her driveway, "No car?" Unfortunately for Tess, his eyes remained on her face and not on her breasts as she had planned.

She shook her head, her mouth pouting just enough to look pathetic, yet not desperate. HE LIKES MEN, pronounced the voice. With those three words, Tess suddenly became aware of the black clawed tattoo on his forearm. She stopped all flirtation with the bear of a man and focused all her energy on getting him to take all the bags that morning. JENNY'S AWAY, the voice prodded. Tess pointed to the end of Jenny's driveway, "Hey, how about we pretend that these two bags are over there and they belong to my neighbor? Would that work?"

He watched her for a few moments and then gave in, wagging his finger at her, "Sure. But only this one time. You hear me, Ma'am?"

"Yes, yes. I do hear you." Tess's heart jumped higher than she did. "Oh, thank you so much." She held up three fingers, giving a stern oath, "Never again, I promise." Quickly picking up the first bag, she handed it to him, "Lots of calf bones in this one." Happy to see his quizzical expression, she added more to the lie, "A farmer friend gave us a pile of calf bones thinking I'd use them for soups. But now they've been thawed too long. Shame too, they made great stock." As she handed him bag after bag, "Last one!" she felt bad about involving such a nice man in her plans. "Thank you for your kindness. Blessings." He threw the bag in the back of the truck and shoved the lever forward, the large inner scoop folded forward, crushing everything contained inside it.

"No problem Ma'am. You have a great day. Stay cool." He climbed aboard the truck and drove down the street to the next pile of garbage bags waiting for him to whisk them away.

While she watched more of Morty being taken away in the garbage, she saw another truck appear, a large auger attached to the back. It pulled up to Jenny's driveway and parked, leaving the motor running while he talked to the site foreman, fingers pointing and lots of nodding. The driver backed his truck up to where the foreman stood and parked it in place. Feeling the harsh sun against her pale exposed skin, Tess headed for the coolness of her house.

What Tess had not seen was Mr. Lo, standing behind a shrub on the corner lot. He was well hidden but could see her house quite clearly. He watched her put out the bags of garbage and wait by them in the heat, her sundress nearly see through in the bright sunlight. When the garbage truck came, he saw her flirt shamelessly with the man, pointing to her neighbor's driveway before he tossed the bags in the truck. Intuition told Mr. Lo he needed to get the whole story on what happened between the garbage man and that married woman. As slyly as he came, he walked back down the same street he had come, disappearing around the corner. There he waited across the street for the garbage truck to come down the opposite side. When it arrived, Mr. Lo approached the driver, asking him what Mrs. Logan had talked to him about. When Mr. Lo heard the garbage man say she was throwing away calf bones for soup, his gut instincts reacted, setting a warning off in his mind. He thanked the man for his time and made his way back to his bench in the shade. Closing his eyes, he contemplated on what he had witnessed. Yes, he would most definitely have to tell Kevin Adams about all her recent suspicious activities.

From her bedroom window, Tess watched the large drill begin to screw soil out of the hole it was making. It was for the pole sitting no more than thirty feet away — light post or maybe electrical, she was not sure. Nor did she care. Sitting on the edge of her bed, Tess finally allowed her body to relax, letting her mind empty of all the schemes and plans. She lay back on the covers, the voice babbling, YOU DID WELL. BUT YOU HAVE A LONG WAY TO GO YET. NO REST FOR YOU. GET BACK TO WORK. YOU HAVE NO TIME TO NAP. PRISON TESS, PRISON.

"Shut up!" she muttered out loud, arguing with the voice. "I'll do what I damned well want." With that, she closed her eyes and rolled over on her side. She forcefully shut down the voice, pushing it to the back of her mind as she drifted off to sleep.

Somewhere in the darkness of her subconscious, she dreamt of fat squirming maggots. Blue white maggots that formed a line along the ground, crawling inch by inch towards something she could not see in the darkened distance, their pincher mouths pulling them forward. She felt compelled to follow the illuminated line of wiggling creatures, to see where they were going and what significance it all meant to her. The further she walked along the line, the brighter the ominous location became. She soon recognized her house and then Jenny's driveway. She stepped carefully, trying her best not to kill any of them as she made her way beside the long slow procession. What she saw before her made her feet freeze in place. The parade of fleshy larva crawled to the edge of the auger hole, each one falling over the brink to their deaths. The seducing energy of the hole pulled at her, forcing her to come forward. Filled with apprehension, she reluctantly walked to the edge, leaning over it, she looked deep down into the darkened hole, a fine trailing of dirt breaking from beneath her feet, spilling to the bottom in a sandy cascade. There in the darkness, she saw two eyes staring up at her, milky dead and lifeless.

With a chest crushing gasp, she woke from her nightmare, sitting straight up in bed. Her heart pound violently in her chest, feeling as though it might burst through her ribs at any second. She took in deep breaths, trying to calm herself. When her heart rate returned to normal, she swung her feet on the floor and sat quiet for the longest moment, replaying the horrible nightmare in her mind.

As if it was a sign, her dream had told her exactly what her next step should be.

She hurried to the window, hoping that the pole was not standing upright inside the hole. To her relief, it was still there, lying on the ground beside the pile of dirt that had been augured out of Jenny's yard. The crew had gone for the day, meaning it was after six o'clock. Disappointed, she had slept longer than she had wanted to, but what did time mean to her these days. Hours ran together, days slipped into nights, never allowing Tess to return to her normal routine.

Not being able to get the intriguing Tess Logan off his ever-curious mind, Mr. Lo made his way back to the same shrub he had used earlier. From where he hid, he saw her in the window, looking out over her neighbor's property. He followed her gaze. Why she was looking at the pole on the ground, he could not comprehend. Maybe Kevin would know. Yes, that's what he should do. Find Officer Adams and let him know what that strange woman was doing.

What exactly she was up to, he didn't know — but he knew she was definitely up to something — he could feel it in his soul.

# Part 16

Waiting until nightfall seemed to take an eternity. Tess spent the remainder of the evening preparing for her plan. In the living room, she had laid out her old black sweat pants and one of Morty's oversized black wool sweaters, the only long sleeved black top in the house. Her black rubber boots sat below them, a pair of soft black gloves and matching toque that she wore during the colder fall months would have to do. The first part of the plan would be her dressing totally in black, in order to blend into the darkness of night. She would overheat in the clothing she had chosen, but they were all she could find. By the garage door stood her kitchen broom and a small flashlight no bigger than her palm. One black garbage bag had been opened, laying on the floor, spread wide like a gaping mouth waiting to be fed.

Tess had tried to eat earlier in the evening to boost her energy. Her tense nerves upset her so much; she simply could not stomach food, pushing away the plate of yellow scrambled eggs and buttered toast. Only sweetened Earl Grey tea would be her energy source for that night. She spent over an hour pacing in her kitchen, going through the steps of her plan in her head, thinking and rethinking each action. Finally, darkness had fallen, and the streets turned quiet as her neighbors ended their day and retired to their bedrooms to sleep. At midnight, she checked outside her window, looking up and down the street for any signs of life. Nothing moved. Feeling confident that the coast was clear, she dressed all in black, immediately scratching at the wool sweater her slim sweating body was drowning in. She rolled up the too long sleeves so they would not be in her way. Carrying her rubber boots, she flipped on the garage light and slipped them on. Clomping to the workbench, she found the keys on their assigned peg and unlocked the freezer's lid. From inside the metal box, she pulled out the hardware store bag that contained Morty's decapitated head. The yellow tinted plastic was stuck to the side of his face, transparent enough for Tess to almost see his staring milky eyes. As soon as she saw them, waves of emotions overwhelmed her. Inhaling deeply, she emptied her mind, shutting herself down, detaching herself from those same emotions. Squashing both the sadness and rage at the same time was difficult, yet she knew she had to focus solely on what she was doing — any slip-ups could cost Tess her freedom. This was a dangerous time for her. If someone saw her outdoors and called the police, there would be no lie to give or door to close. Being outside her house made her completely vulnerable, and Tess knew it. She swallowed down her fears and laid the bag on the freezer's top.

Closing the freezer and locking it, she casually tossed the keys on the work bench. At the garage door, she turned on the tiny flashlight and stood quiet for a few moments, listening for neighborhood sounds while running the plan through her mind one more time.

WHAT ARE YOU WAITING FOR? the voice commanded her, GO DO IT! NOW!

Tess ignored it, using all her energy to focus on her next steps. As planned, she placed Morty's head in the black garbage bag and opened the garage door only high enough for her to slip under; any higher than that and someone might see her slide out into the darkness of the house's shadow. Once in that shadow, she pressed her back against the wall and slid step by step to the end of it, one arm hugging the broom against her ribs. Once there, she turned off the flashlight, tucking it into her bra. Tess stood still until her eyes became accustomed to the darkness. She could feel her racing heart slow somewhat, but the rushing in her ears told her that her heart was still pumping blood faster than it should.

In one fast dash, she made it behind Jenny's new garage and cut across its back wall, staying deep in the shadows. She stopped again, listening for activity in the neighborhood. All that was heard was the sound of summer crickets and the breeze flipping a small tab of plastic attached to the pole. Ducking low to the ground, she cut across the narrow expanse, hiding behind the pile of dirt that sat next to the hole. On her knees, she peeked over the top of the dirt heap, looking through the streets, making sure no one was there. Someone maybe walking a dog or a late-night shift worker.

Being clear, she propped the broom against the pile and in two strides, knelt beside the hole's opening. Placing the garbage bag at her side, it knocked a fine scattering of dirt cascading over the edge, disappearing into the blackness below. For a brief moment, she felt a twinge of remorse, regretting what she was about to do.

WHY HAVE YOU STOPPED? HE WAS A HATEFUL MAN! HE BEAT YOU! DO IT!

Reminded of his abuse, she swallowed down the pain in her heart. "Shut up," was all she answered back. Motionless, she inhaled deeply, holding the air in her lungs, bracing herself. In one sharp tug, she pulled up on the black bag and hung it over the hole. Staring directly at it, she snapped open her hand, allowing it to drop into the dark hole. Morty's head landed with a muffled THUD. A shower of falling dirt trickled on top of the plastic bag. As silence crept in around her, she stared down into the hole, her heart swinging between crushing sadness and peaceful relief. Tess slowly sat down on her haunches, one hand covering her mouth, the other flat against her cheek. Her chest hurt, she could not breathe.

BURY IT! SIX INCHES LIKE I TOLD YOU TO. NOW, BEFORE SOMEONE COMES! It was yelling at her, its tone controlling and degrading.

Tess ignored the voice and sat still, imagining the black bag down in the hole. She felt the impulse to cry, to let go of all the pain she held inside for what she had done — and for the man she had once loved.

WHAT ARE YOU WAITING FOR? JUST DO IT!

"I told you to shut up!" Tess whispered harshly at the voice, "I need to say goodbye." Her wringing hands formed a knotted fist over her aching heart, "Just shut up."

GOODBYE? THE SON OF A BITCH DESERVES DIRT IN HIS FACE, NOT YOUR PITY. HE BEAT YOU ... STARVED YOU ... MADE YOUR LIFE HELL. HE DESERVES TO ROT IN A HOLE SO DEEP, NO ONE WILL EVER FIND HIM. A HOLE NO ONE WILL EVER KNOW ABOUT, ONLY YOU AND ME. DO IT TESS. DO IT!

A tear slid down her cheek, dropping on the dry dirt. Then another came and darkened the same spot. She let the tears flow, sobbing quietly in the darkness.

WHAT IS WRONG WITH YOU? DO YOU WANT TO GET CAUGHT? IS PRISON WHAT YOU WANT? STOP CRYING YOU COWARD AND DO IT!

Tess growled back, "I'm not a coward." She wiped her snotty nose on the back of her glove and bitterly defended herself through clenched teeth, “I am strong. Watch me.” In defiance, her right hand angrily swept dirt in the hole, landing on the plastic below. Another two-handed rake of dirt went in and then another, violently repeated until she was sure there was at least four inches of soil on top of the bag. The sides of her hands crusted with damp dirt, she took the flashlight from her bra and shone it down in the hole. No visible bag and no visible lump, only a layer of fresh dirt. She retreated to where her broom was and using the handle, poked into the side of the dirt pile creating a natural cascade that flowed down into the hole, adding another two inches or more. Being sure she had buried Morty completely, she used the bristle end of the broom to lightly sweep at her footprints, erasing them as she left. Back behind Jenny's garage, she stopped to catch her breath. Her lungs screaming for air, not from running or sweeping, but from the terrifying fear of being discovered, caught in the act.

GET IN THE HOUSE NOW BEFORE SOMEONE SEES YOU!

“Shut Up!” Tess hit the side of her head with her fist, trying to get the voice to stop. "Get ... Out! Go Away!" She hit herself again, making tiny stars dance in her vision. It did not return, but she could still feel its presence lingering somewhere in the back of her mind. Clenching the broom white knuckle tight in her hands, she returned to the garage the same manner she came, sweeping away any footprints she could see in the house’s dark shadow.

Back inside the garage she immediately stripped off her black clothing and carried them to the washing machine. Her brain on autopilot, she washed yet another load of murderous clothes, for the umpteenth time in what seemed to be the longest weeks of her life. Her fingertips she scrubbed clean, not feeling the pain when they bled from the stiff bristle brush, the red drips swirling down the sink's drain in fine streaks.

Her mind still numb, she put on her nightgown and headed for the kitchen to make tea, her stomach growling loudly for food.

I'LL FIX US A CHEESEBURGER

"No, I want pancakes ... with peaches and syrup ... so shut up." In the kitchen, she made her tea, adding a good glug of Morty's brandy. Still on autopilot, she sipped her tea while she made pancakes, adding a large dollop of butter to melt over top of the golden stack. She added sliced peaches from a can, pouring its thick sweet syrup over the entire pile until it oozed into small puddles on her plate. She sat at her table enjoying her late-night meal, enjoying the loss of tension on her shoulders and chest.

As of that night, she only had one piece of Morty left to dispose of — his penis. It was the only item left in her big freezer. She decided she would remove it from the garage and put it in her fridge freezer. She had other plans for it, but that would have to wait until tomorrow. She left her plate where it was, switched freezers and headed to bed.

That night she slept naked, enjoying the cool night air blowing a crossed her skin. She drifted off quickly, the darkness filling her mind, her body for the first time in years, feeling fully relaxed and calm.

Deep inside the blackness, Tess floated on air, her limbs flowing liquid in an unfelt breeze. Her body whirled gently before she landed on her feet, the floor glossy and cold. Still naked, she felt vulnerable to what she could not see beyond the darkness. She sensed someone, or something there, yet couldn't see it. And whatever it was, it felt weighty, ominous. Although she was scared, she felt a pull from a particular spot deep within the darkness. She listened for identifying sounds — there were none. The concentrated silence crushed her ear drums. She covered her ears with her palms, the sharp pain piercing them inside her head.

The voice shrieked, MAKE IT STOP!

Facing upwards, her hands shielding her ears, she shook her head wildly from side to side with horrified agony. On impulse, she began running blindly into the darkness, her body steering itself towards the center of the intense energy. Scurrying, she ran one way, then spun around, running in another. Feeling that she was moving away from the energy, she stopped dead and turned about, manically racing towards it once more. Terrified, tears of panic filled her eyes, making it harder to see out into the vacant expanse. Disoriented in the void, she felt lost and abandoned, desperate to find the source of the beckoning energy, hoping it would help her find her bearings in the black abyss. Within ten steps, she slammed against a hard wall, her body crumbling to the glossy floor in a limp heap. Panic-stricken, she pawed the surface around her, searching frantically for something, anything, to define where she was. Even the wall she had collided with was gone, disappearing completely. Crawling forward on her knees, she swept her arm in front of her, seeking something solid. Behind her sounded a loud BANG, making her twist about, in spot. She lost her balance, falling face first onto the swirling floor again. She lay quiet, listening for any type of sound. The silence still hurt her ears, making her want to scream. Instead, the voice in her head screamed for her, sending a sheering pain through her brain. AAAAAOOOOOOW! The pain was so sharp, it triggered her need to search again, to find relief from the agony. Once more, she swept her hand along the smooth floor; left to right, then back and forth. Further forward she moved, sweeping wildly as she went. Finally, her hand connected with a large hard mass. Instantly, an electrical charge transferred from it to her, binding them together. The startling jolt that ran through her body, it made her sit upright, forcing her to give it all her attention. Using both hands, she reached for the item and held it before her. She rose to her feet, being careful not to drop the glossy sphere she held firmly.

Frightfully, the shiny black ball began to rotate in her hands, turning its opposite side towards her. As soon as she recognized what she was holding, she pulled her hands apart, letting it fall to the floor.

The milky eyes blinked up at her. Its mouth wide as though in pain, blood drooling from one corner. Although spoken as soft as a whisper, the voice roared through the silence, "Why Tess? Why did you do this to me? Didn't you love me anymore?" The voice was that of her husband Morty, filled with pain, begging his murderer for an answer.

Tess could not speak — her mouth moved, but no sound came out.

"Wasn't I good enough for you?" The surface around the eyes changed to that of Morty's face, his expression angry, brows grooved with hate and accusation. "You lazy bitch! Didn't I give you everything you wanted? You Whore!"

His words of hate echoed in her ears, setting her heart rate racing. Panicked and scared, she tried to run away from the terrifying site. She struggled to step away, but her feet would not move, as though glued in spot. It was him. Using their connected energy, he held her in place, making her his victim once again.

The voice exploded, screeching in her mind, STOMP ON HIM! KILL HIM! CRUSH HIM DEAD! DO IT TESS, DO IT!

For once Tess was happy to hear the voice in her head, pulling her from her petrified state. Hate replaced her frozen terror, smashing it into bright shards that burst through the blackness. Unsure her foot would move, she yanked upwards hard. It let go its hold, sending her off balance. She stumbled three steps before she caught herself.

STOP HIM! CRUSH HIM! STOP BEING A COWARD!

"I am not a coward!" she growled through her teeth. Angry at the insult, she spun about, her body taller, stronger as rage filled her body. In two strides, she reached the sphere and stomped down as hard as she could.

She felt her foot connect, felt the hard bones crack on the second stomp, the third disintegrated it like it was fragile egg shells crushed under her foot.

Total silence.

The voice whispered a warning, WE ARE NOT ALONE.

From the inky gloom, a man walked forward, only stopping when Tess held up her halting hand. The body shimmered silver, a liquid mercury shape revealing no details.

"You killed him again." The voice was that of Officer Adams, the chrome figure shifting to his real form. "Come with me. You're going to prison." His image reached for her, handcuffs dangling open.

"No! No! ..." Tess screamed, her head shaking fiercely as she retreated from his grasp, refusing to go.

RUN TESS! RUN!

The cop stepped closer, the metal handcuffs jingling through the silence, "Prison is the place for murderers."

In the distant background, the faint image of Mr. Lo faded in and out of the darkness.

"No, no." Tess stumbled backward, her feet feeling heavy, moving in slow motion.

FREEDOM — RUN TO FREEDOM!

From nowhere, the handle of her little red suitcase materialized in her hand. Identifying the item at the end of her arm, his hold on her vanished. Her feet immediately let go. She turned away from the cop and ran for her life, the darkness enveloping her in cold air.

From behind her, she heard the cop's muffled yell in the distance, "Prison is for murderers! That's where you belong!" She kept running, her lungs burning more than her thighs. "I'm coming for you, Tess Brown. You're mine ... forever!"

*CLANG! CLANG! CLANG!*

The loud clang of metal on metal pulled Tess from her nightmare. Her naked body covered in sweat, her chest heaving with each deep breath she gulped in. Her heart raced so fast; she was sure it would seizure to a stop. The memory of the nightmare rushed through her mind. How did he know her maiden name? And the words 'Mine' and 'Forever' — how did he know about those? Stomach acid rushed up her throat. She ran to the bathroom and vomited in the sink.

*CLANG! CLANG! CLANG!*

The pounding continued outside her bedroom window. Tess slipped on her robe, tied it tight at the waist and staggered to the window. Her hand holding her forehead and her elbow on the wall, she peeked beyond the curtain, her eyes blinking madly from the bright morning light. Outside she witnessed what she had been hoping for — the workers were raising the wooden pole by a small crane, lifting its end over the hole. She watched them let the pole drop into the hole. But they missed; the pole bouncing off the furthest edge, spinning on the chain until one of the workers steadied it with his massive work gloves. Up it went again, high as the small truck crane could pull it. The same worker steadied it from spinning and swaying. Balanced, he stepped back from it and gave the driver the signal. With a single pointed finger at his shoulder, he swept his finger downward, aiming to the dirt below his feet.

Instantaneously, the pole released, dropping into the hole, its end connecting with the bottom. In her head, she heard the sound of Morty's skull crushing under the weight of the pole. The men below didn't react — only she heard the horrible crunch of fracturing bone.

Checking the little tab of plastic on the side of the pole, the foreman yelled, "Drop it again. It's not deep enough."

Tess's stomach tightened. Was what Tess feared most, about to happen? If the pole didn't sink low enough in the hole, they would have to re-auger it, drilling up bits of Morty's ruptured head in the process. She watched wide eyed, her anxious breath held as the pole came slamming down again. To her relief, she heard nothing. A silence that was euphoric to Tess's ears.

The foreman bent down to check the depth, "That did it." He waved his arms to take away the crane, "Fill'er in boys." Chains off and the truck driving away, the workers filled the gap around the pole with shovels, packing down the dirt with a long piece of lumber.

In one hard rush, Tess released her breath, her knees nearly giving out from under her with liberation.

It was over — Morty's head was gone — Forever.

Relieved and exhausted, she stumbled to the bed, stubbing her toe on her red suitcase again.

The voice ordered, PACK IT.

She did not understand, "Why?" The voice failed to answer her, but her inner instinct told her the voice was right in its warning. As calmly as possible she packed the little bag with the essentials she would need — T-shirts, shorts, a pair of jeans, underwear, and socks. When she found the bankbook under her socks, she held it in her hands, staring at it for the longest time, her nightmare running through her mind. As far as she was concerned, that nightmare was a foretelling, an omen of things to come.

Panic set in.

She quickly dressed in whatever was on top of the drawers. She rushed through brushing her teeth and fixing her hair. Tess looked in the mirror and laughed at her bizarre reflection. Her faded lime green t-shirt didn't quite go with her burgundy shorts. But it was her very messy ponytail stuck up wildly, that added the look of a fool's crown. Tess didn't care. Her instincts were telling her to go to the bank no matter what she looked like. Slipping on her flip-flops, she locked the door, her sandals slapping loudly with each hurried stride.

Reaching the bank, she lined up behind an old woman, grey-haired and half hunched over with age. The line moved forward, the old lady limping behind the person in front of her. Tess stepped in place, feeling the slight blast of heat coming in from outside. She spun back to see who would be lining up behind her. "Fuck!" she didn't mean to say the word out loud but by the old woman's tisk-tisking tongue said she had.

"Really!" the woman commented in her direction.

"Sorry." Tess's face went fiery red — more from anger than being caught cursing in public.

"Well hello, Mrs. Logan. How are you today?" asked the one person she did not want to see —Kevin Adams.

She could not believe it. Why was he here? Of all the people she was hoping to avoid, it was him. She suppressed the anger that was rising inside and put on a bright phony smile.

Although not in uniform, the old woman scoffed, "Being rude. That's what she's doing Kevin."

"Mrs. Tyler. I didn't see you there." He smiled kindly at her, "How's that dog of yours doing?" The line moved forward, and so did they, the old lady being next to be served.

"He's dead ... that's how he's doing." The teller yelled Next! and the senior shuffled forward, not bothering to look back their way.

"Oops," Kevin joked, "Guess that was the wrong question to ask." Tess kept her back to him, not responding to his comment. He not only felt the impulse to talk to her but more of an urge to be physically closer to her. He stepped closer, silently inhaling her scent. But what he smelled was something different than what a female should smell like. Lavender and a slight pungency of something the cop could not quite put his finger on. The odd scent seemed familiar, yet not easily identified.

Next!

It was Tess's turn. She walked to the teller and asked as quietly as possible, "I'd like to take out everything ... but one hundred dollars." Adding the final bit at the last second. She slid her bank book towards the teller and waited, her index finger tapping irritably.

"Sorry, what was that?" The teller was terse, impatient to get through the long line up.

"I'd like to take out all my money except one hundred dollars."

"All of it?" the teller's question was loud enough that others looked their way.

TELL HER TO SHUT UP AND GIVE US THE FUCKIN' MONEY.

Tess tried to suppress the woman's loud words, "Shhh! Keep it down. Respect my privacy please."

Offended by Tess's instructions, she huffed at Tess and simply did what she wanted. "Bernice, I need some assistance with this customer." Bernice stopped what she as doing behind her desk and walked their way — Kevin Adams watching every step she made.

"Is there a problem here?" Then Bernice saw who the customer was. "Oh, hey ya Tess. How's that husband of yours? Haven't seen him around lately."

Tess's stomach fell to the floor. Of all the subjects to bring up, Morty was not the one she wanted to hear. She plastered another pleasant smile on her face, and to not cause a scene, went with the flow. "He's good. Staying at his sister's for a while." She let her face become forlorn and whispered the rest, "I needed a break from him. Taking care of him day and night has taken its toll on my health. Doctor suggested I take a break so I don't get too run down."

"Oh Hun, good for you." She patted the back of Tess's hand, "So many caregivers neglect themselves and end up just as sick as the ones they're taking care of." She turned to the other teller, "So what seems to be the problem here, Helen?"

Obviously, the teller was hard of hearing since she seemed to yell at Bernice as well. "She wants to take out all her money except one hundred dollars."

"So? What's the problem?"

"The only money being put in that account is her husband's disability cheques."

"Again, what's the problem?" Bernice was getting annoyed with her nonsense.

"Can she do that?" Much to the mortification of Tess, Helen's voice seems to carry to every corner of the bank. Everyone was looking at the trio.

"Is her name on the account?" Bernice, of course, knew the answer. She was the one who set it up for Morty and Tess in the first place.

Tess knew it as well, but she tried her hardest not to smile in triumph. From the corner of her eye, she could see the cop, watching them intently while his teller counted out his withdrawal.

"Yes, both their names are on the joint account," the teller answered sheepishly, realizing her mistake.

Bernice rolled her eyes at the blushing teller, "Then, by all means, give Mrs. Logan her money."

He raised his head high, "Is there a problem over there Bernice?"

Tess's mind growled, Great! He's sticking his nose where it does not belong ... again. Will that man ever leave me alone?

Bernice had finally lost all patience with everyone, "Nothing's wrong. Just a wee misunderstanding about our banking policies, is all." Before she turned her pursed lips towards Helen, she added, "And you're off duty, so you hush up."

That scolding made Tess snort. But she covered it with a fake cough. No point in making things worse by pissing off the cop. "And can I have it in an envelope." The whole situation was making her so nervous, she nearly forgot her manners, "Please."

"Of course, you can. Right, Helen?" It was not a question, it was unspoken order.

Begrudgingly, Helen did as she was told. She counted out the bills and coins from her till and then counted it out for Tess. Everyone in the place heard her counting the amount out, her voice loud and somewhat resentful.

Tess could feel the cop waiting for her by the door. His larger than life presence blocking the doorway. Helen stopped counting and retrieved the stack of cash, jammed it in an envelope and slapped it back in front of Tess. "There you go." Without a 'thank you' or 'have a nice day,' Helen looked Tess in the eyes and bluntly yelled, "Next!"

Hiding her contempt for the woman's hostile attitude, Tess spun about and stuffed the envelope in her tote bag on her way to the bank's only exit. He was still there, waiting patiently for her to be finished. He smiled brightly at her but didn't let her pass. "You have a lot of money the. You want a ride home? Wouldn't want you to get robbed in the streets."

Tess let out a laugh and mocked his words, "Some cop you are. They're your streets. Aren't they safe enough to walk down in broad daylight?"

They both heard Bernice snort at Tess's come back. He blushed, "Guess I deserved that one."

She shrugged her right shoulder with indifference, "I'm taking a taxi home," she reassured him, "And I'm locking it in my husband's safe when I get there. Exactly like Morty told me to do when he called me this morning." She added the last bit as an alibi, making it appear that Morty was still alive and at his sister's.

He held the door open for her, "Then I won't hold you up any longer."

Tess skirted past him, walked through the doorway and down the street towards the taxi stand, one block south.

But Officer Adams did not leave the bank. When she was out of sight, he went to Bernice's desk and sat down in the chair meant for customers. "Bernice, I need some answers. Police type answers." His face showed he meant business, "I have an uneasy feeling about that woman, and anything you can tell me would be of great help."

Bernice pursed her lips again, "Kevin, you know I can't discuss our clientele's financial information without a warrant." She folded her hands in front of her on the desktop, "I'd love to help ya Kev, but we have rules."

"I get that, but what can you tell me about her and her husband that's not financial business?" His face implored her to give him something, anything, to work with.

She told him about the arrangements made so that Tess could do the banking with her husband's disability cheques. She talked about the accident and how it changed her for better while he was in the hospital. But beyond that, they kept to themselves so there wasn't much that Bernice knew about them outside of the bank itself.

It was Kevin's teller that spoke up, "Um, my brother worked for Morty Logan down at the plant. And he used to tell me what a nasty man he was." She said it quietly so others didn't hear, "I kinda feel bad for her." She laid down a sheet of paper for Bernice to sign. She looked at Kevin with a tilted head, "Funny thing, though. I grew up in this town and I don't remember Morty ever having a sister." She retrieved the paper and headed back to her wicket and waiting customer.

Her last sentence hit Officer Adams in the gut like a hammer.

Without saying goodbye, he jumped to his feet and raced out of the bank, visually searching the streets for any sign of Tess Logan. However, she was nowhere to be found, "Damn it!"

Tess waited patiently in the drugstore line up. The old woman in front of her opened up another change purse to count out pennies.

HURRY UP YA OLD BAT! growled the voice.

Tess ignored its disrespect and mentally told it to shut up, pushing it deep in the recesses of her mind. She paid the cashier and left with the newly purchased box in her tote. Her next stop was to the same second-hand store she bought the grinder from. She purchased a woman's black business suit, a sleek style she would not normally wear. And a pair of high heels to match. From there Tess took her time, trying her best to not look harried, pretending she was enjoying the cool shade of the trees along the street. To avoid overheating, she did take a taxi home. And as promised, she hid the money safe from robbers — tucking the envelope holding $5,149.00 beneath the underwear of her packed suitcase and shoved it back under the bed.

The day had been exhausting for Tess. The intense heat. The incident at the bank. All the while using every ounce of energy to stay calm, trying her best to not react to the cop knowing her every damn move she made. She lay on the bed and closed her eyes. But she did not dare to sleep, for sleep brought on horrifying nightmares, her already frayed nerves could no longer endure.

Officer Adams was getting close, and she knew it.

Tomorrow she would carry out the plan she had contrived in her mind. But first, she needed to rest — night would be here soon enough and she needed to be fully energized when the right moment came.

"That's what he said Kevin." Old Mr. Lo recounted what the garbage man had told him. "Calf bones." He shook his cane in the air, "Who uses calf bones? No one ... That's who!"

"I know what you're saying. I already submitted a warrant request from Judge O'Neil. And if I know him, he'll sign it straight away. I'm still not sure about the bones connection. Guess we'll soon find out." But why calf bones — why so specific? Why had she made a point of mentioning that the bones were calf bones to the garbage man? An image rushed at him. Smaller, slimmer bones! The size of a human's bones! That's when it hit him. He said nothing to Mr. Lo, for fear he would overreact and make matters worse. His brow frowned in disbelief, "I still can't believe it. Not from her. She's so ... so timid ... so frail."

"But that's what she wants us to believe." He held his chin high, "I knew there was something not right with that young woman the first time I saw her throw those blue bags in the trash. Can you imagine, being so discourteous as to dump your household garbage in a street bin?"

Kevin had not heard the old man mention any blue bags before that day, "What are you talking about?"

He pointed with his cane, "Over there. She would drop in blue bags as she walked by. Or should I say, she pretended to not throw away the bags."

"That one?" Kevin pointed across the street.

"Yes." Before he could say anymore, the cop was already halfway to the other side of the street.

He looked down in the trash can, but it was nearly empty, only a few coffee cups and a torn deli container inside. He spun on his heels and strode back to the old man. "Do you remember what day that was?" He really wasn't expecting him to recall at his old age.

"Which time?"

He stared wide-eyed at him, "You mean there was more than once?"

"Oh yes. I'd say at least four times in that one week."

Becoming aggravated, the cop questioned him further, "And you never thought to tell me about it?"

"It didn't seem that important at the time. It was just trash, nothing more. I checked."

Officer Adams was thinking it was more than 'just trash.' "Anything else you haven't told me about?" his tone accusatory.

"Now wait a minute. I told you about everything else I saw." He was insulted by the cop's accusation of him hiding information and showed his exasperation by shutting his mouth tightly. A warning Kevin knew all too well.

He patted the senior's shoulder and gave him a well-deserved compliment, "You're right, you did. Sorry. I'm so frustrated by all this ... my nerves are rattled."

Mr. Lo nodded his forgiveness and added, "No sister? That's bad news. Where is her husband then?"

"That's what we're about to find out. Once I get that warrant in my hot hands, we'll raid her place. Tossing it top to bottom until I find out what she's up to and where Morty Logan is. I gotta get in that house."

"Can I come?"

"No."

"Why not? I helped, didn't I?"

He squinted at the old man's face, "Because you're not a cop ... and it's dangerous. She's dangerous." His eyes shone with tenderness, "And I'd feel horrible if anything happened to my best friend." Those words of kindness seemed to appease Mr. Lo's offended soul. "Jesus, I can't just sit here. I'm going to go bug O'Neil again, put a fire under his ass."

Don smiled widely. He spoke the answer even before Kevin asked. His tone was as-a-matter-of-fact, "It's Wednesday, so he's having lunch at the strip club out on the highway. He thinks he's hidden if he takes it out of town. He doesn't return to the courthouse until he's fed ...

and um, happy." He let Kevin fill in the blanks on the last narrative.

Kevin grinned at him, "Jesus, my sister's right ... you do know everything about everyone."

He shrugged with a smirk, "I try."

Just then the radio crackled in the cruiser. He lightly slapped the old man's shoulder, "Gotta go. Thanks, my friend." Before he climbed in the cruiser, he yelled over the radio's noise, "We'll get her. My gut says so."

# Part 17

Although she had not planned on sleeping, her body had won her over, pulling her into sleep it desperately needed. Darkness outside her window told her she had slept for hours, yet that time, no nightmare came to terrify her. She stretched her body out long, releasing the last bit of tension held in her muscles. She made her way to the kitchen and began preparing her final meal before her long night of work. The clock on the kitchen wall read ten minutes after midnight.

She took the time to hand cut a large potato for French fries that would go nicely with her cheeseburger. She put on her pot of cooking oil, heating it for the rinsed potato strips. The burger she fried in a separate pan, adding spices the way she liked it. She added the fries to the basket and checked for the slight ripples in the oil to tell her it was finally hot enough. She slipped the basket in the rolling oil and flipped the burger. While they cooked, she sliced tomato, dill pickle and cheese for garnish, placing them on the little plate with the hand painted roses in the center. She even filled up a crystal goblet with the remainder of Morty's brandy, shaking out the last drops.

Tess was very aware that this might be her last full meal for some time to come, so she created it of all the things she enjoyed most. A small pot of powdered gravy completed her final food want. When the fries were golden crisp, she tossed them with salt and poured them out on a kitchen towel. She built her burger — a thick slice of tomato, extra cheese, and a giant dollop of mayonnaise — and pickles on top.

She ate her meal in relative silence. Looking around her kitchen, reminiscing about the better times she and Morty enjoyed in their little home. If a painful memory tried to slip in, she shut it down in her mind, replacing it with a happier one. Finally, with enough brandy in her, she found herself staring at the pot of cooling oil on the stove. That was the solution she had been looking for. With a delighted smile, she popped the last morsel of her burger in her mouth. Her fries swam in the thick brown sauce; Tess had always been a sucker for chemical gravy. Finishing her meal, she left the plates where they were. No point in cleaning them up — she would not be there tomorrow.

She took her favorite mug from the dish tray, hugging it to herself. In the living room, she took down the photos of her mother and father, hugging those as well. She stopped at the one of Morty and her standing outside their house, a big fake smile on her face. She remembered that day clearly. He had hired a friend to take anniversary photographs, a gift from him to her. But in the end, he became jealous and accused her of flirting with the photographer. She also remembered the beating she received after the friend had left. That photo she took from the wall and with one hand, threw across the room, hitting the wall with an angry crash. Not wanting any of the other framed lies, she climbed the stairs for the final phase.

In the bathroom, she removed her clothes and stood naked before the mirror. Opening the drawer, she took out the shears she used to trim Morty's hair and set them on the counter. She smoothed her long silky hair with her fingers, feeling the blonde strands against her shoulders and chest. She waited for the voice to tell her what to do. But it did not speak. It was gone. It had left after she tucked it away in the dark corner of her subconscious. She did not need it anymore.

Picking up the shears, she pulled a handful of her hair together and brutally chopped it off. The long honey strands she let fall in the sink, taking another handful, and repeating the same method. Clump by clump she shortened her hair until it was time to trim it to a proper female cut. She carefully styled the sides to look corporate, yet left it flirty in the front. She left everything where it lay, not bothering to sweep or tidy. In the shower, she opened the box of hair color and snipped the packet, adding it to the solution. In less than an hour, Tess went from being a long-haired blonde to a short-haired sexy brunette. After blow drying her hair, she saw herself in the mirror. Her bright blue eyes contrasted sharply against her new sable colored hair. To make room, she pushed everything off the counter onto the floor. With each piece of makeup she used, she stashed it in a blue baggy until the entire look was complete.

She had taken the time to darken her brows, so they were no longer pale yellow. She applied her lipstick in a manner that made her lips appear thinner than they normally were. A neutral pink softened her mouth. A technique she had read about in the physiotherapy waiting room. She even contoured her face adding high cheek bones and a narrower nose. Happy with the reflection in the mirror, she packed away her makeup and all the other essentials she would need in the future.

In the bedroom, she laid out the new suit, replacing the cruel memories of Morty with its feminine styling. Looking at the clock on the nightstand, she knew she had to hurry. Sunrise came early in the summer, and she wanted to be ready when the sun appeared over the horizon. She pulled Morty's suitcase from the closet and laid it on the bed beside her red one. She quickly packed the remainder of the clothes she wished to take with her, the rest she did not care about — they could burn for all she cared. Her jewelry went in next, along with shoes and a rain coat. Zipped up, she slid it to the floor and rolled it to the doorway.

She dressed in the new suit, the long legs tailored as though it had been made for her. Stepping into her glossy high heels, she suddenly felt different. Stronger, more confident — more alive than she could ever recall. She admired herself in the mirror, her shoulders held back and her body slender and tall. "Well, hello Elizabeth ... Nice to meet you, Ms. Waters." She could not believe the dramatic change she had created in such a short time. Even she did not recognize the person she would become.

Pleased with her new appearance, she collected her red suitcase and walked to the bedroom doorway. She took one last look around the room, making sure she left nothing behind she may miss someday. To her disappointed heart, there was nothing more she wanted. It was all Morty and nothing of her. She brought both cases down stairs and parked them by the front door. She took one last gulp from the goblet, the brandy burning her dry throat on the way down. She had to hurry now. It would be daylight soon.

In two strides, she stood before her gas stove, placing the pot of oil back on the burner. Click, tick, tick, tick. She turned on the gas flame to the highest setting and stepped away. She looked around her kitchen, and for the last time touched her yellow gingham curtains and felt the soft leaves of the African violets on the open window sill. She would miss her little kitchen. Daylight seeped in through the clouds, spreading the first light of the day through the window. Melancholy, she pulled herself away and walked to the front door and opened it. It was time to go.

But when she was about to step through the open door, she stopped dead in her tracks and spun about on her high heels. As quickly as she could, she went to the fridge freezer and pulled out the one remaining piece that was once Morty's — his frozen penis. She carefully slipped it in the hot oil, trying not to splash her suit. From behind her, she could hear the ice crystals spit in the hot oil. With a satisfied chuckle, she walked out the front door with both cases.

Within yards from the house, the smoke alarm beeped nonstop, and smoke began to billow out of the kitchen window. By the time she reached the end of the block, she could hear the sirens erupt in the distance. They were coming to put out her fire.

She hoped it all burned down, erasing her life there forever.

She stood, watching the first fire truck arrive, the firefighters frantic to save the burning building. Behind the large red truck, she witnessed Officer Adams race forward, his hand on his gun as though ready to shoot from the hip.

At that exact moment, the morning sun broke through the clouds behind Tess, silhouetting her body.

Kevin Adams froze in spot, his eyes squinting against the sun's brilliance. He could not tell who was standing on the hill top, but he was certain it was not the woman he was looking for. Tess's hair was long and blonde. And she was definitely no business woman. When it came to Tess Logan, there was only one thing he knew for sure — she was a murderer. The long shadow lingered, watching him in return. People began to show up on the street, forcing him to return to his job of protecting the public. Behind him, flames burst through the roof, licking at the sky. He had no choice but to turn away from the figure in the distance.

The fiery sight before her made her happy. Happier than she had been her whole life. She smiled softly to herself. Soon it would all vanish. Tess simply turned around and walked away, disappearing behind the house on the corner, red suitcase in one hand, pulling the other behind her.

She was free.
Elizabeth's new life awaited her.

Did you enjoy this book?
Please leave me a review.
I would love to hear your feedback.

*Thank you* for purchasing my product.
Your support is greatly appreciated.

**Kay D Johnson**

Be sure
to look for
Kay's previous book,
***Life on the Lawn***
now on sale.

This is the story of four, lifelong, best friends - Fran, Pearl, Ruby and Violet, who attend the auction of Henry Phillips, the husband of their late-friend, Virginia. Henry, no longer able to take care of himself, he is forced to leave the farm life behind and retire into a nursing home. With his unwanted transition, comes the selling of his remaining possessions in a simple country action. Treasures and heirlooms that his greedy children do not care to inherit.

As the sale proceeds, these elderly Southern ladies share with each other the memories and adventures that are connected to many of the items up for auction. Tales of apple pies, lost lovers, and murder. Many of the local folk and neighbours gather to bid on the household items at hand, but it's Emmett, the worldly auctioneer, who is downright curious about the quiet outsider. Why is someone as sophisticated as him at a small town auction? Who is this unknown wealthy Frenchman? And why is he watching the four ladies so intently?

This is the story of one simple day,
at a not so simple auction.

## Kay D Johnson

Be sure
to look for
**Kay's newest book**
First Page Last Page
now on sale.

**Nitra Zupan** faces the one crisis all writers' fear most, losing their entire hand written manuscript weeks before a looming deadline. Worse, she is unable to recapture the essences of her first page, the one she considers to be the most significant page of the entire book. After losing her manuscript to Mother Nature's wrath, she places an ad in the local newspaper offering a reward to have her pages returned to her.

Follow their tense adventure as they encounter the assortment of people who return the pages of her work, only to find them all, except for one. Neither, Nitra nor her house keeper, Wallaçe McPhee, is aware that the other has feelings that run deeper than their employer, employee relationship. That is, until they encounter the mysterious woman wearing gaudy red lipstick.

The comedic banter between Nitra and Wallace, along with the fast paced adventure, will bring you to the dramatic end of their search for Nitra's first page, the last page.

Be sure to
look for
Kay's previous book
**MARKED**
now on sale.

George Oscar Dack, a white warlock, is on the verge of shaking up his dull, predictable life. With the help of his sarcastic cat, Darius and a strange old woman, he conducts his experiment using precise elements and implements, to cast a spell upon a Canadian two dollar bill.

Writing his initials across the bill's front as part of the spell, it allows him to observe the bill's travels throughout the day, revealing what effects, either good or corrupt, it has on those who possess it, both young and old characters alike. Some have happy encounters, while others definitely do not.

Come join George and follow the bill's many adventures through his ordinary little town and discover the true connection between him and the old woman who enters into his life.

Be sure
to look for
Kay's previous book

**In the hunt for ...**
**The Perfect Martini!**

With a new job and a new life,
middle-aged Izzy Abbott finds herself
lonely and terribly bored.

Each evening, to spice up her life,
she disguises herself in an entirely new identity and visits a different bar, looking for fun, men, and her version of a dirty dry martini — her perfect martini.

Even though she is having a blast
on her nightly outings, the recent unsolved murder of a woman in the city lingers in her mind while she party's. Should she feel secure or watch out for her safety with a killer on the loose?

Meet the quirky patrons and peculiar bartenders she encounters in the eclectic drinking establishments she visits.

Come join Izzy in
her zany adventures ... in the hunt for
... the perfect martini.

*Be sure to look for* **Kay's** *previous Book*

# Lovage

When single mom, Charlotte Thomas, moved into her new house, she had no idea that the man living across the street would take such offense to her scraping all the grass off her yard with a bulldozer. Against his friendly advice, she was determined to landscape her yard the way she wanted, no matter how much the good-looking Jack Lawson protested. Out came the grass — In went the stone, pea gravel and an abundance of vegetation, finally giving her lovage plant a permanent home.

But it was the elderly lady next door, along with her teenaged daughter, that quickly became very persistent matchmakers. Nicky and dear old Dottie were convinced that her mother needed a man to help Charlie create the garden of her dreams. A man that would eventually fall head over heels for the natural beauty of the stubborn blonde.

Come follow the romantic adventure of Charlotte and her neighbours, as they landscape her little wartime home. Who knows, you might learn some new gardening techniques along the way.

Be sure
to look for
Kay's previous book

# *The Last Motel*

Constantly on the run, Gabriel Carr was already exhausted when his headlights fell upon the neon sign that would dictate the next leg of his grueling escape. Through the heavy rain, he read, The Last Motel for 99 Miles. Finally able to elude the two mobsters hunting him down, he paid for a room to rest both his body and his mind. Depressed and drained of all energy to live, he took refuge inside the room, locking himself away from the world.

Gord, the motel's owner, knew right from the start that Gabriel would bring trouble to his peaceful motel. And when the stranger began spending time with Maizie, the secret love of Gord's life, he didn't like it one damned bit. Even so, he promised himself he would protect her and the others when that trouble did arrive.

It was Maizie, the housekeeper, that drew Gabriel out of his room and introduced him to her little town in Northern Ontario. His time spent with the beautiful and optimistic Maizie changed his mind about ending his life. Instead, he switched his focus on the mission started by his slain girlfriend, Heather.

Gabriel's new plans were going well — until the two hit men appeared, both prepared to eliminate Gabriel Carr, the only witness to the murder they committed. The end result being a dramatic gunfight and ending, no one could have predicted.

***Be sure to look for Kay's previous book***

## *An Angel Named Topaz*

In the winter of 1977, Mickey Backus hires a Private Investigator to follow his wife Rosie, who he suspects is cheating on him. Not only did he want proof of the affair, he was also curious as to who was dumb enough to fool around with the wife of Belleville's notorious mobster.
Thank goodness, Mickey still had his beloved blue lined angel fish to talk to.

When Bernie, Mickey's right-hand man, also hires a Private Investigator, the competition heats up with everyone trying to get the photos the mobster wants. But when all is revealed by the Private Investigators, the identity of Rosie's lover both shocks and angers Mickey, setting off a chain of unexpected events that no one could have predicted, especially those of hookers and murder.

Come follow the bizarre string of episodes that entangle the even odder cast of characters — one being An Angel Named Topaz

www.ingramcontent.com/pod-product-compliance
Lightning Source LLC
LaVergne TN
LVHW091036080826
845145LV00002B/519